⇥ First Fangs Club ⇤

USA Today Bestselling Author
KRISTEN PAINTER

Sucker Punch:
A Paranormal Women's Fiction Novel
First Fangs Club • Book Three

Copyright © 2020 Kristen Painter

All rights reserved. No part of this book may be reproduced in any form or by any electronic or mechanical means, including information storage and retrieval systems—except in the case of brief quotations embodied in critical articles or reviews—without permission in writing from the author.

This book is a work of fiction. The characters, events, and places portrayed in this book are products of the author's imagination and are either fictitious or are used fictitiously. Any similarity to real person, living or dead, is purely coincidental and not intended by the author.

Published in the United States of America.

Newly appointed vampire governor of New Jersey, Belladonna Barrone is fast discovering that life as a vampire isn't much easier than life as a mobster's wife. But that experience certainly taught her some things about how to handle the problems that come with being governor. That is until a friend is kidnapped by the fae and his life put in danger, all because of her actions.

Figuring out how to save him feels very much above her paygrade, but she's the boss and the decision about how to handle this potentially deadly situation is completely up to her. With the clock ticking, she has no choice but to attempt a rescue.

Thankfully, she has the help of her team and some impressive new friends. But going to battle with the fae has painfully real consequences and the outcome of their mission leaves them all reeling. While dealing with the fallout from the fight, Donna once again becomes the target of a jealous vampire rival, which puts her future in question. Somehow, she has to find the strength to keep going and overcome these new attacks.

But there's only so much a woman can handle. Or is there? With new resolve, Donna knows her only option is to fight back. Who else is going to protect her family and friends? She's never been one to run from her problems.

Even when her problems feel like a supernatural sucker punch.

For my State of Survival alliance, CFS.

Thanks for inspiring me in more ways than you know, and thanks to Ishalan for the use of his name.

Chapter 1

With dawn fast approaching, Belladonna Barrone stood in the living room of her home, the governor's penthouse, surrounded by her trusted team: Pierce Harrison, her personal assistant and the attorney who'd saved her life. Charlene "Charlie" Rollins, her administrative assistant. Temo Danielson, her driver and head of security.

His cousin, Penina, was also there, due to her helping out as part-time security.

Next to her stood Rixaline, the teenage dhamfir Donna had given sanctuary to. Rixaline had returned the favor by using her skills of finding lost things to locate Donna's supposed-to-be-dead mob husband, which made it possible to capture him and turn him over to the FBI.

But none of those people could stop the pit that opened up in Donna's stomach as she watched the newly arrived video on her phone. Temo, Pierce, and Charlie had gotten it too.

The sight of friend and FBI agent Rico Medina in the clutches of the fae was unbearably awful. Sounds started to go tinny, the floor beneath her tilted, and for a second, Donna thought she might pass out. Or retch. Or punch something. Maybe all three. But not in that order.

Instead of doing any of that, she did her best to pull herself together. But not in time to stop a curse that would have made Big Tony, head of the Villachi crime family, proud. She stared at her phone's screen for a second longer, then finally raised her head and uttered a sentence she knew was the result of denial. "That can't be him. Please tell me that's not him."

Her team looked at her with the same kind of sinking despair she felt.

Temo shook his head slowly. "Pretty sure it is, boss."

Pierce came to her side. "I'm sorry, but it's definitely Rico."

Donna swallowed, but the bitter taste in her mouth went nowhere. "I know. I just don't want it to be him."

Penina picked up her purse. "I should go. You all have a lot to deal with, and I don't want to be in the way. If you need me, I'm just a phone call away."

Donna nodded. "Thank you for helping out."

"Anytime. I'm so sorry." She looked at Temo. "Talk to you later, cousin."

"Later," he answered.

As Penina left, Donna glanced down at her phone again. "As much as I don't want to, I need to watch that again."

"Hang on," Charlie said. She grabbed the TV remote and changed the channel from the movie Penina and Rixaline had been watching, then tapped her phone screen a few times. A couple of seconds later, the video started playing on the television.

With her hand pressed flat to her stomach, Donna watched, unable to look away. Forcing herself to be analytical and search for anything that might be useful.

The same dimly lit holding cell appeared, all in muted shades of gray because of the low light. The walls and floor looked like stone.

"The dungeons," Rixaline breathed. "I would know them anywhere."

A man was bound to a wooden chair in the center of the cell, head down. Donna recognized his T-shirt and jeans as the same ones Rico had worn earlier at FBI headquarters to take custody of Joe and his accomplice girlfriend, Carmella.

A fae walked into view and grabbed a handful of Rico's hair as he talked to the camera. "We know you have the dhamfir."

Rixaline let out a tiny whimper.

"Return her to us, or your friend dies. You have forty-eight hours."

He pulled the man's head back.

And once again, Donna looked into Rico's face. He looked angry. But also a little scared. She sucked in a breath, unable to stop herself from reacting. It felt like she'd been sucker-punched. "I can't believe they have him."

"Neither can I," Pierce said. "How are they holding a wolf shifter?"

Rixaline spoke softly. "Those ropes are laced with silver threads."

Donna turned to her. "That cell is in the fae headquarters?"

She nodded. "Yes, in the stronghold's dungeons."

Donna's vampire nature flared like a can of gasoline that had just been thrown into a fire. It came over her with the same sudden surge as the first time she'd slugged her mobster husband, Joe, in the face. "I'm going to kill them all."

"I don't think that's such a good idea," Charlie said.

"Really?" Donna snapped. "Because it seems like a freakin' fabulous idea to me."

Rixaline's skin, normally a dusky gray green, seemed paler and greener than usual. "This is my fault. I'm so sorry."

Donna couldn't really argue with that. This *had* happened because of Rixaline, but Donna alone had made the decision to offer the teenager sanctuary. From that point on, any and all consequences were hers to deal with. "No one forced them to kidnap Rico. And if there's blame to be had, it's mine for giving you sanctuary. Doesn't mean I'd change my decision. Or that I have any regrets, other than what's happened to Rico, obviously."

Rixaline's distress seemed to stay the same. Her arms hugged her thin torso. "When do you want to leave?"

"Leave?" Donna frowned. "For where?"

"To take me back to King Dredward."

Donna barked out a sharp laugh. "That is the last place you're going. You really think I'd turn you over to that lunatic? Child, you do not yet understand the kind of woman I am."

Charlie glanced out the penthouse windows, making Donna look too. Dull indigo light edged the horizon, and the stars were nearly gone. "It's almost dawn. The fae will be asleep soon. Hopefully, that means Rico will be left to sleep too."

Donna shifted her gaze to her admin. "We have a lot to do in a short amount of time. Let's start with drafting an email to Artemis. We'll let her know about Rixaline first and then this situation. I can't have the queen finding out secondhand that my sanctuary case has turned into something bigger. I need to get ahead of this."

Charlie nodded as she headed for her office. "On it."

Donna put her phone back in her evening bag. "Rixaline?"

"Yes, ma'am?"

"You remember how to get to the fae stronghold?"

She swallowed. "I do."

"Excellent. Draw me a map. Show me how to get to the dungeons too."

Rixaline hesitated. "It won't do you any good."

"Why not?" Donna didn't have time for games.

Rixaline tugged at her ear. "Only those with fae blood or under the control of the fae can see the stronghold. That's how their protective magic works."

"That's an unfortunate complication, but if magic is doing that, then magic should be able to undo it. But we'll discuss that some more later. In the meantime, draw me that map. Get whatever supplies you need from Charlie."

"Yes, ma'am." Rixaline headed off toward the admin's office.

Donna looked at Temo next. "We're going to need a daylight-capable team."

Pierce frowned. "You're going to run a daylight raid?"

"Seems like the best time to do it, since the fae will be the most vulnerable then."

"But your secret won't be a secret after that."

She'd been doing her best to keep her UV immunity under wraps, but that no longer seemed important now. She thought for a moment. "There has to be a way a vampire can temporarily daywalk, right?"

"If a vampire is well covered enough, they can get away with a short daywalk. But you're talking about something that would explain being out for several hours. That doesn't exist."

"There has to be something."

He didn't look convinced. "I'll see what I can figure out."

"Thank you. Now, Temo. About that team. Put together the best you've got or that money can buy. No expense spared. If we need to hire mercenaries, do it, just make sure they know what they're going up against. No humans. If you want to get Penina to help again, that would be great. Oh, and, Temo?"

His dark brows rose. "Yes, boss?"

"Your fae connections. Reach out to them. See if you can find out anything more about this situation that might be useful. Anything about the layout of the stronghold, the kind of security, anything. No detail is worthless at this point."

"Will do." He gave both her and Pierce a nod before taking off toward the stairs that led to the staff penthouse one floor below.

She turned to Pierce, shaking her head and sighing at the awfulness of Rico's capture. "I can't believe this."

"Me neither." Lines of concern bracketed his eyes. "What else can I do? Just tell me what you need, and I'm on it."

"Tell me this is going to be okay. Tell me we're going to get Rico back. Alive."

He smiled with effort, but it was comforting all the same. "We will."

She took a deep breath, closing her eyes for a second to get a handle on her emotions. "I really do want to kill them."

"You're not alone in that," he said. "You may get the chance."

"This feels...like more than I can handle. This is a man's life at stake here. Getting him back means basically standing up a military operation." She put her hand to her forehead. "I don't have that kind of knowledge. I was a housewife, not a mob boss."

"For one thing, you've already done a great job getting started. For another, Temo does have that kind of knowledge, thanks to his Special Ops days. On top of that, you have all of us to help you. You're not in this alone."

"I know. You're right. But I feel like I'm forgetting something. We need to get as organized as possible. And get some more help. Nothing can fall between the cracks."

"We will get it all done, I promise." His smile took on a gentler curve. "But first, you might want to change out of that dress and that necklace that's worth half a mil."

Her hand went to her throat, landing on the borrowed diamond and ruby sparkler she'd worn to the party they'd just left. "I totally forgot about it."

Not just any party either. The most incredible party she'd ever been to, thrown by Francine, one of the most amazing vampires Donna had met since being turned a couple of weeks ago. And all in Donna's honor. Despite her unfortunate run-in with the vampire governor of New York, Hawke Fitzhugh, the night had been one to remember. "To think just an hour ago, we were happy and laughing and having the time of our lives. Now this."

"Life is funny that way."

She glanced down at her gorgeous red dress, then back at him in his tux. "We should both change. Then set up camp in the dining room. And you should maybe get some ice for that hand." He'd punched Fitzhugh. With good reason. But she didn't want Pierce to suffer for that any more than he already had. "It's going to be a long day."

"It's feeling better already." He flexed his hand, the knuckles red and swollen. "You sure you don't want to set up in the conference room?"

She shook her head. "I like being close to the kitchen. We're going to need sustenance and coffee. By sustenance, I mean pie."

"Good thing we have some left. There's cake too."

"Excellent."

"Meet you in the kitchen, then."

She nodded as she went in the direction of her bedroom. "In ten."

"You got it."

She shut the bedroom door behind her and leaned against it, the enormity of Rico's plight hitting her like a crashing wave.

She could not let him die. He was a friend and an ally, but more than that, he was a stand-up guy who'd dedicated his life to the battle between good and evil. To sticking up for the underdog. To saving those who couldn't save themselves. Like her.

But the fae were a very different kind of evil.

The kind that wanted to turn every vampire they could catch into dinner.

What did that mean for Rico, a werewolf? She wasn't sure what the fae-werewolf relationship was. Would they drain him too? The fae loved vampire blood. She didn't know how they felt about werewolf blood.

She shuddered and burst into action, stripping off the evening gown, high heels, and ridiculously expensive borrowed jewels. There was so much to do that if she allowed herself to dwell on it all, she'd be overwhelmed.

This was one of those times when she just had to let the big picture blur a little so she could focus on the now. Get each small thing done before moving on to the next one. All while somehow keeping the big picture in mind.

There had been moments like this when she'd been married to Joe. Like the time he'd come home suddenly in the middle of the day, thrown money at her, and told her to get out of town with the kids until he let her know it was okay to come home. Thank God the kids had been small enough to think they were just going on a vacation with Mommy.

But this was a lot more serious than anything she'd dealt with before.

She pulled her blessed crucifix from her bra and secured it around her neck. She kissed the cross and said a quick prayer that she'd be able to handle this. More than ever, she wished she could talk to Cammie, her sister who was an actual sister. Sister Mary Lazarus Immaculata, to be exact. But Cammie was in Nicaragua with the rest of her fellow nuns, working at an orphanage.

Donna shook her head at the very idea of such sacrifice. Cammie was such a good person. And not just because she was a nun. She'd want nothing to do with this, though that didn't stop Donna from wanting to talk to her. Even if only to ask her to pray.

Donna dressed in thick leggings, a T-shirt, and a big cardigan. She added a pair of woolly slippers. Comfortable clothes for an uncomfortable day. And not just because of the task at hand. Dawn had just about arrived, and with it, more snow flurries.

She didn't feel cold, and the penthouse was certainly at a pleasant temperature, but something about the gray, snowy day—and the terrible situation with Rico—made her want to bundle up. She pulled the cardigan around her and went to the kitchen to make some coffee.

Pierce showed up a few minutes later as her cup finished brewing. He'd probably hung up his tux instead of just throwing it on the bed like she had with her gown.

She added cream and sugar, then leaned against the counter to drink some while he made a cup for himself. "We really need Temo and Charlie at the table with us."

He nodded. "I'm sure they can bring their laptops in here."

With perfect timing, Charlie strode back in, still in her off-the-shoulder evening gown and borrowed diamond necklace. "Letter's drafted."

"That was fast. Thank you." And of course she'd done it while still in her party clothes. "Why don't you bring your laptop in here and work with us after you change? I'm sure Van Marten's will want their jewels back too. Can we get that taken care of? That would be one less thing to worry about."

"Absolutely. I'll call them on my way to change and tell them they can send a messenger anytime. Back in a few."

"Thanks, Charlie. And ask Temo to join us when he can as well. Tell him to change too. I'm sure he'd like to get out of that suit."

Charlie nodded. "Will do."

"Oh! Sorry, one more thing. I want to bring Jerabeth in on this. Rixaline said fae magic was involved at the stronghold, so I thought maybe Jerabeth could help with that. You have any objections to including her?"

"Not at all. But..." At the mention of the elemental witch who worked as the governor's gardener, Charlie hesitated, but only to look at the time. "She won't be in the greenhouse yet. Still pretty early for her. I could call her and see if she could come in sooner."

"Do you think she'll be useful? Because if you don't, tell me now."

"She knows about your...special abilities, and she's definitely skilled. She could absolutely be an asset."

"Any downside?"

Charlie thought for a second, then shook her head. "At worst, she might not be able to help. But I don't believe that will be the case."

"If you trust her, then that's good enough for me. Bring her in."

She pulled her phone out. "Sending her a text right now."

"Thanks. See you when you get back."

Charlie nodded as she walked out, thumbs flying over the screen.

Donna went back to her coffee. Pierce fixed his cup, then put the creamer back in the fridge. "You're going to need to feed soon if you don't sleep."

She nodded, her mug cradled between her hands. "I know. But that can wait a little longer."

He gave her a look that said he wasn't going to let her forget. She smiled, despite everything else. As if there was any other way to respond to the dedication he showed in looking after her.

The door chimes rang.

She straightened and stared at him. "Who could that be? Security didn't call up that anyone was coming."

He put his cup down. "Then it has to be someone who's on the vetted list. I'll get it."

"I'm coming with you. If they're on the list, then they can't be an enemy, right? At least I'd hope not."

He glanced at her, frowned, but said nothing.

"You're thinking about Fitzhugh, I can tell. Hey, maybe he's come to apologize."

"In the state he was in, I'm guessing he's passed out somewhere."

She didn't argue as she followed him to the door. Fitzhugh had been pretty drunk. She stayed back a little as Pierce reached for the handle.

He opened the door, revealing two women who looked like they could be Italian or Hispanic. One was probably a decade older than Donna and had a definite chip-on-her-shoulder vibe. The other one was another decade or so beyond the first, more like Francine's age. They were petite, well dressed, and looked like they could hold their own in a fight. Or start one.

Pierce greeted them with a smile. "Can I help you ladies?"

The younger one looked past him to nod at Donna. "You're the governor? Belladonna Barrone?"

She took a few steps closer. "I am. How can I help you?"

The older woman answered, an icy-blue, othernatural light flashing in her eyes as she lifted her chin. "I am Louisa Valentina Medina." That was a mouthful. And she shared a last name with Rico. Coincidence? Donna didn't think so. "I am the alpha of the New Jersey pack. In case you don't know, that means I'm the leader, vampire."

Donna canted her head slightly. "I know what alpha means."

"Good. One more thing. I am also Rico Medina's grandmother."

Chapter 2

Louisa Valentina gestured to the younger woman beside her. "This is the pack's alpha-elect, Maria Antonella."

Maria Antonella's eyes narrowed, and the same othernatural light sparked in them. "I'm Rico's *mother*. LV and I would like to have a word with you."

Donna nodded, a little stunned that the women at her door weren't just werewolves, but also Rico's grandmother and mother. *And* they were the leaders of the New Jersey pack. She'd been right about it not being coincidental, but it also seemed like a thing Rico might have mentioned.

But if being married to the mob had taught her anything, it was how to deal with the unexpected. "Please, come in. It's good you came, actually. I would have called you in a little while anyway."

Maria Antonella made a face. "You would have called us?"

"Absolutely. We're just getting ourselves organized here. I didn't know you knew already."

Donna's answer did nothing to erase the look on Maria Antonella's face.

Pierce stepped back, opening the door wider. They came in, studying the penthouse as if it had secrets to share. Their nostrils flared, and they seemed to be sniffing the air.

No, they were *definitely* sniffing the air.

"He's not here," Maria Antonella said to LV.

"I don't think he has been either." LV finally made eye contact with Donna again, scanning her like something on her person might be of interest.

Donna felt like she'd missed something. Did they think Rico was here? Unless there was someone else they were talking about, but that seemed highly unlikely. "You're talking about Rico, right?"

Maria Antonella glared. "Who else would we be talking about?"

Pierce shut the door, then rejoined them. "Can I get you something to drink? Coffee? Water? Juice?"

"Black coffee, two sugars," LV answered.

"How about my son?" Maria Antonella shot back.

"Toni," LV chided as Pierce went off to the kitchen.

Donna did her best not to react too strongly. "I understand you're upset. I am too."

LV's dark, penciled brows lifted. "What do you have to be upset about? That he isn't here? That you can't get to whatever love nest you have him stashed in?"

Donna slowly closed her mouth but continued staring at the woman. "Um...you think I have him stashed in a love nest? We need to back this conversation up. There's been some misinformation somewhere."

"Listen, vampire, I know what I know. He's sweet on you and now this," Maria Antonella snarled.

Rico liked her? That was news. Donna blinked as she tried to process the rest of the situation. "And by 'this,' you mean—"

"He didn't show up for the pack run last night," Maria Antonella said. "He isn't answering his phone or his texts either. We figured he's shacked up with you. We know you two have been working closely together. We know he has feelings for you. And we know the allure of a strong, virile male wolf to the female vampire. So where is he?"

Donna took a breath. This was worse than she'd thought. "There is nothing going on between us except a working relationship. I promise you he's not here or in a love nest. But I know where he is."

"Where?" LV asked.

"Yeah, where?" Maria Antonella relaxed a tiny bit.

Donna gestured toward the kitchen. "Why don't you come in and sit down so I can explain?"

Thankfully, they seemed amenable to that. Donna led them in, then let them pick their seats before choosing one herself. Pierce brought LV's coffee over with another for Donna, which she was definitely about to need. He returned a second later with sugar, creamer, and spoons.

Donna let LV fix her coffee first, then helped

herself to the cream and sugar as she selected her words carefully. "I wish we were meeting under different circumstances. I also wish I had something different to tell you than what I'm about to."

She looked up at the women, making careful eye contact. "Rico has been kidnapped by the fae. He's being held at their stronghold. I highly suspect King Dredward is behind this."

The color drained from both women's faces. Maria Antonella let out a little gasp and crossed herself. "How did this happen? How do you know this?"

"It happened because I took in a young girl who's half fae, half vampire and—"

"Dhamfir," LV whispered.

Donna nodded. "Yes. I gave her sanctuary. The fae were treating her terribly. But King Dredward wants her back, so he had Rico kidnapped to use as leverage. I know this because the fae sent us a video. The girl, Rixaline, recognized the holding cell as the dungeons in the stronghold. We have forty-eight hours to rescue him."

Charlie walked into the kitchen, now in a gray knit tracksuit. She stopped when she saw the two women.

Maria Antonella's lips were firmly pressed together, maybe to stop them from quivering. "Show us the video."

Donna glanced at her admin. "Charlie, this is Louisa Valentina Medina, the alpha of the New Jersey pack, and the alpha-elect, Maria Antonella

Medina. They are Rico's grandmother and mother. Ladies, Charlie is my very capable admin."

"Call me Toni," Maria Antonella muttered. "And you can call my mother LV." She shook her head as she looked at Donna. "I'm sorry for what I accused you of."

"Don't give it another thought. I'm a mother. I would probably act the same way if my son went missing. We're all stressed right now," Donna answered. She looked at Charlie again. "Can you play the video on the television like you did before? Our guests need to see it."

"Of course."

She went into the living room. Donna stood. "Ladies, if you'd like to follow Charlie, she'll set it to play in there."

A few minutes later, a stone-faced LV stared at the frozen image of her grandson on the screen. Toni had tears streaming down her face even as her hands were clenched in fists at her sides.

LV finally turned away from the television to look at Donna. "Have you already made a plan to get him back?"

"We're in the early stages of doing that now. We only just got this video within the hour. But we're working on a strategy. I hope you'll join us."

She nodded. "Your financial abilities exceed anything the wolves can offer, but we are greater in number. And the sunlight doesn't affect us."

"I welcome whatever help you're willing to give. For a long time, your grandson was the only hope

I had of escaping my terrible life. I owe him." Donna held her hand out. "Thank you."

LV shook her hand, then inhaled deeply. "We have a lot to do and a short time to do it."

The sound of rapid footsteps was followed by Temo returning. He glanced at the two women, then Donna. "Boss."

Donna introduced him. "Ladies, please meet Temo Danielson, my very skilled head of security. Temo, this is LV Medina, alpha of the New Jersey werewolves, and Toni Medina, alpha-elect. They're Rico's grandmother and mother, and they're joining with us to rescue him."

"A pleasure to meet you both." Temo smiled and nodded, rubbing his hands together. "This is very good."

Donna clapped her hands. "Let's get to work."

They all settled in at the dining room table, Temo at one end, Charlie and Donna at the other, LV and Toni in the middle. Pierce got more coffees and a few glasses of water. When that was done, he took a seat across from the alphas.

Donna put her hand on his arm as she looked at LV and Toni. "I'm sorry, I failed to introduce my assistant and my attorney, Pierce Harrison."

Toni nodded, and the hint of a sly smile bent her mouth. "I heard about you. You're the one who saved her from the council. Rico told us about that."

Pierce tipped his head in acknowledgment. "That was me. But his testimony was pivotal. I like Rico very much. I wish there was more I could do personally to help with this situation."

A knock at the door interrupted them. Charlie got to her feet. "That's probably Jerabeth. I'll get it."

A moment later, the two women returned to the dining room, introductions were made, and another seat at the table was filled.

As the conversation turned toward the best time to launch the rescue, movement caught Donna's eye. She turned to see Rixaline hovering at the end of the hall, a sheet of paper in her hands. She motioned to the girl. "Come in."

Then she held her hand out in Rixaline's direction and spoke to the werewolves. "This is Rixaline, the dhamfir I told you about. She's the key to our plan because she knows how to get to the fae stronghold."

LV shook her head. "King Dredward is supposed to be impossible to find."

"Nothing is impossible for Rixaline to find. That's why the fae want her back so badly. Plus, she was held at that stronghold, so she knows it better than anyone." Donna looked up at the girl, who now stood timidly beside her. "You drew the map?"

She nodded and held the paper out. She swallowed as she stuck near Donna.

"Thank you so much." Was it the presence of the wolves that frightened Rix? Donna wasn't sure, but something had the teenager on edge. She took the map and laid it flat on the table. "You did a good job."

"Charlie gave me the colored pencils," Rixaline said quietly.

"Smart choice." It was actually a pretty decent rendering with trees in green, paths in gray, water in blue. The fortress was a dark purple square with a small rectangle just in front of it. That rectangle was labeled as a gate. "The stronghold is in a forest?"

Rixaline nodded. "Yes." She tapped a small brown square near the top of the map. "There's a castle here, but the fae call it the folly because it's just for show. That's not where the fae are. They're in the big purple square. Although the stronghold isn't really a square. I don't know the real shape."

Donna looked closer as everyone else did the same.

"A castle that's just for show?" Pierce leaned over her shoulder to see the map. "Wait a minute. Those paths look familiar. In fact, this all looks very much like the Ramble in Central Park." He straightened to see Rixaline better. "Are you telling me the fae stronghold is in the middle of Manhattan?"

"That sounds...right," Rixaline said as she tipped her head in thought. "The woods is surrounded by city. I know because that's part of what helped me escape. I disappeared into the crowds, and they didn't dare take me with all those people around."

Toni shook her head. "How is that possible? I've never heard of any kind of fortress in the park besides Belvedere Castle, which is what I'm guessing the folly is."

Pierce nodded. "Has to be."

"Y-you can't see the stronghold." Rixaline twisted her fingers together. "Unless you have fae blood or are under fae control."

"Fae magic is a remarkable thing," Donna said.

Rixaline nodded.

LV frowned but spoke softly. Like a grandmother. "What does that mean, child? Under fae control?"

Everyone looked at Rixaline.

She seemed to shrink in on herself. "I'm not sure. I think if a fae has ahold of you. Like actually touching you. Or you are under their power in some way. Rico is under their control, so I'm sure he can see the stronghold around him. That's just how fae magic works. I don't know more than that."

"Thank you," Donna said. "That was helpful."

Jerabeth raised a finger, the first time she'd interjected since arriving. "I think I have a solution for that. But...I'm going to need some pretty difficult-to-get ingredients. At least one toughie anyway."

Donna turned toward the witch. "And that would be?"

Jerabeth grimaced. "A live fairy. Because I need their blood."

Chapter 3

Donna groaned softly. "You said difficult, but a live fae sounds impossible."

Toni shook her head as she sat up straighter. "There has to be another way."

"I'm sure there is," Jerabeth said. "But I don't know what it would be."

Rixaline stuck her arm out. "You can have my blood."

Jerabeth's smile was sympathetic. "That's a kind offer, but you're only half fae. I'm not sure it would work. And this doesn't seem like a situation where we're going to get a second chance."

"I agree," LV said. "We have to do this right the first time, or they'll kill him. I have no doubt. And that would lead to war, because I assure you I would not let the murder of my grandson go unavenged."

Donna leaned her head into her hand, her fingers over her left temple. "I hate to say this, but we need to tell the vampire governor of New York what's about to happen in his state."

Toni curled her lip. "A better governor wouldn't let those fae run rampant."

With a sigh, Charlie said to Donna, "You're right, Governor. I hate it, too, but you're right. I can't imagine what Fitzhugh's reaction would be, but I can guess how he'd react if you ran a raid in his state without telling him first."

Donna groaned softly. "Maybe we'll get lucky, and he will ignore us."

Pierce snorted. "Sure."

Charlie started scribbling something on the legal pad in front of her. "I'm making a note to draft an email to him. Although…" She stopped writing. "A phone call might be better. Considering what happened at the party, the personal touch might go a long way. And then he can't say he didn't get the email."

"Good thinking." Donna sipped her coffee. "Except a call might make him think I've forgiven him. I do not want him thinking everything's copacetic between us. Because it isn't."

Charlie nodded slowly. "I understand wanting to let him stew, but remember he can still press charges against Pierce."

Donna looked at LV and Toni, who were clearly lost. "Fitzhugh insulted me at a party we attended last night, and Pierce punched him in the mouth."

Both women smiled. Toni gave Pierce a thumbs-up. "Good job. That jerkwad's needed a punch in the kisser for a long time."

Donna's brows rose. "He's got quite the reputation, doesn't he?"

LV huffed out a breath. "No one likes him any more than what's necessary to get things done. Thankfully, we almost never have to deal with him, since we're not in his state, but I can promise you the New York pack wants nothing to do with him."

"Interesting." She took a moment to organize her thoughts. "Back to the topic of needing the blood from a live fairy. Jerabeth, I'm assuming that's for a spell?"

Jerabeth nodded. "Basically. I told you it was a difficult ingredient."

"You weren't lying. How much will you need?"

Jerabeth looked around the table. "To be effective, anyone who's going on this raid needs to be able to see the stronghold, which means I have to make enough for everyone involved. I'd say at least three vials. Although once the wolves shift, they won't need the potion. Fae magic generally seems to be focused on human-based life forms."

"All right." Donna followed Temo's gaze. He was staring at a spot on the table like he was lost in thought. "Temo? What's on your mind?"

He blinked and looked up. "I *might* know someone who'd be willing to donate, but he's going to want something in return. It won't be a small something either."

"He's a full-blooded fae?"

He nodded. "We're not bros or anything, but he's been a reliable source so far."

"When you say he's going to want something, are we talking money? Favors? Something else?"

He sighed. "I won't know until we talk to him. That's the other thing. I don't think this is a deal he'll agree to without a face-to-face with you. He'll want your personal guarantee."

Donna sat back. A personal meeting with one of the creatures who considered her kind little more than walking entrées. "Have you met with him in person before?"

"I have."

"You think it's safe for me to meet him?"

"I hate to say that and then things go poorly, but he's probably the safest one you could meet with." He frowned. "I don't know any other way."

Donna didn't hesitate. Rico's life was at stake. "Set it up. But under no circumstances will I meet with him alone. I want you and at least one other person with me. Which reminds me…" She turned to Charlie. "I need some iron bracelets. Something that doesn't look like I'm wearing shackles."

"Right away."

"Jerabeth, get me those empty vials, but bring me five."

"You got it."

Donna's stomach growled, but it wasn't necessarily for food.

LV smiled knowingly. "You're up too late, vampire. You're going to need something more than coffee to keep you going."

"I'll be fine, but we should get something to eat.

Coffee isn't going to sustain any of us for long."

Charlie opened up her laptop. "I can take care of that. I'll order us something to be delivered." She started typing, then stopped and looked up. "Anyone have any food allergies I should know about?"

LV and Toni shook their heads.

An hour later, after they'd come up with a few strategies for approaching the stronghold and rescuing Rico, security called up that their order had arrived.

Charlie and Pierce went down to get the food, returning a short while later. Pierce was carrying a stack of enormous, covered platters, and Charlie held a couple of bags in each hand.

They set the food out on the kitchen counter buffet style and let everyone help themselves. Donna stood and gestured toward the spread as she spoke to LV and Toni. "Please. You're our guests."

She followed behind them. It was an impressive array. Croissant breakfast sandwiches, a platter of bacon and sausage links, another of crispy hash-brown-style potato cakes, a large bowl of fresh fruit, sliced bagels with three flavors of cream cheese, and a tray of sweets that included mini danishes, doughnuts, and rugelach.

LV paused while filling her plate. "Thank you. I expected one thing when I was on my way here, and that's not what I got. Although, now I wish Rico *was* here with you."

"I wish he was too." Donna added a couple of strips of bacon beside her sausage, egg, and cheese croissant. There was more food here than they'd eat in three days. Which was perfect. She wanted the wolves to know she wasn't going to skimp on anything, whether it was feeding them or rescuing Rico.

"Would you like one of us to accompany you to the meeting with the fae?"

That was a kind offer. Even if it might also be the wolves' way of keeping an eye on her. "I might take you up on that."

"Let me know. We'll send one of our sentries. They're very strong, loyal to the death, and ready at a moment's notice."

"Thank you. That sounds good."

Temo came up to her. "Meeting's set. Tonight. Soon as the sun sets. But it's just you and me. He wouldn't agree to more."

Not much she could do about that. "Where?"

"Bus station just north of here."

She mulled that over for a moment. "At least it's public."

"You want a couple sentries?" LV asked.

"Maybe you could put a few there. Undercover."

Temo sucked air between his teeth. "He'll sense them."

Donna shrugged. "Werewolves can't travel by bus?"

LV narrowed her eyes. "I have a married couple I can send. They'll blend in better and be less obvious that way. And then, if you need them, they'll be a shout away."

"Okay, that works." She looked at Temo again. "You sure we can't take Charlie?"

"Just you and me, boss. He'll spook if he sees more."

"Then I'm definitely glad for the sentries." She took a deep breath. "Let's eat and get back to work. There's a lot still to do."

Thankfully, there wasn't as much to do as Donna had anticipated, mostly because they hit a brick wall at a certain point. Until she met with Temo's fae contact and made the deal for his blood so that Jerabeth could use it for her spell, they were stuck.

She said goodbye to LV and Toni, approved the email to Artemis, then decided to finally get some sleep. She made Pierce, Charlie, and Temo do the same. They'd been up as long as she had.

Sleeping was hard to do with the thought of Rico being held captive and possibly being tortured. She focused on the way he'd looked in the video. Angry, but not injured. She clung to that because without sleep she'd be useless during the rescue.

She drank a pint of blood, then collapsed onto her bed, unable to do much more than stare at the ceiling and pray he was all right.

Surprisingly, she finally drifted off. She slept hard but woke suddenly, shocked out of sleep by a nightmare in which Rico had been served as the main course at a fae banquet.

She bolted upright in the darkness. Her heart pounded. She made herself breathe. "It was just a dream."

But it didn't feel that way. It felt like a terrible premonition of what was to come. She shook her head, refusing to believe that. Rico was going to be okay.

Or LV was going to be right. War would come.

Donna sat in the dark for a few moments longer as she woke up fully. The nightmare was gone, but the feeling remained like a shadow on her spirit. She grabbed her phone and dialed. It was after 4 p.m., and Cammie might be unreachable in Nicaragua, but at least Donna could hear her voice on her answering message. That was better than nothing.

"Hello?"

"Cammie? Is that you? I didn't think you'd be able to get calls when you were in another country."

"I can't. But I'm home."

"You are? When did you get back?"

Dead air answered. Finally, Cammie exhaled softly. "Sooner than expected."

"Is that good? You sound...odd."

"It's definitely good. I'm just tired. What's new with you? How's your new job going?"

Donna wasn't totally convinced Cammie was being completely honest. Which would be highly unlike her. Nuns tended to shy away from lying. "It's never dull, that's for sure." She let out a long sigh of her own. "Rico's been taken hostage by the fae king because of something I did."

"What?"

"Yeah. I gave sanctuary to a teenage girl who's half fae, half vampire—"

"Dhamfir," Cammie whispered.

Did everyone know that word except for her? Apparently. "Yes. Anyone with a heart would have done it. Poor kid. Anyway, King Dredward wants her back, and in retaliation, he had Rico kidnapped. I have forty-eight hours to get him back. Actually closer to forty now."

"How are you going to do that?"

"Oh, you know, storm the stronghold, guns blazing." Donna laughed a little, even though there was nothing amusing about the way she felt or what they were going to do. "Of course, it's more complicated than that, and we do have some strategy and no actual guns, but that's it in a nutshell."

"We?"

"My team and a team from the wolves. Hey, get this. The alpha of the pack is Rico's *grandmother*. And the next in line is Rico's mother. Alpha-elect, they call it. Can you believe that? Crazy, huh?"

"Mm-hmm."

Donna gasped. "Mary and Joseph. You knew that already."

Another long pause. "I did."

"And you never said anything?"

"It wasn't deemed necessary."

"By who? The mother superior?"

"It's...more complex than that."

Suddenly, Donna wasn't sure she knew everything there was to know about her sister.

Chapter 4

Donna made a face at the phone. "You know that 'it's more complex than that' is the kind of answer that only makes more questions, right?"

"I get that." Cammie sighed. "Listen, even with your team and some wolves, it's a bad idea to storm that stronghold. For one thing, you don't know where it is."

"I've got that handled."

"Okay, let's say you do. You won't be able to see it."

"Working on having that handled." But how did Cammie know that?

"Donna, the fae are deadly. They're killers."

"Technically, so am I. And I am not going to abandon Rico. I understand your concern, but I'm not just Belladonna Barrone, mob wife, anymore. I'm a freakin' vampire, Cammie. I have skills."

"And the fae think you're a delicious snack." She let out a noise that was somewhere between a groan and a sigh. "Look, I need to take care of something right now, but don't do anything until I call you back. Okay?"

"By 'don't do anything,' you mean don't storm the stronghold?"

"Right."

"Okay, but the something you have to take care of better not take too long. Rico's clock is ticking."

"I understand. It won't."

"All right. I'll get a shower while I wait."

"Perfect. I'll call you back as soon as I can. I love you."

"I love you too." Donna hung up, then got out of bed, walked to the bathroom and flipped on the light.

It was shockingly bright, and for the first time since she'd been turned, she looked like a wreck. Mostly because she'd fallen asleep with her makeup on, and there was no magical vampire skill that could overcome that.

"Ugh." She cranked on the shower, pulled her nightgown off, and got under the hot water. She stood there for a long while, just letting it stream over her. Finally, she soaped up with the amazing verbena body wash Charlie had supplied her with.

The smell alone was enough to perk her up. But not so much that she forgot about her conversation with Cammie. How did Cammie know so much, like who was in charge of the wolves? And why hadn't she shared that information before? Might have been nice to know.

Although, it really wouldn't have changed anything. Rico would have still been Agent Medina to Donna right up to the point that he took custody of Joe and his skanky girlfriend, Carmella.

She tipped her head back and washed her hair. Poor Rico. She said another prayer of protection over him. She wasn't sure how well received her prayers were these days, but since the pope-blessed crucifix she'd been wearing when she was turned continued to make her immune to the sun, she liked to think they were still getting through.

She slathered on conditioner, then scrubbed her face as she let that sit. LV had said they could bring a good number of wolves with them. What did that mean? Was a *good number* twenty? Or a hundred? How many wolves were in the New Jersey pack?

Cammie probably knew.

Donna frowned as she washed off the cleanser. Once again, she was behind the eight ball of knowledge because she'd been thrust into this position with virtually no experience and little time to learn. She still couldn't believe that winning the case against Claudette, her negligent sire and the previous vampire governor, had resulted in *her* becoming the new vampire governor of New Jersey.

A final rinse and she was done. She wrapped up in a towel and went into her closet to figure out what to wear to meet with Temo's contact. Instinct said it was best to cover up as much skin as possible, so she went with black jeans, a black turtleneck sweater, and a Gucci belt—because hello, fashion.

She also picked out a slate-gray wool coat that came to midthigh. She added flat boots and decided the only jewelry would be her hidden crucifix and the iron bracelets Charlie said she'd get.

Which hopefully she had.

Donna didn't like the thought of meeting a fae without any iron on her. She kept her makeup simple. Eyeliner, mascara, and a nude lip. This was a clandestine meeting, not a fun night out with the girls.

She tucked her phone in her back pocket, threw her coat over her arm, and walked out into the kitchen.

It was empty.

She hung her coat over one of the chairs and went down to the office. Charlie was at her computer.

She looked up. "I was just wondering if I should wake you. How are you feeling?"

Donna shook her head. "I don't know."

Charlie's brows lifted slightly. "And yet, I completely understand."

Donna held out her arms. "Do you think this is all right for a clandestine meeting with a fae contact?"

Charlie pursed her lips and tilted her head, an act of serious consideration if ever there was one. "It's close. I have just the thing you're missing." She pointed to the console table behind Donna that held the printers. "Look in that box."

Donna turned to find a dove-gray box about the size of a briefcase sitting there. The center of the box was marked with a large gold F and a small e inside of an ornate filigree oval. It looked like the kind of packaging a couturier might use, but she doubted that box held an evening gown. Not with the symbol for iron on the front. "What's this?"

"Open it and see."

Donna pulled the top off. Inside was dark red tissue paper sealed with a gold sticker bearing the same Fe logo. She broke the seal and lifted the tissue. "Well, now. How about that?"

She lifted out the most exquisite merlot-colored leather jacket she'd ever seen. It had some motorcycle-style detailing, but it was longer, almost to midthigh, and had additional elements, like quilting on the shoulders and elbows and several interior and exterior pockets. At least three of the slim exterior pockets were actually sheaths that already contained blades. "I am in deep love with this."

"Good, because that's your armor."

"That explains why it weighs a thousand pounds."

"It won't after you put it on and read the incantation that comes with it."

Donna flicked her gaze to her admin. "Say what now?"

Charlie got up from her desk. "This is a Ferris & Coven custom jacket. It's got iron sandwiched between the leather and the lining in various places. Enough so that you'll be fae-proof. But yes, that makes it heavy. Which is why the company also includes an incantation specific to this jacket that will not only fit it to you, but invoke a spell that reduces the weight by a significant amount."

Donna blinked, a little lost for words. Mouth open, she tried to speak, but the questions in her head got tangled together on the way to her mouth.

Charlie grinned. "Ferris & Coven is a family-owned business. A father and his three daughters, who are all witches. Well, one is…not entirely a witch."

"And they just decided to get into the handmade leather jacket business?"

"He was already in the leather business but mostly catered to bikers. He also dabbled in blacksmithing. Then one of his daughters fell in love with a vampire. And that vampire was killed by the fae." Her grin flipped to a frown. "The rest, as they say, is history."

"Wow."

She nodded. "There should be more in the box. Like a set of bracelets for you to wear when the coat is too much. Or in addition, if you want."

"How did you get all of this done in the time I was asleep?"

Charlie laughed. "This jacket was ordered for you after our first meeting. It's standard-issue for most governors. Claudette took hers when she left. Ferris & Coven always have the bracelets on hand. I just had them add a pair to the delivery, which worked out to be today."

"It's amazing."

"You should visit the shop sometime. If for no other reason than to meet William Ferris and his daughters. He's quite the character. Think Santa, if Santa was hot and rode with the Reapers, but also did charity work and rescued cats as a hobby."

"Okay, yeah, I need to meet him. And the women."

"Ready to get fitted?"

"Sure. Why not? Then I can wear this tonight."

"Perfect."

Donna pulled the coat on, struggling a little under the weight. "Do I need to zip it?"

"Yes. Otherwise, it could end up too tight."

Donna got it zipped. "It's definitely too big. Not terrible, but with the weight..."

"I know." Charlie pointed at the coat. "There should be a slip of paper in the right pocket."

Donna stuck her hand in, found a little card, and looked at it. "Looks like Latin."

"Might be."

"Do I just read it out loud, or is there something else I need to do?"

"Just read it. And don't freak out."

"You mean because it's going to get tighter?"

"Right."

"Okay, here goes." She held the card up. "*Aptus perfectum.*"

For a second, nothing happened. Then warmth spread out from the center of the garment over the chest and down the sleeves, back and front.

It quivered slightly. Then began to contract. The temperature increased too.

Donna tensed. It was an unsettling feeling, as if the coat had come alive and was crawling all over her with tiny, fiery insect feet. She knew that wasn't what was happening, but the sensation remained.

She lifted her chin as if she could stretch away from it, grimacing. "This is very unnerving."

"So I've heard."

The sleeves shortened to the perfect length as the rest of the coat shrank around her. She almost held her breath. "This is going to stop, right? Because if it doesn't…"

"It will," Charlie said.

And then it did.

Donna held still. "Do you think it's done?"

Charlie looked her over. "I can't imagine it fitting any better than it does. How does it feel weightwise?"

Donna shrugged her shoulders, testing the weight. "Like a normal coat. Which is amazing."

"Then I think it's done."

Donna stretched her arms out. "It feels like it was made for me. I guess because it was." She grinned as she smoothed her hands over the leather. "This has to be one of the coolest pieces of clothing I've ever owned. And I wore custom-bedazzled Jimmy Choos on my wedding day. Thank you."

"You're welcome." Charlie put her hands on her hips. "Now I'd say you're ready for that meeting. I can let Temo know if you want, but I didn't think you were leaving this early."

"I'm sure we're not. Unfortunately, that means I have time to call Fitzhugh." She unzipped the coat and took it off for now.

Charlie made a face. "I don't envy you that. Do you know what you're going to tell him?"

Donna sat in her desk chair and planted her feet. "I'm going to stick to the facts. My call is a courtesy to let him know the fae are holding a hostage we're going to liberate, and it's happening in his territory. My plan is to keep it brief. I don't want to talk to him longer than I have to."

"I hear that." She put her hand on the phone. "Why don't you let me get him on the line for you? Keep it all official."

"All right."

Charlie picked up the cordless desk phone and dialed. After a moment, she spoke. "Good evening, this is Charlene Rollins calling on behalf of Governor Barrone. Is Governor Fitzhugh available to speak? Thank you. I'm transferring to Governor Barrone now."

She gave Donna a nod and handed her the phone.

Donna did a big, cleansing exhale before putting the phone to her ear. A second later, Hawke's voice came through. "This is Fitzhugh. Call to apologize?"

She grimaced. That wasn't a good start. She ignored the question and went on with her plan, keeping things professional. "Hello, Governor. I'm calling as a courtesy to let you know the fae have taken a hostage who's important to us. They've got him at their stronghold, and my people are going to rescue him. I thought you should know since this is all happening in your state. I wouldn't want you to hear about it secondhand."

Silence answered her, as if he was surprised that she'd bother. "I...appreciate that. Thank you."

"You're welcome. Have a good night." She cut off the call and handed the phone back to Charlie. "I probably shouldn't have hung up so quickly, but since he opened the conversation by asking if I'd called to apologize, I went with my gut."

"You did what you needed to do. That's all that matters." The security light on the intercom lit up. "Are you expecting anyone? Or a delivery?"

"Nope."

Charlie pressed the button. "This is Charlene. What can I do for you?"

"There's a visitor for the governor." The man's voice was low, like he didn't want anyone else to hear. "A woman who says she's the governor's sister, but she's dressed like a nun."

Brows bent in consternation, Charlie glanced at Donna. "What do you make of that?"

"That my sister has decided to pay me an unexpected visit. And that that we need to put her on the approved-visitors list." She rose from the chair. "Send her up."

Chapter 5

Donna went straight to the door and opened it before the elevator arrived. She leaned on the jamb, watching as the numbers above the doors lit up to show the car's progress.

At last, the doors opened, and Cammie stepped out in her traditional black and white habit. Her eyes brightened when she saw Donna.

"This is a welcome surprise." Donna held her arms out. "It's so nice to see you."

Cammie walked into the embrace and hugged her back. "You too. I hope this is a good time."

"It's always a good time and never a good time, but that's what being governor is all about. Doesn't matter, though. For you, I'll make whatever time you need. Well, as best I can."

As Cammie pulled away, she held on to Donna by the shoulders and looked into her eyes. "I'm glad to hear that, because we have to talk."

"You look and sound very serious."

"I am. Because it is." She smiled. "But it's nothing that can't be managed, I promise."

"That's good to hear. I should tell you I do have to leave in about an hour. I hope that works?"

"More than enough time," Cammie said.

Donna's interest was certainly piqued. She couldn't imagine what Cammie wanted to discuss. "Come on in. Hey, you haven't seen the penthouse yet."

They walked into the space, and Donna spread her arms like a spokesmodel. "What do you think?"

Cammie stared ahead at the wall of windows. Across the Hudson River, Manhattan was twinkling to life as dusk approached. "That's a very impressive view. Seems fitting for a governor."

"The view is definitely amazing. Come on, I'll show you the rest."

Charlie was in the kitchen, fixing a cup of tea. Temo was at the dining table, typing on his phone. He gave them a quick glance, blinked once at Cammie, then put the phone down and got to his feet.

"This is my admin, Charlene Rollins, and my head of security, Temo Danielson. Charlie, Temo, this is my sister, Sister Mary Lazarus Immaculata. Formerly known as Camille, so if you hear me call her Cammie, that's why."

Temo's brow rose slightly as he smiled. "Very nice to meet you, Sister."

Charlie stirred a spoonful of sugar into her tea. "It's a pleasure to meet you."

"You too," Cammie said. "Both of you."

Charlie set the spoon aside. "Would you like some tea? I'd be happy to make you a cup."

"No, I'm fine, thank you."

Charlie picked up her cup. "If you'll excuse me. Work to do. Governor, I'll be in the office if you need me."

Temo edged toward the downstairs steps. "I should go make sure the car is ready. I'll be back in a few, boss."

"Sounds good." Donna was sure Temo had already prepped the car, but her team seemed to understand she needed time alone with her sister. She turned to Cammie and hooked her thumb over her shoulder. "There's a sitting room. We could go in there and talk."

"That sounds perfect."

Once they were in, Donna shut the door and sat across from Cammie. This was the same room where she'd first met Fitzhugh. But this would be a very different conversation. With him it had been all about gaining the upper hand. With Cammie, well, no matter what the topic, no matter how serious, she and Cammie were family. Sisters. Equals. "So, what do you want to talk about?"

Cammie smiled briefly, then her face settled into a grave, no-nonsense expression. "What I'm about to tell you needs to stay between us."

Donna nodded. "Of course."

"Swear on your crucifix."

Donna wriggled the chain and cross out from under her turtleneck so she could hold it in her hand. "I swear to keep secret whatever you're about to share with me."

Cammie relaxed a bit, taking a deep breath. "I didn't go to Nicaragua to work at an orphanage. I went there to clean out a nest of rogue vampires that were preying on nearby villages."

The crucifix fell from Donna's fingers. She stared at her sister. Her hundred-and-thirty-pound, pacifist, married-to-God sister. "It really sounded just now like you said you went to clean out a nest of vampires."

Cammie nodded. "Because that *is* what I said. *Rogue* vampires, actually."

Donna blinked a few times as she processed. "I know you knew about vampires before I did, and you said that the church produces a lot of hunters, but are you telling me that *you* are a...vampire hunter?"

Her smile was terse, but Donna imagined Cammie meant it to be reassuring. "I am. Among other things."

Other things? What else could there be? "But you're also still a nun?"

"Yes. The Sisters of the Holy Rosary is one of many specialized convents around the world that train and deploy hunters wherever they're needed. You also need to keep that to yourself."

"Specialized? I think you're underselling it." Donna sat back and gave herself a little time to process. "This explains how you knew so much more about vampires than I did. But why are you telling me all of this? Especially when it's such secret stuff."

Cammie bent her head for a moment. When she

looked up, there was fear in her eyes. "I'm telling you this so you'll understand the next thing I have to say to you."

Now Donna was worried. "Which is?"

"This...battle you're about to engage in with the fae?" She shook her head. "It can't happen. At least not with you attached to it."

Donna frowned. "It's not up for discussion. I have to do it. Rico needs my help. He's being held hostage because of me."

"The wolves can handle it. Let them."

Donna spread her arms in disbelief that her sister would say such a thing. "Let me repeat. *He's there because of me.*"

"I understand that. But please don't go."

"Camille. You're asking me to abandon a friend. Potentially to his death. That doesn't sound like you. Or at least the you I thought I knew."

Cammie wiped her hand over her mouth. "If you do this, it will probably cause a war. And if that happens, there is a standing kill order for *all* vampires and fae. The order will not allow humans to become collateral damage, which is what would happen if war breaks out."

A little shiver ran down Donna's spine. "I'm your sister. The mother of your beloved niece and nephew. Are you saying you would—"

"*No.* Of course not." Cammie looked toward the river. "But there are plenty of others in the order who would." She glanced down at her hands, folded in her lap. "And I would be helpless to stop them."

Heat built up in Donna's eyes as a knot formed in her throat. Both signs that tears weren't far behind. But then, it wasn't every day that your dear sister told you your death might be imminent. She got up and walked to the windows. Heavy gray clouds blocked the stars. More snow was on the way, it seemed. "I don't know what to say."

"Say you won't go."

"I can't." Donna put her hand on the glass. The cold felt good. She wanted to press her forehead against it.

"Can you at least tell me when you plan on going?"

She put her hands in her pockets and looked over her shoulder. "Why? So you can stop me?"

Cammie stood. "No. So I can try to protect you."

This was a deciding moment. Donna felt it. She'd always trusted Cammie. Always felt safe telling her secrets, never doubted Cammie's love for her. Cammie had been her protector at times. Was Cammie still that same person?

There was only one way to find out. Tell Cammie the truth and then see what she did with the information and what she did to Donna. Defend her? Or betray her?

She turned to face her sister. "Probably tomorrow morning at first light. The fae will be asleep and at their most vulnerable."

"But you can't go out in the…" Realization dawned on Cammie's face. "Except you can, can't you? That's why you asked me about the crucifix and what it might be able to do." She let out a breathy little laugh. "You know, I had that crucifix specifically blessed to protect you *from* vampires."

"It did its job. In a way."

"I suppose." Cammie's eyes narrowed. "So you can daywalk, huh? I don't think you know how rare that is."

"I have an idea. But I would appreciate you keeping that information to yourself. If that's even possible. Considering what you've told me, a little quid pro quo should be in order."

"Donna, I'm not your enemy. But I've been a hunter a lot longer than you've been a vampire. It's been my life. You can't expect me to ignore the training I've been doing since I joined the convent."

"No, I don't suppose I can." She tried to smile, but the result was weak. "I can't believe you didn't tell me you were a hunter sooner."

"I thought about it, but I didn't want to worry you when you were already dealing with so much."

Donna nodded. "Is this a done deal then?"

"I can't stop them from doing what they think is right." Cammie took a breath. "If it makes you feel any better, they won't just target vampires and fae. The order will apply to any supernatural that appears to be a threat to mankind."

"Good to know equality exists among hunters."

Cammie sighed. "I love you. I hope you know how hard this is for me."

"I love you too. I hope when this is over we can move past this."

Cammie nodded. "Me too." She lifted her finger toward the door. "I can see myself out."

Donna nodded. Under any other circumstances, she would have walked her sister out, but for the first time in forever, she needed a moment to think and digest. She dropped onto the couch and hung her head in her hands as a few tears leaked out. Cammie was her rock. How was she supposed to get through the rest of her life knowing that her sister might be ordered to kill her?

A soft knock on the open door was followed by, "Boss?"

Donna wiped the tears off her face as she lifted her head. "Time to go, I guess."

"Not quite," Temo said. "You okay?"

She stood up, keeping her gaze on the windows. "Looks like snow, huh?"

"Boss."

She sighed. "No. I'm not okay. But I'll be fine to do this meeting."

"You want to talk about it?"

She smiled and finally looked at him. "I can't. I've been sworn to secrecy."

He nodded. "I understand. I hope everything will be all right, whatever it is."

"Thanks, but I'm not sure." She swallowed. The knot was still there. "You think you know someone…"

"Your sister isn't who you thought she was?"

"You might say that. She's turned out to be a lot more than I thought she was."

"Does she know how much more you are?"

"Yes." Donna sat down again. "That's part of the problem."

He came in and took the seat across from her. "What convent is she with?"

"Sisters of the Holy Rosary."

"Is there, uh, any chance she's Venari?"

Donna pushed a strand of hair out of her face. "I don't know what that is."

"I don't want to freak you out, but the SHR is a known front for one of the Church's hunter schools. As in vampire hunters."

Donna sat up a little straighter. This was one of those times when it didn't bother her that someone knew more than she did. "Tell me what you know."

"The Venari, an ancient order of nuns and priests, are trained in the art of killing vampires and demons. Actually, pretty much any supernatural that goes rogue and becomes a problem, the Venari are equipped to take down. The SHR is the local chapter. How long has your sister belonged there?"

"Pretty much all her adult life."

"Then she has to know about it. She may just be an ordinary nun, but she has to at least be aware of what really goes on there. And having a sister who's a vampire? That can't be easy for her. All things considered. But maybe I'm way off base here."

"You're not." Donna had sworn not to say a word, but telling Temo he was right didn't seem like a violation of that promise.

"Sorry. This has to be pretty hard for both of you."

"It is. And I can't really say more, but she let me know that if things don't go well with the fae, there could be consequences."

"I'm not surprised. The Venari tend to be about as understanding as the vampire council."

"That's comforting." She ran both hands through her hair, scratching her nails over her scalp. There was work to be done. Whatever happened with Cammie was out of Donna's control. Unless Donna chose to skip the raid. But how could she? Rico's time was running out. "Let me get my coat from the office, and we can go meet your contact. I don't want to be late and screw this up."

"He'll wait. He's very interested in meeting you." Temo got up. "I already pulled the car around."

"Okay." She went to the office and put on her Ferris & Coven coat.

Charlie pointed to it. "The vials you asked for are in the interior breast pocket, and I sent you an email with a link to the banking app you'll need to install to pay this guy if he wants money. The account number's in the second email."

"Thanks, I'll install it in the car."

Charlie frowned. "Everything all right?"

"No." Donna smiled. "But then, what's new?"

Chapter 6

The ride to the bus station took them into an older neighborhood that could have used a couple million for a rehab. But then, maybe *neighborhood* wasn't the right word. Calling it a commercial district might have been closer, since quite a few of the buildings looked like they'd been used for industrial purposes. Those industries were gone now, leaving behind empty warehouses with broken-out windows and brick walls darkened by age and grime.

At least the graffiti added a pop of color.

Temo slowed as they approached the bus station, one of the only brightly lit buildings in the area, along with a bodega, a small neighborhood convenience store, and a liquor store across the street. Proof that there was some residential life here. He did a U-turn at the light and parked near the bodega.

"Is the car going to be okay if we leave it?" She didn't want to risk losing their way out, should things turn bad.

"Should be." Temo unhooked his seat belt. "I'm going to give Alvaro a couple bills to keep an eye on it. He owns the bodega."

"So you've been here before?"

"The bus station is where we usually meet."

"Good. That makes me feel better." She took her seat belt off as well.

He smiled. "Don't worry, boss. I do my homework."

"I know you do. I'm not worried about that."

"Nervous to meet the fae up close?"

She nodded as she took a breath. "Very. Despite everything I've been through in my life, the fae freak me out. I'll be okay, though."

He held out his fist. "I know you will be. You're Belladonna Barrone. And I've got your back."

She laughed softly and bumped her fist against his. "Thanks. I appreciate that."

"Plus, there are two sentries inside the station, according to LV."

"Right. I wonder if we'll be able to tell who they are."

"I guess we'll know when we get in there."

"You lead. I'm ready."

"Then let's do this." They got out. He locked the car, then ran into the bodega to quickly speak to the owner. He came out nodding, indicating that the deal to watch the car had been handled. Together, they headed across the street.

She couldn't shake her nerves. "You think this is going to go all right?"

"I do now, boss. After speaking to my contact, I mean. He seemed eager. And that's not a reaction I've gotten from him before. For some reason, this whole situation is very interesting to him."

"I'm sure he has his motivations."

"I'm sure he does. No idea what they are, but I'd guess they go beyond just what he stands to make by doing this. Maybe we'll find out. Or not. Fae aren't known for being overly chatty about personal things."

"Fine with me." The trash cans outside the bus station were overflowing, and people stood around smoking. "I'm not looking to get chummy with this guy."

"I hear that." Temo pulled the door open for her.

Inside, the bus station retained all the trappings of the year it had been built, which was probably in the late '70s based on the abundance of avocado green. The yellow-tinged lighting didn't help, highlighting the years of wear evident on the hard plastic seats and dingy linoleum floor.

Didn't seem to be keeping anyone away, however. More people filled the station than she'd expected, but then, last time she'd traveled by bus, she'd been in college and trying to get home for the weekend.

Some people sat, while others stood looking at the arrival and departure boards. A few browsed the selections at the newsstand. Most had a weary air about them. As if they'd rather be anywhere but here. She understood that. She studied the ones who appeared to be paired off, trying to discern any wolfy traits in them.

But they all seemed human to her. Maybe that was her inexperience showing. Or maybe werewolves were really good at blending in when they needed to. She wondered if, in a less-crowded situation, she'd be able to pick them up by their scent. Right now, all she smelled was cleaning fluid, body odor, and smoke.

"This way," Temo said.

She kept up with him as he threaded through the small crowd and took them to the far side of the station, where banks of lockers stood in little alcoves. An overhead grate diffused the light. He went a little farther until they were in another section of lockers marked with a sign that said Long-Term. One of the lockers had a missing door, and another had a hole where the lock should have been.

This alcove had lockers on three sides and a single row of the same hard plastic, avocado-green seats in the middle. On the other side was a sign for the restrooms.

A man rose from the seats as they entered. He was lean and tall enough that his long coat must have been custom made, since it reached nearly to his ankles. A wool newsboy cap was pulled low over his eyes, and a thick scarf swathed his neck, but none of that could hide the dusky skin or angular ears that peeked out.

She couldn't see his back, but she wondered if the outline of his wings was visible through the fabric of his coat, or if it was as specially made as hers was.

Temo nodded at him. "Sorry if you had to wait."

The man's nostrils flared as he inhaled deeply. His nose wrinkled a second later. Had he smelled the iron embedded in Donna's coat or the bracelets she'd slipped on? "I haven't been here long."

Temo kept himself slightly between Donna and the fae as he spoke. "Governor, this is Ishalan."

The fae's eyes narrowed, and he smiled without opening his mouth, which made the skin over his sharp cheekbones wrinkle. "Governor. What a pleasure."

Donna couldn't bring herself to smile. Not yet. "Ishalan. It's kind of you to help us." Although she knew kindness had little to do with it. But it wouldn't hurt to give him the benefit of the doubt.

His smile broadened with amusement, and he chuckled. "I believe we both understand that if I help you it has nothing to do with what can only be described as the weakest of human emotions."

"Yes, we do." She didn't like him already. Being kind did *not* make a person weak. In fact, it took great strength to care about others. It required a person to think about more than themselves. But then again, he was fae. Was the word *kindness* even in their vocabulary? "What do you want to make this deal happen?"

"You realize what a dear thing you ask of me."

"Your blood is dear? Then what is my blood?"

Temo bristled, shifting into a much more protective stance. She was sure he didn't like the direction this was going, but Donna had to let this fae know she wasn't a soft target. That was something she'd learned from life in the Villachi family. Soft targets got hit first.

Ishalan's tight-lipped smile turned bitter at having his words turned around. "Fae blood is much more powerful, Governor."

"Maybe it is. Maybe it isn't." She shrugged like the whole matter was quickly losing its importance. "If you aren't interested in making this deal…"

Ishalan dropped his patronizing smile. "I'm only saying that I expect you to understand that the compensation must be equivalent."

So much buildup. His ask was going to be big. She could feel it. The mob often worked the same way. "Why don't you tell me what you want, and we can discuss it? How can I say yes or no when I don't know what you're asking?"

"Very true." He looked at Temo, who'd relaxed slightly. "She is as smart and direct as you said she'd be." His attention came back to her. "There are two things I desire."

"And they are?"

"I am in need of funds. As I'm sure Temo told you, I have been cast out." He held his hands up. "For the unforgivable sin of disagreeing with so much of what my brethren do. But being on my own is hard. Some financial help would make that easier."

What was Rico's life worth to her? There was really no amount too high, but the negotiation had to be done properly, or the fae would believe he had the upper hand. "What figure do you have in mind?"

"Perhaps you'd like to offer what you think is best."

She hesitated as if she hadn't given this any thought. "Ten thousand."

He hissed. "Do you think I am a charity?"

"Hey," Temo said. "That's good money for someone with no skin in the game."

"Said like a man who knows where his next meal is coming from," Ishalan snapped.

Donna didn't believe Ishalan was destitute. His clothes didn't bear that up. Even his shoes looked new. And expensive. After being married to Joe, she knew men's shoes. This was just a game to the fae. "What's your counteroffer?"

The fae scrubbed a hand over his chin like he was thinking. "Fifty thousand. In cash."

She shook her head. "Twenty-five, and we don't have time for cash. I need the blood right now. If you can't accept a direct deposit, then we'll go talk to the next fae on our list."

Ishalan groused under his breath. "Fine. I'll take the deposit. But since I am forced to compromise, I can't accept less than forty."

Donna looked at Temo, thankful he was smart enough to play along. "Your other contact didn't even bring up money, did he?"

Temo barely moved. "Nope."

Ishalan grunted. "Twenty-five is not enough."

"Thirty, and I'm done negotiating the number."

The fae frowned but nodded. "I accept. But I now want two more things from you instead of one more."

She crossed her arms over her chest. Gently. The vials were glass, and she could feel them through the leather. "What else?"

"I want to go with you when you raid the stronghold."

"I'll think about it." But at first blush, that seemed like a bad idea. "What's the second thing?"

"I want a favor from you that I may call in at a later date. A future favor, it you will." He smiled, revealing a mouth full of pointed teeth.

Donna didn't like that. He could ask anything of her. At any time. She shook her head. "Too open-ended."

"I promise it will not be anything you'd find distasteful. But you are asking me to betray my kind. Giving you my blood could get me killed."

"And you're asking me to trust you, the fae willingly doing that betraying." It *was* a precarious position to put him in. But he could have said no. "I'm not forcing you to do anything. And I'm paying you a considerable sum."

"I realize that. But let's be honest. Time is of the essence, is it not? Besides, you'd be hard-pressed to come by what I'm offering anywhere else."

Was he calling her bluff about the other volunteer? "I'll need seven vials from you."

"Seven?" The word screeched out of him, turning

heads in the main waiting room. "You ask too much, vampire."

"Five, then. And you'll have your favor and your money."

"Three, and I'll still have my favor, my money, *and* my place at the raid."

She stared at him long and hard with the kind of stony face she knew Big Tony had used when he wanted the person across from him to question their decisions. The longer she stared, the more Ishalan's look of fierce determination faded.

When he spoke again, there was a softer tone to his voice. "I am not your enemy, Governor."

That's exactly what he was, but she said nothing and continued to stare. Finally, she spoke. "Temo, text your other contact. Tell him we're on our way."

Temo pulled out his phone. "You got it, boss."

Ishalan sighed in harsh frustration. "Four vials. But I want all three things."

"Four, and you'll have your money and your favor with my right to deny that favor if it would cause me trouble. As for including you in the raid, why should I allow that? I don't know you, and I certainly don't trust you. This deal doesn't make us friends or allies."

"I swear to you that if you allow me to come, I will not get in your way or do anything that could hamper the rescue of your friend." Such earnestness in his words. "In fact, anything I do will only be to your benefit."

"Why should I believe that?"

"Because…" He hesitated, shaking his head and looking away. "I would not lie about this."

"I don't know that. I need a reason to trust you. Something more than promises and platitudes."

"I know things. Things that could be very useful. I know the layout of the stronghold. I can take you straight to where they're holding your friend."

"That would be useful, if I needed that kind of help. But I don't, and it's still not a reason to trust you."

Temo put his phone away. "She's right. You want the vampire governor to trust you? You need to be upfront now. Tell her the truth about why you're willing to go against your own kind. I've been dealing with you for years, and I still don't know."

Ishalan let out a whistling sigh. "Dredward is a terrible king."

Donna uncrossed her arms. They were getting nowhere. "He seems equivalent to the beings he rules."

Ishalan frowned, pulling the skin taut over his knife-edged chin. "It's true. The fae are a harsh breed. But Dredward only encourages that."

She leaned in slightly. "Harsh? The fae hunt down my kind indiscriminately and drain us of our blood. And you're asking me, a vampire, to trust you, a fae, without any concrete reason beyond King Dredward sucks. I already knew that."

He lifted his cap to rake his long, slender fingers through his shaggy hair. "You have to take my word. I am…on your side."

"Why? Tell me now, or we're leaving."

A muscle in his jaw ticked, and he shifted as though he was in pain. "Because. Dredward is my brother."

Chapter 7

Donna hadn't been expecting that. From the look on Temo's face, neither had he.

Ishalan leaned closer. "You understand now?"

She nodded. "I think so. Your own brother cast you out."

"Yes. Well, no." Another sigh. "I left because he tried to kill me. Any threat gets eliminated, but then, you already knew that."

Did she? "I suppose I did."

"Well, you're harboring the dhamfir. Why else would you give her sanctuary?"

"Because she's a child, half vampire, and the fae were searching for her with the intention of returning her to a life of servitude. Hunting my kind. What other reason is there?"

Ishalan's slim brows rose as his mouth pursed in a sort of cat-with-the-canary expression. "You don't know."

"Know what?"

"Just that...Dredward wants her dead."

"Of course I know that." She also knew he was

lying. He'd suddenly decided not to tell them whatever he'd been about to share. So what was it? Did she really care? This didn't feel like the time to call him out on that. Not with Rico's time ticking away. She pulled four vials from her interior coat pocket and held them out. "Fill these, and I'll have your money deposited."

He took the vials and glanced at the sign for the men's washroom.

"No," she said. "Here. Where I can watch you."

"You don't trust me."

"I believe we already established that."

"I don't fault you for that distrust."

"I'll sleep better at night knowing that."

Temo snorted.

Ishalan sat down, uncapped the first vial, then put his finger to his mouth and nipped the skin with his jagged teeth. Blood welled up. It was nearly purple, and the rich, metallic scent was so powerful Donna's fangs descended like the dinner bell had been rung. What would fae blood taste like? What would it do to her? Had any vampire tried it? They must have. Seemed only fair since the fae drank of them with abandon.

Whoa. She was spiraling into a deep hunger way too fast. Enough.

She swallowed the saliva pooling in her mouth and turned slightly to face Temo more. He kept his eyes on Ishalan, as if understanding the battle Donna was fighting. He probably did know. He'd been around vampires long enough.

Seconds ticked into minutes, but before much longer, the vials were filled. Ishalan stayed seated as he held them out, sucking on his fingertip.

Temo took them, saving her from feeling the warmth of the blood through the glass.

Ishalan took his finger from his mouth and inspected it. There wasn't a trace of the puncture. So the fae healed like vampires did. Interesting. He looked at her, his brows disappearing beneath his cap. "My money?"

Donna nodded. "Right." She pulled her phone out and opened up the banking app Charlie'd had her install, which Donna had done on the ride here. She logged in and clicked on the link to transfer money. "Your account number?"

Ishalan rattled it off. She plugged it in, set the amount, and hit send. "Done."

Still seated, he took his phone out and checked things on his end. A few seconds passed before he nodded. "It's arrived. Thank you."

She looked at him a little closer. He was pale and a little listless. "Temo, go to the newsstand and get Ishalan some juice and some cookies."

"On it." He left them alone, but Donna wasn't worried about her safety with the fae any longer.

"That is...*kind* of you," Ishalan said.

"I'm glad such a display of weakness doesn't bother you."

He smiled without any malice, shifting his gaze to look at her without moving his head. "You're the most interesting vampire I've ever met."

"Have you met many?"

"Enough." He finally lifted his chin. "You're not afraid of me, are you?"

"Not until I have a reason to be."

Temo returned with a plastic bottle of orange juice and a bag of chocolate chip cookies. He handed them to Ishalan, who took both but ignored the cookies to drink half the bottle in one long gulp. His color returned almost instantly. Apparently, even the fae needed a little something after giving blood.

He opened the bag of cookies and dumped half of them into his mouth. His sharp teeth must have pulverized them, because a second later he swallowed, then drank the rest of the juice. He stood and tossed the empty bottle into a nearby trash can. "You don't like me, but you helped me."

"Is that a question or an observation?" Donna asked.

He looked at Temo. "Your boss is a strange one. But I like her."

"So do I," Temo answered.

Ishalan shifted his gaze to Donna. "Will you allow me to join you for the raid?"

"Yes." Better to have him there with her than have him there on his own, feeling like he could do whatever he wanted without repercussions. Also, it would be incredibly helpful to have an actual guide inside the stronghold. Rixaline had only been there as a prisoner. Ishalan had been free-roaming.

He nodded. "Thank you."

"You're not desperate to come because you want to kill the king, are you?"

His eyes narrowed slightly. "Whatever would give you that idea? That would start a war."

Yes, it would. Cammie had already told her that. But Donna didn't know how much she trusted Ishalan's words. "Temo will text you the details." She shot him a glance. "We should go."

Temo jerked his chin at the fae. "Later, Ish."

With a grunt, Ishalan turned and disappeared into thin air in about three steps.

"Well, that's interesting," Donna said. "I didn't know fae could do that."

"They can't. Not all of them. It's like how vampires sometimes develop secondary gifts after they've been turned for a bit. But that disappearing thing only lasts for a short while. Long enough for him to get outside, I'd say. But as party tricks go, it's pretty good."

"I'd say. I wouldn't mind being able to do that myself."

They headed for the car.

"Does your friend Alvaro sell anything good to eat in that bodega? I'm hungry all of a sudden."

Temo grinned. "You ever have a chimichurri burger?"

"Can't say that I have."

"Prepare to have your mind blown."

Three burgers and two beers later, Temo (who'd eaten two of the three burgers) and Donna were back in the car. Thanks to their metabolisms, the beers had no more impact than a soda, but Temo had insisted they were the best thing to drink with the spicy and very delicious burgers. He'd been right too.

He turned the SUV toward the Wellman Towers. Even with the burgers, the whole thing had taken less than an hour. "Can I ask you something, boss?"

"Sure."

"Why four vials of blood when Jerabeth only needs three?"

"Because I could." She laughed softly. "I just figured it might be good to have backup. And when are we going to get access to fae blood again? I mean, in a situation where we can easily collect it. Why? Do you think I pushed too much?"

"No. I think it was very smart." He glanced at her. "You're pretty good with the negotiating. Not just with the money, but asking for five and all that. I gotta be honest, I thought you started too low with the money, but you really handled it. And now he knows better than to try to get over on you. I'm learning some things. I like it."

"I guess being married to the mob for so long wasn't a complete waste." The lights of the city were beautiful beyond the river.

"Is that how your husband did business?"

"Almost all the time. Ask for more than you want but expect less." She snorted. "Not that Joe or Big Tony usually got less. Most people didn't have the plums to stand up to those two." Herself included. How she'd changed.

"You're going to get that same kind of reputation. But in a good way. Because you're fair."

She smiled. "Thanks."

"I know going into that meeting with Ishalan that you were scared, but it didn't show. You're good at that too. Same thing when we paid the Russians a visit. I admire your ability to compartmentalize like that. Not everyone can do it. It's the trait of a warrior."

His kind words filled her with pride. "I don't know if I'm a warrior, but I just remembered what I was there for. *Who* I was there for. That helped me a lot. So did having you at my side. Hard things are always easier when you don't have to face them alone."

"Very true." He stopped in front of the Wellman Towers lobby doors, then reached into his jacket and retrieved the four vials to give to her. "See you upstairs in a while. I need to go gas up."

She took them with a nod and stuck them in her pocket. "Thanks. Be safe."

"Always." He waited until she was inside before he pulled away.

She walked to the penthouse elevator. Beside her, at the main elevator, stood a very large man. He was young and attractive, despite the amount of sweat covering him. He looked like he'd just come in from a run, based on how he was dressed. Somehow, the only smell coming off him was a hint of citrusy aftershave.

He glanced at her, then at the elevator she was standing in front of. "You must be the new governor."

No alarms went off in her head, but it was odd to be recognized when she didn't have a clue who he was. But then, most people in the building had to know a new resident had moved into the governor's penthouse. He wasn't a vampire, though. She knew that much. She kept her face blank. "I am."

"Congrats on the job."

"Thanks." His elevator doors opened first, then hers arrived a second later.

They each stepped onto their respective cars, and that was that. She arrived at the penthouse seconds later, still wondering who he was. And what kind of creature he might be, since Artemis had told her pretty much everyone who lived in the building was some variety of supernatural.

The other thing that stuck in her head was how long it had been since she'd had any exercise. Running, especially, which had once been her go-to stress-burner.

She walked into the penthouse, her mind working. Charlie and Rixaline were in the living room, watching a movie and eating a giant plate of very gooey nachos. Lucky was lounging next to Rixaline. The nachos seemed to be all Rixaline's. So was the movie. Charlie had a cup of tea on the coffee table next to a half-eaten blueberry muffin the size of a softball, and she was typing away on her phone.

Lucky meowed when he saw Donna. "Hi, big man. Still working, Charlie?"

She looked up. "Just answering an email. Which reminds me, some flowers came for you. They're on the kitchen counter." She got off the couch and came around to Donna's side. "How'd it go?"

Donna pulled the vials out of her pocket. "Mission accomplished."

"Four, huh?" Charlie smiled. "Way to go, boss."

"Let's call it a backup. Or future insurance."

"Either way, good to have." She took the vials. "Jerabeth's hanging out downstairs, waiting. I'll get these to her immediately."

"Good. Hopefully, she can do what she needs to do in time."

"She will."

"Who are the flowers from?"

"I don't know. The card is sealed."

"Okay, I'll have a look in a second. There's a gym on the second floor, right?"

"Yes. And an indoor pool, a big Jacuzzi, a steam room, and a sauna. There's a pair of racquetball courts too. But the pool is really great. It's not just this big rectangle. They designed it to feel like you're at a resort. I'm always surprised it doesn't get used more, but most of the time you have it all to yourself."

Donna had been planning to hit the gym and put some serious miles on one of the treadmills, but after hearing about the pool, she changed her mind. "You know what? I'm going to check it out. A swim might do me good. I feel like I have all this nervous energy that has no place to go right now. That might be just the thing. Unless I'm needed here?"

"We're kind of on hold until Jerabeth works out this spell, so go enjoy! There are pool towels down there, but we have some beach towels in the hall linen closet too. Pierce is sleeping, but I could wake him up if you want company."

"No, let him sleep. We all need to prepare for tomorrow as best we can."

Donna went into the kitchen to see who'd sent her flowers. They were beautiful. White roses, pale pink hydrangeas, branches laden with red bittersweet berries, and lots of greenery. She plucked out the card and opened it. Blank.

That was odd. Had the florist forgotten to fill it out? She looked at the name of the shop on the envelope. It was local. Maybe Charlie could call them in the morning and see if they could correct the error. She leaned in to smell one of the roses, although she didn't really need to lean. The bouquet was huge, just begging to be inhaled.

The flower's perfume was incredibly strong. Interesting, too, with a spicy undertone. Maybe from the bittersweet. Her nose twitched like a sneeze was pending. She wiggled it and sniffed hard to get rid of the sensation. That seemed to do the trick.

She left the bouquet on the counter so she'd remember to ask Charlie about calling the florist and went to her room to see what she had in the way of swimsuits. Not much, she was afraid, but there was one suit that ought to fit.

She'd bought it a few summers back for a long girls' weekend to the Jersey Shore. All of the mob wives had rented a big house for the getaway. It wasn't something Donna had wanted to do. She hadn't liked being around most of the other wives. It had always turned into a big competition over who had the most expensive purse or the best nails or the newest designer whatever.

And then there was the husband talk. Big Tony's wife and Donna's sister-in-law, Lucinda, never went. Which was a blessing, but it made Donna the next most influential wife there. Really, it was a blessing *and* a curse. Some of the wives treated her like she held the keys to the kingdom. But others acted like it was their job to take her down a peg and remind her that their husbands could just as easily take Joe's place.

Wasn't true. Joe was Lucinda's brother, meaning Joe's spot in the Villachi family was set in concrete. But that didn't stop the jealousy or one-upmanship.

Because of that, Donna had to show up on point. Joe would have had a fit if she'd done otherwise, as it would have made him look bad. Like he wasn't doing well enough for his wife to be at her best for the trip. That meant new threads, hair and nails done, everything waxed and tightened and plucked to perfection.

The shopping trip beforehand was exhausting enough, but then to spend four whole days and nights with those women? There wasn't a vineyard in the world that made a strong enough wine. And on those trips, they drank enough to know.

All that drinking led to some pretty interesting evenings. After they spent a day in the sun by the pool or on the beach, knocking back a significant amount of vino tended to exacerbate the women's natural state beyond what the usual wine with dinner might do. The mopey ones turned sullen. The cranky ones got mean. The bubbly ones danced topless on the pool table. Or sang dreadful karaoke. Also sometimes topless.

Inevitably, things were said, tears were shed, and fights broke out. All of it exhausting and stressful and the opposite of what a vacation should be.

The only upsides were the new clothes and accessories. Now, she peered up at the top shelf of her closet for the boxes marked Summer Clothes. When she'd moved here, she'd sorted through most of her clothes, but a lot of the summer stuff she'd just dumped into those two boxes to be dealt with later.

There were two boxes the suit could be in. She got the stepstool out and took them both down, then put them on her bed to dig through.

She found the suit in question at the bottom of the second box. It seemed in good condition. What there was of it. For a one-piece, it was surprisingly low on fabric. High on gold hardware, however, in typical Versace style.

She'd chosen Versace because if there was ever a designer who knew how to dress a mob wife, he was the one. She'd paired the strappy black suit with Versace's Grecian slides and billowing black chiffon coverup and big straw hat trimmed in black.

It had been an absolute winner as far as the wives were concerned. Total fail when it came to not spending every upright moment sucking in her stomach so it didn't pooch out between the straps.

Not to mention the weird tan lines all that criss-crossed fabric had left her with.

But the pool she was headed to now was indoors, and all that mattered was that she had a suit. The upside of this suit was that it was extremely secure. Or at least it had been that first time she'd worn it. Her new vampire self was a little smaller.

She undressed and got into the suit, which took a minute because she accidentally put her left arm through the straps that crossed over the shoulder and her right leg though an open space on the left part of the torso. Honestly, the suit needed an instruction manual.

When she had it situated, she went to take a look in the mirror.

Okay, the suit was still hot. She looked pretty decent in it too. Might have been better when she'd filled it out a little more, but at least now she didn't have to suck in her stomach.

One more perk to being a middle-aged vampire. And with the way things were going, she'd take every perk she could get.

Chapter 8

Hair in a clip and dressed in her Versace suit, her bathrobe, and a pair of flip-flops, she hopped in the elevator and pressed two for the pool level. Her phone was in the pocket of the bathrobe, and she'd told Charlie not to hesitate to call.

Donna was going to the pool to work off some stress, but if things blew up, she wanted to know. In fact, if she was needed for any reason, good or bad, she wanted to know. Burning off stress came in a distant second to anything that might move them closer to freeing Rico.

Just thinking about him in that cell made her stomach knot and her body tense. The physical reaction was so strong she worried that being so on edge might cause her to do something stupid during the raid. One wrong move, one mistake, and things could take a desperately bad turn.

If she was the reason for that, she'd never be able to live with herself. Just thinking about it was almost enough to make her weepy. She sniffed, surprised at how hard the new mood had hit her.

The doors opened, and the tang of chlorine greeted her. The smell took her back to some of her early memories of childhood, back when her dad had still been around. They'd had enough money to belong to the country club then, mostly because that's where her father did a lot of business and it was a write-off.

But her mother had taken her and Cammie there to swim. The pool was a good babysitter, and her mother liked the appearance of going to the country club.

Bygones. And not worth thinking about anymore. It had been ages since the memory had crossed her mind anyway.

She stepped off the elevator, inhaling the warm, damp air that permeated the small lobby. To the left was the entrance to the exercise facilities. Straight ahead were men's and women's locker rooms, and to the right was a set of frosted glass doors with the word Pool on them in letters so large only two fit on each door.

She pulled one open and went in. It had to be ten degrees warmer in here than the penthouse. Considering it was about to snow outside, that was a good thing.

The floor-to-ceiling windows were steamed up, making the world outside seem farther away than usual. The lights of Manhattan, crisp and clear from the penthouse, were just blurry spots of brightness here.

Charlie had been on target when she'd said the pool had been designed with a resort feeling. While the main pool area was big enough for swimming laps, there was also a sort of lazy-river part that wound off it, disappearing into a jungle of tropical plants, palms, and rocky grottos with gentle waterfalls. She couldn't see it all, but the river reconnected at the other end and seemed to be driven by jets, because it definitely had a current.

Soft spalike music accompanied by nature sounds, mostly birds chirping, or maybe they were frogs, played in the background. With the gurgling of the water, it was just the right level of white noise.

Soft lighting around the seating areas and in the pool itself gave the entire space a soft, underwater glow. The place was spectacular.

How was there no one else here? Once things calmed down, she could see herself spending a lot of time here. Whoever had designed this had obviously done so with the UV-sensitive paranormal in mind, because it felt like a tropical oasis.

Her kids would love this.

She took a towel from the stand, then walked around to the far side, where she found a chaise closer to the pool steps. She claimed it with her towel and phone, then toed off her flip-flops before going to test the water.

No point in taking off her robe until she knew if she was actually going in.

She swished her toes through the water and was pleasantly surprised at the temperature. Warm enough to be inviting but not a hot tub either. Props to whoever was in charge of that. No one wanted to get into a cold pool with flurries about to come down outside.

She draped her robe over the back of the chaise and returned to the water's edge. Now that she didn't necessarily need to breathe, it might be interesting to see if she could make it all the way across underwater just swimming at a normal human speed.

She took a breath and dove.

The water was glorious. She loved the feel of it, the buoyancy, the warmth, the way her body slid through it. She kept her hands out in front of her until she started to slow, then swam froggy-style the rest of the way.

She touched the wall a few seconds later and came up for air. She'd made it across and ended up at the entrance to the lazy river. A short stack of tubes sat nearby, but she decided to try floating on her own.

Flipping onto her back, she went feet-first into the opening, then let the current take her. There were definitely jets. She could see them spaced evenly enough to keep her moving. She steered with her hands, occasionally pushing off the wall with her foot if she got too close.

The surroundings really did seem like an oasis. All kinds of well-manicured plants and flowers decorated the banks of the river. She passed under a rock arch that had a couple of orchids growing off it.

Farther along, she came to one of the waterfall grottos, but she didn't go in. Looked like a cool place to hang out, but she wanted to see the whole thing, then swim some laps and get back to the penthouse.

She'd just started to make the bend when she heard a splash. Not a big one, but enough that she knew she wasn't alone anymore. She wondered who'd shown up. Pierce maybe. She turned onto her stomach and swam toward the end of the river.

She stopped before she got dumped out into the pool. She didn't see anyone for a moment, then realized that was because whoever had dived in was underwater, swimming across the pool just like she'd done.

He surfaced a few seconds later, turned to take the next lap, and caught sight of her. Not Pierce. "Governor."

She was so busy staring at his body that it took her a second to recognize that her company was the same man she'd seen in the lobby. The one who'd just come back from a run.

The one who looked like he'd been chiseled from a block of fine Italian marble. She swallowed, realized she was staring, lifted her gaze, and nodded. "Hi."

Wow. He was...wow. The kind of hot that made her gums ache. Also parts lower. That was new. The gums, not the lower bits. She was forty-nine, not frozen.

He smiled, which filled her stomach with butterflies. "I guess we both had the same idea."

"I guess so." His gaze dipped briefly, reminding her of the suit she had on. She sucked in her stomach, then remembered she didn't need to do that anymore and relaxed. Human habits died hard. "I've never been here before, but seeing you in the lobby made me realize it had been a while since I'd been out for a run, but then my admin suggested I check out the pool, and here I am."

Why was she rambling? She didn't ramble. She'd almost giggled, too, which *really* wasn't like her. Her head felt a little odd on top of it. Kind of thick and floaty.

"Fortunately, there's plenty of room for both of us to do that."

"It's a big pool." Mary and Joseph, she couldn't stop staring. How did a man end up looking like that? She needed to stop ogling his body, or he was going to think she was a creeper. And not just because he was probably half her age. "I'm Donna, by the way."

"I'm Kace. I live two floors up from this one."

"Nice to meet you, neighbor." Now she was flirting. Was she turning into a cougar? "I live in the penthouse."

"I know."

"Of course you do." She laughed, even though it wasn't that funny. What was going on with her? Why was she acting like this?

His gaze shifted again, and he gave her a little nod. "Nice suit."

"Thanks." She licked her bottom lip and took a few steps from the river into the pool. "Is it impolite to ask what you are? I know there aren't many humans who live in this building, so..." She shrugged. He was definitely no mere mortal.

He chuckled, stretching one arm out to lean on the side of the pool. Was he showing off for her sake? Who cared? She'd take it. His arm had more muscles than her entire body. "I'm an FTS."

"Sorry, I'm pretty new to all this. I have no idea what that means."

"Right, I heard that about you. You've been a vampire what, like two weeks?"

"Something like that. So what's an FTS?"

"Fairy-tale shifter. It's slang for those of us who shift into things that aren't considered real by humans. Dragons, griffons, basilisks, mermaids, yetis—"

"Wouldn't vampires fall into that category?"

Still smiling, he shook his head. "You'd be surprised how many humans believe vampires are real. No, FTS are generally considered more mythological than just made up. It's a fine line, I suppose."

"So which one are you?" Somehow, she was another foot closer.

"Gargoyle."

"Really? Wow." Oh boy. Now she wanted to touch him. "I never would have guessed that was a thing. Not that you're a thing." A hot thing, maybe. Okay, what was going on with her? "You know what I mean."

"I do."

A soft chirping that wasn't a bird or a tree frog caught her attention. Her phone. Someone had terrible timing. She pointed toward the chaise where her stuff was. "That's my cell, and I need to get that. Plus, you probably want to swim laps. Nice meeting you."

"You, too, Governor Barrone."

She dove under and swam for the other side but still reached her phone too late to get the call. She stood there, dripping, trying not to get water on the phone as she checked to see whose call she'd missed. Charlie.

That couldn't be good. She hit the call-back button and put the phone to her ear, glancing at Kace to see how his laps were going.

"Governor?"

"Yep. Sorry, I couldn't get to the phone in time."

"I hate to cut your swim short, but you should probably come back to the penthouse."

Donna tensed, anticipating the reason. "What's going on?"

"It's nothing too terrible. But if you could return at your earliest convenience, that would be great."

She grabbed her towel and dried herself off as best she could while still on the phone. "What aren't you telling me? And why aren't you telling me?"

"Because it might be nothing."

"Charlie."

"Do you mind telling me whose name was on the card that came with the flowers?"

"The card was blank. In fact, I was going to ask you to call the shop that sent them and see if they could give us that info."

"Did you smell the flowers?"

"Yes. They smell amazing. I don't see what that has to do with anything."

Donna could hear her talking to someone else. "Yes, she smelled the flowers." That person answered Charlie, but with the music and the water, not even her vampire hearing could make out the words.

Then Charlie's long, unsettled exhale filled the phone, followed by much more urgent words. "You need to come back now."

Donna stuck her feet into her flip-flops, then pulled on one arm of her robe. "I'm coming, but what is going on?"

"Jerabeth came up to get a sample of Rixaline's blood for comparison and noticed the flowers on the counter. She leaned in to smell them, and long story short, she thinks they may have been used to drug you in some capacity."

Donna switched the phone to her other ear so she could get the rest of herself into the robe. "That's crazy. I feel fine. I feel great, actually. Super great."

"It may not have hit you yet. Wait, did you just say 'super great'?"

"Yeah, so?" Donna picked up her towel to put it in the used-towel bin, facing the pool as she went. Kace was at the wall again, about to make a turn. He smiled at her.

"That doesn't sound like you, that's all."

Donna smiled back, giving him a wink. Maybe she should invite him to…whoa. A cold chill swept through her. *A wink?* That wasn't her style. Neither was all this flirting or thinking about her childhood, and what was that lingering feeling of fluffy headedness? "You know what? I think it might have hit me after all. Something has. Whatever. I'm on my way."

CHAPTER 9

Donna couldn't get back to the penthouse fast enough. She practically ran into the kitchen.

Charlie was on the phone. "Yes, ma'am, thank you. I very much appreciate your help. Good night."

She hung up and shook her head. "That was Miriam Pasternak, owner of Beautiful Buds, where the flowers came from. Fortunately, the shop doesn't close until eight, so I was able to get her. She said the order came in over the internet, and it specified that a blank card was to be included."

"Why would someone do that?"

"Probably to make the flower delivery look less suspicious. If those flowers had come without a card, I definitely would have wondered about them. Probably would have questioned security about who delivered them. Instead, I assumed the shop forgot to sign the card, and then I brought them into the penthouse and told you about them without a second thought."

"So the blank card got them through the door. That was a smart move."

"It was." She frowned. "How are you feeling, by the way?"

"Pretty much fine, except it seems all of my emotions have been cranked up to eleven. I got weepy in the elevator on the way down to the pool, then I had flashbacks of my childhood just because of the smell of chlorine, then I...may have flirted with a very handsome man who came to swim." Donna pinched the bridge of her nose. "Calling him a man makes it sound okay, but I'm pretty sure he was half my age. Mary and Joseph, he was hot."

Charlie snorted. "Did you get a name?"

"Kace. He's a gargoyle. Lives two floors above the pool." Donna groaned as she continued to pinch the bridge of her nose and hide behind her hand. "I winked at him, Charlie. *Winked.*"

A little laugh answered her. "He's not half your age. He's thirty-seven, and he is definitely hot."

Donna looked up. "Single?" She squeezed her eyes shut. "Don't answer that. I don't care." Except she did. Or at least the drugs were making her think she did.

"As far as I know, yes. But look, we need to get you tested. If this is some trick by the fae, which we suspect it is, then we need to find an antidote."

"How would drugging me like this benefit them? Do they think if I'm super emotional that I'll suddenly give in to their demands?"

"Maybe. Or maybe they're anticipating your rescue attempt and think this will throw you off your game."

"It could. I can't trust my reactions right now."

Rixaline left her movie to join them. "There's a third possibility."

Donna looked at her, eager for any insight the girl might have. "What's that?"

"I'm guessing you didn't respond to the video they sent?"

"No," Donna said. "I haven't."

"I'm sure King Dredward didn't like that. He's used to people asking how high when he says jump. If the fae did drug you with those flowers, it could be…well…" She chewed on one of her fingernails.

"Just say it. You're not going to get into trouble. You know that."

Rixaline nodded. "It just that…they might have used something very poisonous. Something deadly. And they might not give you the antidote until you turn me over." She sniffed. "I don't want you to be sick."

Donna gave the girl a reassuring smile. "They aren't the only ones with smart people on their side. We have Jerabeth. She'll figure it out. I'm certainly not going to give you to them, even if they're trying to make me sick."

"But what if she can't figure it out? What if getting the cure from the fae is the only solution?"

Donna reached out and grabbed her hand. "Hey, you don't have to worry about me. There's only going to be one winner in this battle. And it's not going to be King Dredward. You have my word on that. Now, you just go watch your show, and don't worry about it, okay?"

"Okay." Rixaline went back to the living room, where she picked Lucky up and cradled him against her chest.

Donna softened her voice as she spoke to her admin, despite the intense anger welling up inside her. "I'm going to burn that stronghold to the ground. The fae are a menace. They deserve to be eradicated. I hope I get to kill Dredward myself."

Charlie's eyes narrowed. "I don't know if that's you, or you on drugs."

Donna blew out a breath. "If the rage I'm feeling is any indication, it's the drugs. I mean, it's me, too, but this anger is deep. I swear I could put my fist through the wall without a second thought. It has to be the drugs. I don't have a temper this bad." It was getting worse too. She could feel how easy it would be to go on a rampage.

Or ride down to the fourth floor and start knocking on doors until she found Kace and used him to burn off a very different kind of energy. She swallowed as her face heated up. "I'm going to need a way to settle myself down, or I might do something I regret before Jerabeth comes up with a fix."

"She should be back up here soon. She took the flowers to see if she could work out what's in them, but she mentioned she might need a blood sample from you."

"Not a problem, but let's call Dr. Fox too. I know Jerabeth's on top of this, but it can't hurt to have a medical professional on the case as well. Any help he can give would be great. Plus, he might be able to flush whatever this is out of my system if it comes to that."

"Excellent idea. I'll get him now." She picked up her phone again.

"Thank you. I'm going to take a quick shower and change." Donna went to her bedroom and did just that, getting out of her wet suit and under the hot spray. Cold water might have been a better idea, but she couldn't convince herself of that. She rinsed the chlorine from her hair, then got out, towel-dried it, and twisted it back up in a clip. It could dry the rest of the way on its own.

She dressed in comfortable clothes, the leggings, T-shirt, and big cardigan that were becoming her around-the-house uniform, then went back out to see if Charlie had been able to reach Dr. Fox.

Donna supposed being the physician to the vampire governor meant he was pretty much on call at all hours.

Charlie was making a new cup of tea to go with a plate of cookies that had appeared on the counter. She smiled weakly when she saw Donna. "I'm a stress eater."

"No worries. I should probably feed. Can't hurt with whatever's going on, don't you think?"

"I don't know. I think it would probably be fine, but what if a feeding only gives the drugs more fuel? The fae could have designed it that way, anticipating that feeding is exactly what you'd do. Maybe you should wait until Jerabeth knows more about what you were dosed with. Or until Dr. Fox gets here. He promised less than half an hour."

"Okay, I can wait." Donna took a seat at the counter and helped herself to a cookie from the plate, a square of crumbly shortbread. "Do you think we should have responded to Dredward after that video?"

Charlie stirred some sugar into her tea. "And said what? 'You're going to pay for this'? 'You're all in big trouble'? I don't know what we could have told Dredward that would have made things any better. Or different."

Donna nodded as she chewed the bite of shortbread she'd taken. "That was my thought too." She glanced toward Pierce's room.

"Thinking about waking him up?"

"No. Better to have him well rested. Temo downstairs?"

"Yes. While you were in the pool, he came up to say he'd be downstairs if you needed him." Charlie smiled. "Pretty sure he was going to FaceTime with Neo."

Such a happy thought in an unhappy time. "They're so cute together."

"They really are." Charlie sipped her tea. "What about you? Thinking about giving Mr. Donovan some more face time?"

Donna frowned. "Mr. Donovan?"

"Kace."

Donna groaned. "I can't be held responsible for

the things I do while I'm under the influence of fae drugs."

"He is quite the specimen. Most gargoyles are. All that rock-hard muscle and those sculpted good looks."

"Hush. I don't need the reminder." Donna shook her head. "I think Pierce would be hurt if he knew I was looking at another man."

"You've looked at Rico, haven't you?"

"Yes." And Pierce definitely knew about him. "But he was around first."

"True. But you don't have any commitment to Pierce, other than your vampire and assistant relationship. You're not sleeping with him. Are you? Sorry, not my place to ask that. I just…ignore that."

Donna couldn't. "No, I'm not. I like Pierce very much. In fact, I love him. He's been amazing to me. And I do find him attractive, but having a romantic relationship with him could turn awkward fast."

Charlie nodded. "It could. Maybe you should talk to him about that."

"Not now. Too much going on. And I'm not about to start dating anyone right this second anyway."

Footsteps preceded Jerabeth's entrance. Her already wild red hair was in a tumultuous knot on top of her head, and she had a rolled leather tool pouch in one hand. "Governor, there you are. I have bad news."

"I already know. Or is this new bad news?"

"New, I'm afraid. Every single rose was laced with a powdered compound. I did a quick analysis of the powder, and it was definitely designed to lower inhibitions and heighten emotions. It seems specifically aimed at the vampire physiology too. I inhaled some, and it's had zero effects on me. How are you feeling?"

"Like my emotions could very easily reach a boiling point."

"That's what I was afraid of. It's not going to get better either." She looked at the cookie in Donna's hand. "Did you feed? Or have you just eaten human food?"

"No blood yet. Charlie thought it might not be a good idea."

Jerabeth's brows rose as she looked at the admin. "Good instincts. The fae were probably counting on you feeding. If you do, you'll only increase the potency of what's in your system. It has to run its course naturally."

"How long is that going to take? If I don't feed, I'm going to weaken. That's going to make me a liability on the raid. More than I already will be with this garbage in my system."

Jerabeth sighed. "Pretty sure that was the point of drugging you. I need a sample of your blood so I can run some tests."

"Fine." Donna stood and took off her cardigan. "I had Charlie call Dr. Fox too. Not that I don't think you're capable of solving this, but it can't hurt to have help. And I'm sure he'll come at it from a different angle."

"I'm good with that. In fact, feel free to call in

whoever you like. I'm not about to turn down help." Jerabeth put the leather roll on the counter, untied it, and opened it up to reveal a variety of syringes and vials.

Donna grimaced. Just because she was a vampire didn't mean she loved needles.

Thankfully, Jerabeth worked quickly taking blood. "Okay, that should do it."

Donna glanced down. The needle mark was already gone. "That reminds me. How's it coming with the fae blood?"

"I'm sorry, Governor. I've had to put that aside to work on this."

"*No*," Donna snapped. The single word reverberated like an explosion.

Rixaline jumped in the other room, and Lucky took off running.

Donna inhaled. "I'm sorry. That came out a lot louder and meaner than I intended. I didn't even know I could be that loud."

Pierce came running out of his room. "What was that?"

"Me," she said. Pierce knew a lot about vampires. Maybe he'd have some insight into her situation. "Sorry about waking you, but now that you're up, you might as well know what's going on. Sit down, and I'll bring you up to speed."

CHAPTER 10

Charlie held her hand up. "Wait. Let's get Temo up here and fill them both in at the same time."

"Already here." Temo walked in. "What was that shout? Sounded like something one of my cousins might have done."

"About that..." Donna, with a little assist from Charlie and Jerabeth, told the two men the whole story.

Temo looked ready to kill. So did Pierce, actually. But Temo spoke first. "Boss, there has to be something we can do to help you."

"I agree," Pierce said. "If nothing else, we have to find a way to get you safely fed. I'm concerned that as you weaken it'll be harder for you to fight off the drugs' effects."

Jerabeth leaned against the kitchen counter. "That's a very real possibility. If she feeds, the drugs' power increases. If she doesn't feed, her ability to resist the drugs' effects decreases. It's a lose-lose. The fae knew what they were doing with this. But then again, they've had many years and many vampire victims to perfect such things on."

Donna growled, barely containing the anger she felt. "I may not kill them all, but Dredward is done."

Pierce looked at Temo. "Do you think your contact had anything to do with this? He knows about the raid."

"No. He gave the boss four vials of his blood. If his fae brothers were to find that out?" Temo grimaced. "Ish doesn't want any more trouble than he's already got."

Charlie crossed her arms. "You're sure about that?"

"As sure as I can be." Temo shrugged. "I've known the man awhile. He's too hurt and bitter about what happened to him to give the fae any help. Especially against someone willing to confront them." He shifted in his seat. "Ishalan probably wants Dredward overthrown more than you do, boss."

Donna gave that some thought. "If that's true, and I believe you, Temo, then I'm glad I gave him the okay to join us on the raid." She paced to the other side of the kitchen, then turned and came back. "In fact, if he really wants to see Dredward go down, maybe he can give us the antidote for these drugs."

Temo pulled out his phone. "You willing to pay for that information? I know he's going to ask."

"Yes," Donna answered. Temo started typing as she spoke. "Offer him ten thousand and tell him I'll let him live when I'm erasing the rest of the fae from the face of the earth."

To Temo's credit, he didn't blink. "You got it."

A wave of heat washed over her with a burning intensity. Exhaling, she fanned the back of her neck. "I thought the hot flashes ended when I was turned."

Jerabeth straightened. "Could be the drugs intensifying."

Sweat began to drip down Donna's spine. "Well, that sucks. We have to find a solution to this and fast."

Pierce stood. "Jerabeth, why don't you take a sample of everyone's blood and see how it interacts with Donna's? Maybe there's one of us she could feed from that wouldn't strengthen the drugs."

Jerabeth nodded. "It's worth a shot."

The door chimes sounded. Charlie headed in that direction. "Probably Dr. Fox."

Donna was on fire, but worse than that, she felt like she was about to snap. She was going to yell or cry or hit something, and what little control she had was quickly slipping from her grasp. She did not want to lose it in front of her team.

She loved these people. Cared what they thought about her. She didn't want them to see her like this. Or to take the brunt of her emotions. Or worse, accidentally hurt one of them if she lost control.

Pierce came over to her. "Come with me."

She glared at him, unable to do anything else with lava flowing through her veins. "I know you mean well, but this isn't the time."

"Shut up and come with me."

She frowned but followed him. He led her into

her bedroom, opened the door to the balcony, and gestured for her to go outside. Tiny flakes drifted on the breeze.

She stepped out into the cold. The relief was almost instant. She grabbed hold of the railing and took deep gulps of the icy air. In less than a minute, she felt almost normal. She looked over her shoulder. He was standing just inside, still wearing his pajamas. He had to be cold. "Thank you. I'm sorry for my reaction. I didn't mean it."

He smiled. "I know. And you're forgiven." He folded his arms over his chest. Definitely cold. "I have to confess something."

She chewed on her lower lip. "I can't take any more bad news."

"It's not bad."

"Then what is it?"

He glanced down for a second. "I overheard your conversation with Charlie. About me. I just want you to know that you're right. A relationship between us could make things very awkward. If you want to date someone, you should do it."

"Pierce—"

"No, I mean it. Look, I don't want to stand in the way of your happiness."

She had no doubt that was true, but the smug look on his face said he thought it was very unlikely another man was going to make her as happy as he could. He was probably right. "That's kind of you."

He shrugged. "What we have is already amazing and intensely special. Nothing's going to change that, outside of death or marriage. And I don't see any vows in my future. You?"

"No way. Never again." Truer words had never been spoken.

"Then go have fun, Donna. I'm not going to love you or care for you any less. You spent most of your adult life married to a man who never put you first. It would be strange if you didn't want to sow some wild oats."

Was he just saying this to give her an out? They'd never played those kinds of games before, so why would they start now? He'd always been extremely honest with her. She could feel herself getting weepy again. "Do you really mean that? Or are you putting my happiness ahead of your own?"

His smile perked up a little. "As you know, I can leave whenever I want. The only thing that keeps me with you is my desire to be here. I gain nothing by lying to you."

It was frightening to think of life without him. Her mood turned blue, and she fought it with humor. "You'd lose that fat salary if you left."

He laughed. "True, but I wasn't exactly destitute when you met me."

"No, you weren't." She came back inside, cupped his face, and kissed him on the mouth. There was nothing much romantic about it, more like a kiss between friends. Who maybe, possibly, might someday be more. "I'd be lost without you."

His grin beamed bright. "No, you wouldn't. You're the most capable woman I know. But I appreciate the thought. And I'm not going anywhere."

A knock on her door turned both their heads. "Governor?" Charlie called. "Dr. Fox is here. I didn't know if you wanted to see him before he goes to work with Jerabeth."

"Coming," Donna answered. She gave Pierce's hand a squeeze, then shut the balcony door. "Let's hope he can help."

In about twenty minutes, blood samples had been taken from everyone, including Jerabeth and Dr. Fox, who'd volunteered immediately when he'd been given the details about what was going on.

He tucked the last vial safely into his medical bag. "Normally, I'd want to do this work in my lab, but I have a good bit of equipment in my car. I packed everything I thought I might need when you called, Charlene. I'll just need to bring those things up, then Jerabeth and I can get to work. Do you mind if we set up in the salon?"

"It's all yours," Donna said. "And I'm sure Temo and Pierce can help you bring up your equipment."

Both men stood, nodding.

Jerabeth hooked her thumb toward the stairs. "I'll go get my supplies as well and meet you in the salon, Doctor. We can start testing immediately."

"Wonderful," Donna said.

Charlie picked up her cup of tea. "Governor, if you don't need me, I should go check email."

"Sure." That left Donna and Rixaline. She put her arm around the girl. "You okay?"

She nodded. "I might go read. Or maybe take Lucky to my room and see if he wants to play. Actually, I should probably brush him. He never seems to get enough of that."

"Nope. That cat could be brushed all day, I think."

Rixaline grabbed Lucky and headed to her room, leaving Donna alone in the kitchen. She had a burning desire to do something, but what? Maybe she should call Dr. Ursula Goldberg. She was the psychologist who ran the First Fangs Club, the support group for women who'd recently been turned.

She'd also been Donna's therapist when Donna had been human, giving the doctor a special insight into Donna's life.

But had La ever dealt with anything fae-related like this? Somehow, Donna didn't think so.

That left the women from the group. But which of them would be most likely able to help? Francine, the older and utterly unstoppable matriarch who'd just thrown Donna the most amazing party? Neo, the younger, streetwise computer programmer who, thanks to her help as security backup recently, was quickly capturing Temo's heart? Bunni, the slightly ditzy bottle blonde who seemed to mostly want revenge on the boyfriend who'd abandoned her to a nest of vampires? Or one of the other women Donna had met only recently—LaToya, the vivacious single mom, or Meghan, the supermodel?

The problem was that reaching out to Francine, Neo, or Bunni would most likely mean they'd want to help. They were those kinds of people. Well, maybe not Bunni, but then again, she didn't seem like someone who'd back down from a brawl.

That was a problem because Donna didn't really want her new friends involved in the fight with the fae. It was too dangerous. And it wasn't their battle. She'd be devastated if something happened to them.

She wasn't sure about LaToya or Meghan, but a single mother didn't need to be putting her life on the line for Donna. And an injury, no matter how fast she healed, might sideline Meghan at a perilous time in her career. The poor girl was already being called a diva for agreeing to shoot only at night.

None of that stopped Donna from wanting those women around her. They were good people. And they understood the trials and hardships of being a newly turned vampire.

What they might know about the fae remained to be seen. She went to the windows to stare out at the river. She hated everything about this situation. She wanted Rico safe. And the fae to stop being such enormous pains in the—

"We're back," Temo announced as he, Dr. Fox, and Pierce stormed into the penthouse, arms loaded.

Dr. Fox hadn't been kidding when he said he'd brought some equipment. "You need any help with that stuff?"

"No," Pierce said. "But you could shut the door. I didn't have a free hand."

"Sure." She closed the penthouse door, then followed them back to the salon room to see if anything needed moving out of the way. It didn't.

She stood by the wall and watched the flurry of activity as equipment was unpacked and set up according to Dr. Fox's orders. Jerabeth showed up, too, with her own supplies.

Donna inched out of the room, feeling very much like she was in the way. She was almost out when Temo caught her eye.

"Boss, I meant to tell you Neo said anything you need, just call. I didn't go into details."

She smiled. "Thanks."

"She said she'd get the girls together in a heartbeat. I think she was making a vampire joke. Not sure. But anyway, she's ready to help."

"I knew she would be."

He smiled. "She's all right."

"Yes, she is." Maybe Donna would call her after all. Couldn't hurt to let her know what was going on.

A new thought came to her. It absolutely could hurt. How was she going to tell them about the daytime raid on the fae stronghold without exposing her immunity to UV light? She needed a plausible explanation for that.

It seemed like a new problem awaited her around every corner.

Charlie poked her head in. "Governor?"

"Yes?"

Charlie's brow furrowed. "Queen Artemis is on line one in the office for you."

"Let me guess, she's not calling to wish me good luck on the raid either."

"I don't know. But that wouldn't be my guess, no." She frowned. "Sorry."

Donna took a deep breath. Maybe she'd broken some unknown rule and would be relieved of her duties as governor. That would solve a few problems. And create more. No, she needed this job. At least until Rico was safe and Rixaline was no longer in danger.

Then she could quit. Or resign. Or step down. Whatever governors were supposed to do.

She went straight to the office, shut the door behind her, and picked up the phone. "This is Governor Barrone."

"Hello, Belladonna. I got your email. I understand things have escalated between you and the fae."

A new and interesting wave of emotion overcame Donna. One that suddenly left her feeling fearless and unable to give a flying fig what the queen thought. "I wouldn't say that exactly. 'Escalated' implies there was already something going on, and I really had no beef with them. Taking the FBI agent hostage, however, was an act of aggression, plain and simple."

"*Because* you gave the dhamfir sanctuary."

Donna rolled her eyes, but that did nothing to change her mood or keep the edge from her voice. "Are you suggesting I shouldn't have done that?"

For a moment, Artemis didn't respond. Perhaps she was surprised by Donna's tone. Or that Donna wasn't backing down. Or maybe she was more on Donna's side than Donna realized. Although Donna wasn't so sure about that. Artemis wasn't the enemy, but Donna wasn't about to call her a close friend either.

Regardless, she didn't wait for the answer. "I'm a mother, as you know. I wasn't about to turn a child back out onto the streets, where she was being hunted by our deadliest enemy with plans to use her to track down more of us. Taking her in was the kindest and best decision for all involved."

Artemis cleared her throat softly. "You are certainly not Claudette."

"And for that you should be grateful."

CHAPTER 11

Donna realized instantly that her response had come off a little flippant. Her words were absolutely true, though. The previous governor, who was also Donna's sire, hadn't apparently been all that interested in doing her best. As a sire, she'd been pretty lackluster too.

Despite all of that being true, Donna did a little damage control. "I just mean to say that I care about this position. I'm not taking this job lightly. I want to help the people I serve in whatever way they need."

"No reason to be defensive, Governor." Artemis sounded amused. She was nearly impossible to read at times. "Claudette was…Claudette, and there's no denying that. I simply wanted your take on the current situation. I assume you have a plan?"

"I do. But it might be better if you don't know what that plan is. That way, you have plausible deniability if things go wrong."

"I can't do that. I'm responsible one way or the other. So I need to know what you're going to do and when you're going to do it. I would venture a guess you will not be returning the girl to the fae."

"That's correct. I'm just going to rescue the agent and do my best to make Dredward understand the mistake he made in targeting someone I care about."

"*Just* rescue the agent? You make it sound as though it's going to be a walk in the park. You understand it won't be, correct?"

Did Artemis know the stronghold was in Central Park, or was she just using that expression? "Not only do I understand it, I expect it'll be one of the hardest, most dangerous things I've ever done. And I'm saying that as a woman who spent twenty-seven years married to a high-ranking mobster. I have no illusions about what we're going to face."

"Good. But you said 'we're.' You already have a team, then?"

"It's being assembled." If Artemis thought she was going to get names—

"Do you need another member?"

There was no fast answer as Donna processed the question. After a moment, she found the right words. "Are you asking to join us?"

Artemis laughed. "Is that so hard to believe? There is no vampire with any love toward the fae."

"I would be honored to have you with us." Except Artemis wasn't sun-proof, and that would be a problem. In a couple of ways.

"I feel as though I'm waiting for a but, Governor. Do you have an issue with me accompanying you?"

"No, not at all." Though a few other members of the team might not be so keen on the vampire queen going with them. "It's just that the raid is planned for the morning. When the fae would be asleep."

"Smart. But not easy. How are you going to protect yourself from the sun for that long?"

Donna thought fast. "The gardener who takes care of the rooftop greenhouse is an elemental witch. Jerabeth Smalls?"

"Yes, I know her. And?"

"I'm hoping she can come up with something to give me a few hours of protection." Donna cringed. It was a good on-the-fly answer, but if Artemis wanted some of whatever that fake magical special sauce was, the jig would be up. No sense in avoiding that possibility. "I suppose you'll be wanting some of that, too, if you're going to join us?"

Artemis laughed. "No, I'll be fine. At my age, a few hours of sun have very little effect."

"Really? Good to know that awaits me."

A snort answered her. "You have a long wait. I am ancient, Governor."

"Understood. You look fabulous, though." It was true. Artemis's skin practically glowed.

"Thank you. When in the morning is this raid taking place?"

"Dawn. If everything comes together." Maybe that was too soon, and Artemis wouldn't be able to arrive in time. Donna had no idea where she'd be coming from. Then another thought occurred to Donna. "Ma'am, with all due respect, is this really a good idea? I have no doubt you'd be a valuable asset, but the fae are formidable. What if something goes wrong? Once the fae realize you're with us, they could make you their target. Your presence could start a war."

"No vampire lives forever, Governor. I'm aware of the risks. But I've waited for a day like this when the fae would finally give us good reason to attack."

"I can understand that. But the focus of our raid really is to get the agent free. Although, if Dredward or *any* of the fae end up as casualties, then so be it. A number of wolves from the New Jersey pack will be with us. Rico Medina, the agent who was taken is—"

"Medina? As in Louisa Valentina Medina, the pack alpha? Will she be with you?"

"Yes, ma'am. She's Rico's grandmother. And Maria Antonella, the alpha-elect, is his mother. To say those two women are unhappy with the fae right now would be an understatement."

"I'm sure." Artemis's tone had gone icy. "I don't know if I'll be able to attend or not. I wish you well, Governor. Stay safe."

The line went dead.

Donna blinked and looked at the phone. What had just happened? There was no way Artemis was afraid of the werewolves, so what was it? Bad blood between her and LV or Toni? What could have caused that? Donna had always been under the impression that vampires as a whole were friendly with werewolves, especially considering the attraction that seemed to happen naturally.

Weird. But she didn't have the time or the energy to give it two more seconds. She thought about checking in at the salon to see what progress had been made, but she didn't think Jerabeth or Dr. Fox would want anyone breathing over their shoulder. Wouldn't help the process go any faster either.

Instead, she went to the kitchen and raided the pantry for something sweet. Whatever drugs the fae had gotten into her system, they made her feel like she was going through puberty and menopause at the same freakin' time. Delightful. And since she couldn't feed, she wanted sugar.

A lot of it.

Thankfully, the pantry was well-stocked. Several packages of cookies took up one shelf. Charlie had obviously made up her assortment from these when she'd told Donna earlier she was a stress eater. Shortbread, wafers, chocolate-dipped rounds sprinkled with chopped nuts. They all looked British or Belgian. Maybe one was German.

In addition to those, there were some standard American selections, like Oreos and Fig Newtons.

The next shelf was dedicated to candy. M&M's in both the plain and peanut varieties, then an assortment of gummy candies and a couple of boxes of fancy truffles. Beside them were stacks of assorted chocolate bars, baskets of peppermint patties and peanut butter cups, and a big package of cherry Twizzlers. There was even a tub of chocolate-covered espresso beans.

On yet another shelf were bags of caramel corn, marshmallows in two sizes and three flavors, and animal crackers. The placement of those next to tubs of frosting made it seem like they were there for dipping. There were also jars of peanut butter, Nutella, Marshmallow Fluff, and an assortment of jams.

Donna's mouth watered as the aroma of the sweets filled her senses. Her stomach rumbled.

"Hungry?" Charlie asked.

Donna looked over her shoulder. "I can't feed, so I need to indulge in something." She went back to looking. "Sugar seems like the next best thing. Good thing we have a lot of it. Why *do* we have so much?"

"Claudette loved sugar. But I also adjusted the grocery order when Rixaline joined us. Being a teenager and all that."

"Good call."

"Did you see what's on the left?"

Donna turned to look. A row of boxed cake and brownie mixes. Nearby sat a basket of add-ins, like chocolate chips, toffee chips, coconut flakes, and chopped nuts. The selections overflowed.

She shook her head. "I can't wait for any of those to bake. I need something now."

"Hopefully, you'll be able to feed soon."

Donna grabbed a small bag each of regular and peanut M&M's, the Twizzlers, and a Three Musketeers bar. "That would be great. It would be even better if we had an antidote for whatever this is."

Charlie nodded. "Yes."

Jerabeth and Dr. Fox ran into the kitchen. He held up a test tube. "We've made a little progress."

"And?"

"We're not there yet, but we're getting close. We really need some new samples to test."

Donna's brows shot up. "You mean blood from different people?"

Jerabeth nodded. "Yes. Mine and Charlie's came close to working, but not enough for us to think it was safe."

Donna sighed. "I don't know who else to ask."

"That's okay," Charlie said. "I do. There's a reason we live in a building filled with supernaturals. There's an unwritten rule that says the tenants of Wellman Towers stick together." She glanced at the doctor and Jerabeth. "Come on. We've got work to do."

"Wait a second," Donna said. "Are you seriously going to ask people in the building to donate blood?"

"Yes. Believe it or not, it won't be the first time. It also won't be the strangest request that's been made in this building."

"But I don't want to be beholden to however many people live here."

"Governor, come spring, when warm weather arrives, you can throw a blowout party on the roof and invite everyone. That will be repayment enough."

"You're sure?"

She smiled. "Have I steered you wrong yet?"

"No, you have not."

"Back in a bit."

Dr. Fox raised his hand. "If I may, this is going to take some time. Until then, we have no real way to combat the drugs. It might be best if you tried to sleep. For a vampire, it's the next best thing to feeding. Not to mention, you have the raid coming up. Crashing then would not be good."

"No, it wouldn't be. And I'm happy to try. I just don't think I *can* sleep with so much going on."

Jerabeth stepped closer. "I can help with that. If you want help."

"Sure. Worth a shot."

"We should go to your bedroom."

"Okay." Donna headed in that direction, Jerabeth at her side.

"Thank you for including me in this," Jerabeth said. "I know you're unsure about me because of what happened on the roof, but I promise I will never betray you."

"I know you won't." Donna glanced at the witch. "You're welcome too. And thank you for agreeing to help." She went into her bedroom.

Jerabeth followed, closing the door behind her. "Just lie down and get comfortable."

Donna sat on the bed but went no further. "Can I ask what you're going to do?"

"I'm going to make the air warm—body temperature, actually—and heavy. I know that sounds like a bad combination for sleeping, but trust me. You'll see."

"I'm game." Donna stretched out.

Jerabeth held out her hands and spoke so quietly Donna almost couldn't hear her. The soft, whispered sounds started to lull her on their own.

The air warmed slowly. A minute or so later, a strange sensation came over her. She could no longer tell where she ended and the air began. It was like she was floating. Except she wasn't.

Then the air changed again, pressing down on her slightly. Keeping her in place, like some ethereal cocoon. Giving her a sense of security. And making her sleepy. Very...sleepy...

Knocking woke her up. Mary and Joseph. Jerabeth's magic had actually worked. She glanced at her phone to see the time. It was almost midnight. Squinting, she looked in the direction of the knocking. "I'm up. What's going on?"

Charlie opened the door and stuck her head in. "Sorry to wake you, but we found a donor whose blood won't exacerbate the drug in your system."

"That's good." Donna squinted at her. "Why are you smiling like that?"

"Because you're not going to like who it is, but I'm finding it pretty entertaining."

"I don't know what that means. Who's the donor?"

Charlie's grin somehow got bigger. "Mr. Tall, Dark, and Stony himself. Kace Donovan."

"Ha ha, very funny. Who is it really?"

Charlie snorted. "Sorry, Governor. I'm not making that up. His blood is the only one Dr. Fox and Jerabeth have tested that has not made the drugs worse. You can feed from him."

Donna groaned and fell back on the bed. "How do I explain that to him? How do I face him? Of all the people... He probably won't even agree, so there's no point in asking."

"About that." Charlie sucked air in through her teeth. "He's already in the living room, so that seems pretty agreeable to me."

Donna noted that despite being known as the undead, vampires could still suffer from absolute mortification. She was proof of that. "I'd ask you to kill me, but there's no point since it wouldn't solve anything."

"Nope. Shall I tell him you'll be out shortly?"

She wanted to say no, but the drugs in her system resisted that response. The thought of sinking her fangs into Kace held infinite appeal to what could be described only as her inner junkie. "I need a minute."

"Whenever you're ready." Charlie closed the door, leaving Donna to fight her internal battle.

She needed to drink from him. She got that. It would strengthen her. She'd be useless at the raid otherwise. She was already feeling weak and tired. Almost mortal, really.

But after all that flirting she'd done at the pool, there was no way this wasn't going to be awkward. Stupid drugs. Stupid fae. She sat up. But the drugs gave her the perfect explanation, didn't they? It was their fault, not hers. It was like being tipsy. He had to understand that, right? Plus, he hadn't exactly shut her down earlier.

Or would he think she was just making excuses?

She took a deep breath. She was about to find out.

Chapter 12

Donna pulled herself together enough so that she looked decent. Her hair had dried in weird waves from being clipped up, but there wasn't much she could do about that beyond running a brush through it.

She might have also added a touch of mascara and combed her brows into place. But that was it.

Too bad there was no vampire superpower for avoiding embarrassment. She walked out to the living room and found Kace chatting with Charlie.

He immediately stood when she entered, looking more serious than he had earlier. Good. Maybe all that flirting was forgotten. "Governor. We meet again."

Or not. Bringing up the pool right away had to mean it was still foremost in his mind. At least he had a shirt on. That made it slightly easier to keep her emotions under control. Still, he made a dress shirt and jeans look incredibly good. The dress shirt helped him look closer to his age too. Which only made him seem like more of a possibility and less like a spring fling.

New heat started to climb her spine. Other bits went tingly. Down, girl. She swallowed. Stupid drugs. "I understand you've been made aware of what's going on?"

He nodded. "Your admin told me that due to special circumstances, you're in need of a new blood source, and mine is apparently a match."

She looked at Charlie. "Special circumstances?"

"I figured this was a need-to-know situation, and that was all he needed to know."

Donna appreciated that. "I think we can tell him a little more. Mr. Donovan, the fae have drugged me in an effort to incapacitate me. The drugs heighten *all* of my emotions while also lessening my inhibitions. I'm sure you can understand how that might affect me."

He scowled. "I'm sorry they did that to you, Governor. How does my blood play into this?"

"Your blood is the only one that tested negatively for increasing the effects of those drugs."

His frown remained. "The fae aren't a problem for my kind, but that doesn't mean I'm a fan. In fact, I'm glad they don't like us, but I know how they hunt vampires, and it's disgusting. I would be pleased to help."

He started to roll up his sleeve.

Donna cleared her throat. "I don't need to drink directly from you. My physician is here. He could easily take your blood, and then—"

Kace shook his head. "I know you're not too familiar with my kind, but that's not possible. There are very few things that can pierce a gargoyle's skin. Certainly no kind of needle or small knife. A sword wielded by a strong opponent? Maybe. But don't expect the sword to be good for much after that." Then he smiled. "Vampire fangs, however, seem to work just fine." A wild, mischievous light danced in his eyes. "You're going to have to bite me, Governor."

Heat spilled through her, turning into need. For blood. And for him. Her fangs shot down. That need coiled out from Donna's center like ink through water, coloring every inch of her until she teetered on the brink of helplessness.

She tore her gaze away from him to look at Charlie, hoping Kace hadn't noticed she was digging her nails into her palms. "Is anyone in the sitting room?"

"No. I'll make sure you're not disturbed." She spoke to Kace. "If you'll follow me? We certainly appreciate your assistance."

"Happy to do it."

They left, giving Donna a chance to breathe and regain her composure. The pain in her palms hadn't helped at all. How was she supposed to bite him and not lose every shred of control?

She was too young a vampire to handle this. She didn't have the practice necessary. She wasn't even that good at drinking directly from the source. Sure, she did it with Pierce, but look what she'd done to the first human she'd ever tasted. Yuri was dead.

Okay, he maybe deserved it a little since he'd intended to either rape her or kill her, or both, but draining her first human wasn't a good precedent. Kace would be only the third mortal she'd bitten. And the first one she'd bitten while under the influence of fae drugs. The kind that heightened all her emotions and impulses. Without realizing it, she'd begun to pace the living room.

"Governor?"

Donna found Charlie standing at the divide between the living room and the kitchen.

"He's waiting on you. Are you okay?"

Donna shook her head. "I'm a little afraid to do this."

"Because of how the drugs are making you feel?"

"Yes. What if I can't stop? What if I do something to embarrass myself?"

"For one thing, if you start to go too far, Kace will stop you himself. And you don't need to worry about embarrassing yourself. He knows you're under the influence of drugs against your will. If anything, he's completely sympathetic to what's happening."

That made her feel only marginally better.

"You know, your control might improve with a good feeding. You know what Dr. Fox said. The weaker you get, the more power the drugs exert over you."

Donna took a deep breath and got ahold of herself. "Then I need to stop stalling and get it done."

"Pretty much."

"Okay. Thank you for doing all this."

Charlie smiled. "Anything you need, Governor. I'll be in the office if you need me."

Donna gave her a nod. As Charlie left, Donna walked toward the sitting room.

The door was closed, but she could feel Kace on the other side. It was like all of her senses were trained on him. She went in.

He was standing by the windows but glanced at her as she entered. His sleeve was no longer rolled up. "Your view is a lot better than mine. But you're a lot higher up too."

She wasn't interested in small talk. "I'm not myself right now. You need to know that. I wasn't myself at the pool either."

He turned around. "Not then either?"

"No."

His grin was lopsided as he shook his head. "I'm embarrassed to say I thought you were flirting with me because you found me attractive. I guess that's the male ego for you."

He was embarrassed? "Oh, I find you very attractive. But the drugs are responsible for my behavior earlier."

"That's too bad."

Was he flirting with her now? A new flush of need went through her. Whether he was or wasn't, her body was responding. "You shouldn't—"

"I just mean you're a beautiful woman. Any man would be crazy not to be interested. But I suppose you know that, being a vampire and all." He came closer, stopping in front of her. "Where do you want me?"

She looked up at him. He was tall and broad and smelled of aftershave, clean and fresh and delicious. Thinking of his features as *chiseled* seemed too on the nose, considering the kind of supernatural he was, but that word stuck in her head.

"Governor?"

"Hmm? Oh, right, sorry." Having a brain and a body that were no longer listening to her was as frustrating as it was exhausting.

The lopsided grin was back. It was the only part of him that wasn't perfect, which made it remarkably endearing. "Hard to concentrate?"

Not on him. "The drugs are making me foggy."

"Is that what it is?"

What was he implying? She frowned. "What else would it be?"

"You don't think there's something between us? My grandmother would call it a spark."

"It's just the drugs." There was no way she would admit to more in her current state.

He nodded slowly, but his expression said he wasn't the least bit convinced. "I'll sit on the couch. Would that be okay?"

Her mouth was dry. And her body was on fire. The perfect mix for combustion. "Yes."

He went to the couch. She followed and sat next to him, her knee touching his. How was she going to do this without making a fool of herself? Doubt crept in.

She scooted back. "I don't think I can do this."

"Why not? What are you afraid of? You can't hurt me."

She gave him a sharp look. "That's *not* what I'm afraid of." Not after Charlie's pep talk.

"Then what?"

"I might do something inappropriate." Like maul him.

He smirked but didn't let it turn into a full smile. "How about I just give you a pass? Whatever happens, happens. We'll just chalk it up to you not being you."

"You're being awfully cavalier about this."

"I'm a consenting adult. I can handle it."

She ran her tongue over her fangs. His eyes tracked every move. "All right, then. Let's do this."

He tipped his head back and to the side, keeping his eyes on her. "I've never been bitten before. This should be interesting."

"If you've never been bitten, how do you know my fangs will puncture your skin?"

"It's just a thing all gargoyles know." He stretched his head back farther, offering himself to her.

She couldn't stop staring at his throat. His pulse thumped through his skin, his heartbeat clanging in her ears like a dinner bell. Her gums ached. "I thought you were, uh, going to give me your arm."

"I decided my neck would probably be easier. The skin's a little thinner there."

He was the one getting bitten, so the choice was

up to him, but sitting beside him made his throat hard to reach. She tucked her knees under her and twisted to face him. Still not the easiest position. She leaned in slowly, trying to work out where to put her hands and how to brace herself, and then he grasped her around the waist and moved her to straddle his lap.

He was quick, giving her no time to do anything but gasp in surprise. He put his hands back on the couch as he straightened his head to look at her. "Isn't that easier?"

It was. She couldn't argue with that. But it was far more intimate than was probably safe. "I wasn't going to... That is, this is very close, and I—"

"You're about to bite me on the neck and drink my blood." He squinted at her, clearly amused. "Close is unavoidable. No reason for things to be harder than they need to."

Fine. If that's how he wanted to do this, like it was a game, she'd play. She put her fingers on his jaw and pushed his head back and to the side. Her senses, understanding what was about to happen, sharpened down to focus on him like he was the only living creature that existed in the world.

She opened her mouth, fangs fully extended, and leaned in. She put her mouth on his wonderfully warm skin and scraped her fangs over his throat, instinctually finding the right spot on the vein. Then she sank her teeth in.

There was resistance she didn't expect. But a second later, she broke through.

He let out a small sound, not exactly one of pain.

She was vaguely aware of his hands taking hold of her legs just above her knees and his fingers digging in, but she was lost to the moment. Kace's blood was very different than Pierce's. She could taste the power in it. Taste that he was something more than human. It wasn't as sweet and easy as Pierce's, though.

It was as different as cold spring water was from dark beer.

Then, just like with Yuri, something murky rose up inside her. Something primal and deep. The drugs twisted it into a hunger that felt unquenchable. It frightened her. Made her feel like if that something decided to drain Kace, he wouldn't stand a chance.

She wasn't going to let that happen, though. She might be young, but she wasn't exactly a newbie either. She knew more than when she'd first bitten Yuri. She dug into her small reserve of self-control and forced the darkness down.

For a second, she was sure she'd won.

Then something new surfaced within her. Desire that had nothing to do with blood and everything to do with the man beneath her.

Time spiraled into a meaningless concept. His pulse filled her head like she was listening to her own heartbeat. The rhythm became part of her. She drank to appease her thirst, while hoping she could take enough to shut down the fresh desire that had arisen.

Abandon danced at the edge of her senses. A kind of wildness that whispered, *Take it all.*

She shoved it away, refusing to give in.

Images filled her brain. Flashes that went by in an instant. Kace in military gear. An explosion. Blood. Bodies. Smoke and shrapnel. An overwhelming sense of loss and pain and grief.

The images vanished as quickly as they'd arrived, and as they left, so did her hunger. It just vanished. Gratefully. Her fangs receded about halfway, and she sat back, a little dazed with the kind of blissful well-being that usually followed a great day at the spa.

Warmth spread through her. The happy kind, not the unbearable kind she'd been feeling all day that made her want to stand under a cold shower.

She leaned in toward him again, this time to run her tongue over the two puncture wounds, healing them like she did with Pierce.

Kace's eyes were closed, his head resting on the back of the couch. "What was that for?"

"To mend the punctures." He was truly gorgeous. "How do you feel?"

The lopsided grin returned. "Like I just woke up on a lazy Sunday morning and know that I can lounge in bed for as long as I want."

She wiped the corners of her mouth just in case she hadn't been as neat as she'd intended. "That sounds like a good thing."

He opened his eyes, straightening his head. "It is. I feel totally relaxed. I didn't count on that. I thought it would hurt more, but it didn't really hurt at all. How do you feel?"

"Good. Better. More in control of what's going on inside me." She started to move off his lap to sit beside him, but he caught her by the arms and pulled her in, kissing her on the mouth.

She was too blissed out to resist. Not that she wanted to. She kissed him back, careful not to graze him with her fangs.

The kiss ended a second later, and she sat back. "What was that for?"

"Because I wanted to. Since I saw you in the pool."

She smiled, unable to help herself, and got off his lap to settle in beside him.

He glanced over. "No comment, but you're smiling. I'll take it."

"Thanks for letting me do what I just did. I really needed that."

"You can do that whenever you need to."

"Good to know. Especially because I may need to again if these drugs stay in my system much longer."

A moment of silence passed. "Why did the fae drug you? Seems like a pretty directed move without motivation."

"Because…" There was no reason not to tell him that she could think of, so she explained what was going on. From Rixaline to Rico, she laid the whole thing out. "They're just awful creatures."

"They're afraid of you."

With a skeptical look, she turned her head to see him better. "I don't think so."

"I do. Why else would they go the trouble of trying to incapacitate you?"

Was he right? She narrowed her eyes, thinking back. "What did you mean when you said earlier that you're glad the fae don't like you?"

"The fae hate gargoyles because they're powerless against us."

"Powerless?"

"With a few exceptions, like your fangs, we're pretty indestructible."

The images she'd seen while drinking from him made sense now. He'd been the only one of his company of soldiers to survive an attack. All because of what he was.

She sat up a little straighter. "Would you like to join my team?"

Chapter 13

Kace grinned. "Help you raid the fae stronghold? I'm all in for that."

"Good." Donna smiled back. He'd be a welcome addition. "I'll introduce you to Temo, my head of security."

"I know Temo."

"You do?"

"I've lived in this building for a few years."

"Oh. Right." That brought a question to Donna's mind. "Do you know Claudette too?"

"I do. Although not in the biblical way, if that's what you're asking."

Her eyes rounded. "It wasn't."

But there was still something very satisfactory in his answer.

He laughed. "I also know Temo because I worked personal security for Claudette a few times. Why she didn't use him, I don't know. But it was no big deal. Went to a couple of parties with her and played bodyguard. She likes that look."

Donna knew why Claudette didn't use Temo.

He'd caught her and Fitzhugh getting overly acquainted in the back of the SUV once, and she'd frozen him out after that. "What do you mean by 'that look'?"

"You know, like she's important enough to need protection. And I'm not saying this job isn't important. It is. But she didn't really do enough as governor to get the kind of attention that might require security. If that makes sense."

"You mean she didn't give any dhamfirs sanctuary."

"Exactly. Nothing even close. In fact, she didn't seem to do much more than hang out with Governor Fitzhugh and throw parties with him. I've done security work for him, too, by the way."

She frowned. "He's a jerk."

"I see you've met."

"My assistant, Pierce, punched him recently."

"Wow." Kace looked impressed. "I'd like to meet that guy. Fitzhugh has had that coming for a while. Any particular reason?"

"Fitzhugh insulted me, basically. He was drunk and spouting off. He wanted me to throw a party with him, too, and I said no. He didn't like me after that." Donna shrugged. "Anyway, let's go find Temo and get you up to speed. I have a lot to take care of."

"I can imagine." He stood and offered her his hand.

She took it, and he helped her up, pulling her against his chest to kiss her again.

After a moment, she reluctantly pushed away.

Only the fact that she'd just fed kept her hormones in check. "No more of that. My system can't take it right now."

"Sorry. I couldn't stop myself. But I won't do it again. Until you're ready for me to do it again."

"Good to know." She made a face at him before heading for the door. He was a great kisser, but maybe a little too young for her. Not to mention that if she wasn't going to get involved with Pierce because of their working relationship, she couldn't very well turn around and start something with the temporary security guy.

Maybe when this was over and Kace was no longer on her payroll, she'd revisit that. Right now, her focus had to be on rescuing Rico. She walked out into the kitchen. "Temo? Are you around?"

"Downstairs, boss," he called up the steps. "You need me?"

"Yes, please," she called back.

Thumping footsteps announced his jog up the stairs. He smiled when he saw Kace. "Hey, bro, what's up?"

"I'm joining the team for the raid."

Temo's brows rose as a curious look crossed his face. "I would have already asked you, but I thought you were done working security for the governor."

"That was the old one." Kace tipped his head toward Donna. "I like the new one a lot better."

"I bet you do." Temo laughed. "Good to have you on board. Come on downstairs, and we can go over the game plan."

Donna stopped him. "Temo, any word from Ishalan on the antidote?"

"Just that he's working on it. That might be a tricky one for him, given that he's so far removed from the inner workings of things."

She sighed. "Worth a shot."

"I'll let you know the moment I hear more."

"Thanks."

They left, and she went to the salon. She stood at the door until there seemed to be a natural break in the activity. "Jerabeth, I hate to interrupt, but could I have a minute of your time?"

"Sure, Governor. Doctor, I'll be right back."

"Take your time." Dr. Fox switched on a machine that started spinning a batch of vials. "We're just waiting on this next set of results."

Jerabeth walked out to the hall. "What can I do for you?"

"Let's talk in the office." A moment later, that's where they were, door closed, Charlie at her computer. Donna sat at her desk, indicating Jerabeth should take a chair too. "You know that I don't have an issue with the sun the way most vampires do."

Jerabeth straightened, tensing. "Yes, but I swear I haven't told a soul."

"I know. That's not why we're having this conversation. We're having it because I need you to come up with a plausible spell or potion or something that might make that possible. I need an explanation."

"Oh." The witch sat back, looking greatly relieved. "Does it actually have to work?"

"That would probably be for the best. In case someone wants to test it." Donna groaned. "I'm asking too much of you. I'm sorry. Your plate is already full, and I just asked you to make room for dessert."

"I could call in some help. If that's okay with you. She wouldn't need to know more than the brief. Create a spell or potion that can keep a vampire safe from the sun for an extended period of time. With you running this raid at dawn, it's completely plausible. Although I have to tell you, this is something vampires have been after witches to create for years. No one's been successful at a long-term potion yet."

"That doesn't make this easy, does it?"

"No. It could also make me a target."

"You know you have my full protection if that becomes an issue."

Jerabeth nodded. "I appreciate that. We just might need to say the formula became unstable or something. Enough that no one wants it."

"Good to know." Donna sat up a little. "Who are you thinking about asking for help?"

"The first witch that comes to mind is Harper Ferris. Harper is a solid potion-maker. I think she could do it. Or possibly her sister Reggie. She has a particular vendetta against the fae anyway, seeing as how her fiancé was killed by one."

"Wait a minute. You're talking about the witches who make the leather goods with their father?"

Donna glanced at Charlie, then back at Jerabeth.

She nodded. "Yes. Ferris & Coven. Daisy, Harper, and Regina are Will Ferris's daughters. I'm sure they'd help, considering the situation."

"The coat they made me is amazing. Please do reach out to them."

Jerabeth got up. "I'll do it immediately."

"Good. Time is short, Jerabeth. I need something believable to cover my daywalking abilities before I leave for the stronghold."

"Understood. I will do my best." She left.

Donna exhaled loudly, propping her elbows on her desk and leaning her head into her hands.

"There are a lot of moving parts, aren't there?" Charlie asked.

Donna nodded. "Do governors get to take vacations? Because I feel like I'm going to need one."

"I bet. Since you're here, do you want to check out the armory and pick out a sword you like for the raid?"

Donna moved one hand so she could turn her head and stare at her admin. "A sword?"

"You're going to need a weapon for this fight. An iron-edged sword is what most vampires favor in close combat with fae. If distance was involved, I'd suggest a crossbow with iron-tipped arrows, but I'm not sure that's right for this."

Donna sat up. "Just one small thing. I don't have a clue how to use a sword."

"I realize you haven't been trained. We'll address that at a future date, but you're a vampire. You have speed and strength. That alone will give you enough skill with a sword to defend yourself. Plus, with the iron-edged sword, you don't have to worry about a fae taking the sword and using it against you. Just touching it would burn them."

"So a sword is just standard-issue."

"Pretty much."

Donna squinted. "We have an armory?"

Charlie smiled and nodded at the louvered doors across from Donna's desk. "Do you think that closet is filled with office supplies?"

"Yes."

Charlie got up and opened the doors wide, revealing an impressive array of weapons, mostly an assortment of blades, short and long, but also several crossbows and a couple of other things Donna didn't know the names of.

"Wow. The last time I saw an arsenal like that, I was in my ex-husband's secret stash room. His were all guns, though."

"We have a few of those too." Charlie pushed a button inside the closet, and the center panels opened, revealing a second layer of firearms and rifles. "These aren't ordinary guns, however. They're specifically designed to deal with certain types of supernaturals. Most take very specific ammo. Bullets made of wood, silver, or salt. Or some combo. We have a rifle that shoots a net, one that shoots sulfur flares meant to draw out certain kinds of demons, another that... Well, you get the idea."

"Loud and clear." Donna whistled and stood up.

"Holy Mother, that's a lot of hardware." She walked over for a better look.

"Here," Charlie said. "Let's go back to the swords so you can pick something out." She pressed the same button, closing the panels and bringing the bladed weapons front and center again.

Donna didn't know where to start. "Are they all iron-edged?"

"No. Just the ones in this right panel. There are also these smaller iron-laced weapons on the side wall. Some throwing stars, a couple daggers, things like that. But your coat already has some small blades in it."

"I remember that."

"Oh, that reminds me. We do have a shotgun that takes iron-pellet ammo. That can be very useful, but again, I'm thinking most of your fighting this time will be done in close quarters. Not the best place to use a shotgun."

Donna remembered a certain grandmother with a shotgun who'd nearly taken off her and Neo's heads. "I'm going to skip that for this raid."

She reached for a medium-size sword with a red leather handle. That was the only fancy thing about it. Otherwise, it looked pretty utilitarian, as swords went. The blade wasn't even that shiny. "How about this one?"

"Up to you. Swing it a few times. See how it feels in your hand."

Donna stepped back so that Charlie was safe and hefted the blade with a firm grip. "Feels all right."

"You've only been holding it for thirty seconds. Give it a few practice blows."

Donna swung the sword in a wide figure eight, then, recalling her days on the high school drill team, spun the sword around in her hand and gave it a few fancy twirls.

Charlie's eyes widened. "I thought you didn't have any sword skills."

"I don't. But I had three years on the Fighting Bulldogs drill team in high school."

Charlie laughed. "I think you're going to do just fine."

"How do I carry this thing?"

"There's a sheath for it. Straps across your body. We'll get it adjusted for your—"

Donna's cell rang. She glanced over at her desk where it was sitting. "I'd better grab that. It's Neo."

"I'll take the sword."

Donna handed the weapon off, then answered her phone. "Hey."

"What's up, mama? Actually, I already know the answer to that. Temo gave me the 411. Are you all right?"

"I'm dealing."

"I can't believe the fae took Rico. What are you going to do?"

Donna hesitated. "I'm not sure talking about this over the phone is the smartest thing to do."

"Oh, right. I'll come up."

Donna's brow crinkled. "Up?"

"I was gonna play like I was home, but look, whatever, I'm downstairs with Temo."

Donna rolled her lips in to keep from laughing. "You are, are you?"

"I'm letting him work, don't worry. But yeah, I'm coming up. Bye."

"Bye." But Neo had already hung up. Donna motioned toward the kitchen. "I'm going to meet Neo in the kitchen. Did you know she's downstairs? You must."

Charlie pursed her lips. "I'm going to plead the Fifth in the name of love."

Donna snorted as she walked out. "I'm all right with that."

Neo was already in the kitchen when Donna got there. She whipped her braids over her shoulder and gave Donna a big hug. "You sure are getting put through it lately. I'm so sorry."

"Thanks, but things are mostly managed. Do you know everything that's going on?"

"You mean how much has my man told me? Just that you got home from the party to find a video showing Rico held captive by the fae. And maybe that the fae have drugged you."

"That's pretty much it. And they have. As you probably also know, Temo's putting together a team, and at dawn, we're raiding the fae stronghold to get Rico back. The New Jersey pack is assisting us, but I still don't know how many wolves they're sending."

Neo got a determined look in her eye. "I'm going with you."

"But we're going at dawn."

"If you can go, so can I. You must have some kind of intense sunscreen, right?"

"Not exactly. I have some witches working on a way to make me temporarily immune. But I'm not subjecting anyone else to that risk. Plus, I really don't want you to get hurt. So thank you. I love you for offering. But no."

"You can't tell me what to do." Neo grinned. "There has to be a way I can help."

"Not unless you can come up with some high-tech thing that kills fae that I don't know about."

Neo's mouth opened. "Yes, girl, that's it."

"What is?"

"Temo!" Neo shouted toward the stairs.

"Yes?" he shouted back.

"You have an SUV that's sunproof?"

"For you, baby, anything."

Neo grinned. "I'm going with you. But I promise to stay in the car."

"So just for moral support, then?"

"Ha, no. This is the perfect time to test out a little project I've been working on. The Skynet 2020." She wiggled her brows. "I just need to run home and get it."

"What kind of a project is this exactly?"

"A weaponized drone with the capability to hunt down fae and blast them with iron filings." Her grin widened. "Technically, weaponized drones aren't legal for civilian use, but we're vampires, and this is war, so…" She shrugged.

"A thing like that had to be incredibly expensive to make." Donna knew Neo was too young a vampire to be independently wealthy from years of smart investing. "Should I even ask where you got the money?"

"Okay, also technically, I'm building it for a stupid-rich vampire client as part of his home defense, but this will be the perfect time to test it out." She nudged Donna with her elbow. "What do you say?"

Having a drone in the air would be a real advantage. Especially against an enemy that could fly. If the drone got damaged or destroyed, Neo would be on the hook for that, though.

Thankfully, the governor's accounts ran deep. "I say you're on the team."

Chapter 14

Temo came upstairs a few moments later. Neo grinned at him. "Hey, baby, I'm on the team. I'm going to stay in the car, though, out of the sun, and fly my killer drone."

Baby. Donna tried not to get silly, but it was so cute. She wanted to hug them both.

"Cool." His smile faded slightly as he looked at Donna. "Boss, bad news. Ishalan can't get the antidote. He said he tried every possible source he has, but no one's talking, and he doesn't know what drugs they used. He feels bad. I could tell."

That brought Donna down to earth. She took a deep breath. "That's about what I expected."

Dr. Fox walked in, looking around. "Do you know where Jerabeth is?"

"She went to talk to some of her associates about working on another project I need done before the raid," Donna said.

He shook his head. "She probably told me she was leaving. I get a little single-minded when I'm in the midst of a project like this."

"Anything new?"

He frowned. "Nothing worth getting excited about. All the same, could you spare a moment to come to the salon with me? There is something I'd like to show you."

"Sure." She looked at Neo. "Back in a bit."

"Don't worry about me. I have to run home to get the drone. I'll be back as soon as I can so I'm ready to go."

"Okay, see you then." Donna followed Dr. Fox back to the salon.

He shut the door, then directed her to the area he'd turned into his workspace. "Watch this."

He took a few drops of blood from a vial and put them in a glass dish. Next, he brought over a small light bar. He turned it on, directed the light over the sample for several long seconds, then turned it off. He set the light aside to open another vial of clear liquid. He sprinkled a few drops of the liquid onto the blood.

He put the vial away and looked at her expectantly. "See?"

Nothing had changed, so Donna was stumped as to what she was expected to learn from the demonstration. "I promise I paid close attention, but I didn't see anything. It looked like nothing happened."

Brows high, he faced her, putting his hands in the pockets of his lab coat. "That's exactly right. Nothing happened. What makes that interesting are the details. That was your blood. Under UV light. And then sprinkled with holy water."

She had a feeling where this was going. Her fingers itched to touch her crucifix. "And?"

"Let me back up. I first tried the UV light thinking I could turn your blood to ash, then do an analysis of what was left behind to give me further insight into what chemicals the fae used. When nothing happened, I tried the holy water."

She swallowed as nonchalantly as possible. "I don't know what all this means." Except she was pretty sure she did.

He peered over the rims of his glasses with an almost palpable excitement. "Governor, I need to run some more tests, but I believe you may be able to daywalk."

She wavered for a moment. "You're my doctor, which means there's a confidentiality agreement, right?"

"I'd never breathe a word of this. And not just because of that, but because I understand how dangerous revealing such information could be for you. Of course, it's just a theory right now, but with some further testing…"

She nodded slowly. "That won't be required. I already know that I can daywalk."

His mouth came open. "You do?"

"I found out by accident."

"Do you have any idea why?"

She hesitated. "Complete confidentiality?"

"To my grave."

She pulled the crucifix from underneath her T-shirt. "This is why."

"I don't know how you're even wearing that. Is there something special about it?"

"My sister, the nun, got me this crucifix during her trip to the Vatican. It was blessed by the pope himself. My sister said she had it blessed to protect me from vampires. I was wearing it when I was bitten and turned. When I wear it, I'm UV immune."

His eyes narrowed. "Your sister had it blessed to protect you from vampires? That's not an ordinary request."

"She's not an ordinary sister."

"Well, as interesting as that all is, I feel confident in telling you that wearing it has nothing to do with your immunity."

"How do you figure that?"

"The blood in that dish was not protected by the crucifix when I tried to turn it to ash. I don't believe that actually wearing the crucifix makes any difference. Seems more likely the important part was that you were wearing it when you were turned."

"So you think I could go out without it? Because I couldn't right after I was turned. I tried."

"You might be able to now." He smiled. "I'd want to do more testing first, obviously. I don't think the raid is any time for you to go without."

She nodded. "Neither do I. But that's really interesting. Maybe we can do that testing after the raid."

Compassion filled his eyes. "About that. Please be careful on the raid, Governor. I like you very much. I don't want to see anything bad happen to you. You're kind and compassionate and tough. You're exactly the person who needs to be in this job. For a long time."

"Thank you. I'll do my best not to get hurt."

"Good. I'm not leaving until you get back, just in case I'm needed. Although I hope that's not the case." A timer started beeping. He reached over and shut it off.

"I appreciate that. I'll let you get back to work." She returned to the office to see Charlie. Donna could almost hear time slipping away as the hour to leave for Central Park drew closer. "Hey, we need to fit a sheath for the sword, right?"

"We do." Charlie got up from her desk. The armory doors were still open. "I got it out already. It's actually called a scabbard." She picked it up with the sword already inside. "This is it. There's a buckle on the strap, so all we need to do is figure out where it's comfortable on you and then adjust it. You want to be able to draw it easily."

Donna took her cardigan off. "It'll go over the coat, I assume."

"Yes. You should put that on first."

"Be right back." Donna went to her bedroom, grabbed her new leather coat, and slipped it on as she returned to the office. She was still amazed at how well it fit and the magic that had made that possible. "All set."

"Okay, put this over your left shoulder like a crossbody bag. You're right-handed, so you want to be able to draw the sword easily with that hand, and that puts the sword's hilt just above your left shoulder."

Donna put the strap over her arm and head and adjusted it across her body so the sword lay flat on her back. "Like this?"

"Yes. Now let's tighten it." Charlie cinched up the buckle. "How's that?"

"Feels snug."

"Draw the sword, and let's make sure the scabbard stays in place."

Donna took a few steps back, then reached back and pulled the blade out. "That worked pretty well, but I'm a little worried about putting it back. Can I wear it on my hip instead?"

"If you'd feel more comfortable with that, sure. All that matters when wearing a sword is your ability to access it easily." She undid the buckle, dropped the strap around Donna's waist, did a few more modifications, then stepped back. "Try it again."

The strap sat low on Donna's hips, out of the way of her arms and just under the hem of the coat. She grabbed the hilt and pulled. She liked the soft metallic hiss that sang out as it came free. Then she grabbed the top of the scabbard and easily guided the sword home again. "Much better. That's how I'm wearing it."

"Good thing we tested that out. We can run a second strap through the scabbard and around your thigh if you'd like."

"That might not be a bad idea. If I have to run, I don't want the sword swinging all over the place."

Charlie made the adjustment with another strap from the armory, then stepped away and put her hands on her hips. "How's that feel?"

"Perfect."

"Then you're all set for the raid."

Sweat dripped down Donna's back and trickled between her cleavage, soaking her T-shirt. Apparently, even though she'd fed, the drug-induced hot flashes weren't going away. "Except for the toxins still in my system." She started unzipping the coat. "I'm about three seconds away from taking everything off. These hot flashes might actually be getting worse. Didn't the Amazons go into battle naked? I might try that."

Charlie moved in to help unbuckle the scabbard. "Governor, it's snowing out and in the low twenties. Not sure naked is the right move. Although the distraction factor would be epic."

"The weather sounds like perfection right now." As soon as Charlie took the sword off, Donna shucked the coat. She pulled her wet T-shirt away from her body and flapped it to get some air flow. "I can't fight like this. The moment I exert any energy, my temperature shoots up, and I feel like I'm being cooked alive." She sighed. "I guess that's what the fae intended. I swear I'm going to end as many of them as I can." She waved the bottom of her T-shirt back and forth a little faster. "If I don't melt before the raid begins. I'm going to stand on the balcony and take advantage of the natural air-conditioning. Just in case you need me."

"Don't freeze to death."

"Unlikely." Donna almost ran to the sliding doors in her bedroom. She wrenched them open and stepped out into the cold, closing her eyes as she inhaled the crisp air. For a moment, it didn't seem like even that was going to work, but at last, she cooled off enough to feel like she was going to make it.

Opening her eyes, she went to the railing. The snow wasn't heavy, but it was drifting down in big, fat flakes that were accumulating. She wasn't sure if that would help or hurt their chances during the raid. Maybe the fae secretly hated snow or cold, though that was unlikely since they'd put their headquarters in a state that got plenty of the white stuff.

She held her hand out, catching a few of the flakes. They lasted only a second on her warm skin. She took one more deep breath, then went back inside.

"Governor?"

"In here, Charlie."

Her admin came in. "Jerabeth is back. With company."

"You mean Reggie Ferris?"

"I mean all of the Ferrises. Will, Regina, Harper, and Daisy. They're in the living room. They want to join the raid."

Donna glanced down at her sweat-damp T-shirt,

leggings, and boot-slippers. "Why do people always show up when I look like I just got done cleaning the house? Let me change, and I'll be right out."

Charlie nodded. "I can make small talk like nobody's business."

"Thank you." Donna wished she had time to shower, but that would be rude. She undressed, gave herself a quick cleanup with a washcloth, and went with dark jeans, a dark patterned blouse, and fresh deodorant. After slipping her feet into a pair of flats, she stuck some earrings on, too, just to jazz things up.

Finally, she walked out to greet her guests. "Welcome to the governor's penthouse."

Jerabeth grinned broadly. "Governor, please meet the Ferrises. When I told them what was going on, they all immediately wanted to help."

William Ferris stepped forward, hand out. "Ma'am, I'm Will Ferris. Pleased to meet you."

He was exactly as Charlie had described him. A hot, muscular Santa in biker's gear of jeans, a T-shirt, and a leather jacket covered in patches. Some kind of wicked-looking hooked knife was clipped to his waistband. Next to that, a chain hung down a few inches, but then disappeared into the pocket of his jeans. A black bandanna tied in the back covered his head. A few braids decorated the silver beard that hung past his collarbones. To her, the beard leaned a little more toward ZZ Top than Santa. Pre-turning, if she'd seen him on the street, she might have found a different route that didn't cross his path.

Donna shook his hand. "The pleasure is mine. The coat you made me is not only beautiful but remarkable. Thank you for that."

He smiled, softening his intimidation factor by several notches. "I'm so glad you like it." He gestured to the statuesque, ice-white platinum blonde on his right. She might have been Donna's age. Or older. "This is my eldest, Daisy."

Donna nodded. "Hi, Daisy." The woman could have easily been a Viking warrior. If she'd had a sword strapped to her and been wearing a horned helmet, Donna wouldn't have blinked.

"Next to her," Will said, referring to the slightly shorter woman at Daisy's side, "is my middle daughter, Regina."

Regina wiggled her fingers in greeting. Her black hair was streaked with cobalt blue. Her nails were painted the same color. "Call me Reggie."

"Reggie it is," Donna said.

Will put his hand on the shoulder of the woman to his left. "And this is my youngest daughter, Harper."

Donna had never seen such gorgeous rose-gold hair in her life. The waves almost looked metallic. If the woman was a day over forty, Donna would have been shocked. "Hello, Harper."

"Ma'am," the woman answered with smile.

Donna shook her head. They were all strikingly attractive and dressed in leather. A walking advertisement, she supposed. They could have been a supernatural version of Charlie's Angels. If the

Angels had been super-fierce witches. "It's so generous of all of you to want to help."

Reggie stepped forward, her expression hard and serious. "With all due respect, Governor, generosity has nothing to do with it. The fae killed my fiancé. Anything I can do to work against them, and I'm in. I understand you need some solid sun protection."

"I do," Donna lied. Then she decided to share some truth as well. "But I may not make the raid at all. The fae have managed to drug me. Without an antidote soon, my presence at the raid might be more of a hindrance than a help."

Reggie glanced at Jerabeth, then back at Donna. "Let me guess. Your emotions are completely out of whack, and your internal temperature is uncontrollable."

"Yes. How did you—"

"You haven't fed, have you? That will only make it worse."

"I did feed, but from a source that was deemed safe."

Reggie shook her head. "I hope that's true. You've got *ageratina altissima* in your system. I'm sure there are other things in there, too, but that's the worst of it. The way the fae use it, the concoction is a deadly poison, but only to vampires. Won't keep the fae from drinking your blood. In fact, it might even make you taste better to those winged psychopaths."

"Tremetol," Jerabeth whispered. "Of course. I should have guessed."

Donna stared at Reggie. "How do you know all this?"

A dark, angry gleam filled her eyes. "It's what the fae used on my fiancé just before they drained him dry."

Chapter 15

Donna put her hand to her heart. The pain in the woman's eyes was evident. "I am so sorry."

"Thank you." After a quick, tight-lipped smile, Reggie continued. "Based on my findings, the fae started using tremetol only in the last couple of years, which makes me think it's a recent discovery for them."

Jerabeth caught Donna's gaze. "Tremetol comes from *ageratina altissima*, or white snakeroot. It's a pretty, flowering plant that looks innocent enough. But Reggie's right in that it's deadly to vampires the way the fae use it, and in its simplest form, it's also deadly to humans. I actually have some growing in my poison garden."

Reggie nodded. "But the fae would never use it on humans. That would catch the attention of the Venari, and the Venari would wipe them out."

Donna made a mental note to clue Cammie in on what the fae had done to her. But all of this new information was promising. She looked at Jerabeth. "Do you have an antidote for tremetol?"

"Not for the fae's version, but I can figure one out, I'm sure," Jerabeth said.

Reggie peeled off her blue leather jacket. "No need. I know how to make it. I've done it before." She grimaced. "I was just too late."

"Come on," Jerabeth said.

"Jerabeth, will you let Dr. Fox know too?"

She nodded, and the two women disappeared.

Donna glanced at Will Ferris. "Now I'm doubly glad you came. I may owe you my life."

"We're happy to help."

Charlie stepped forward. "Can I get you folks something to drink or eat while you wait?"

"Please," Donna said. "Anything you want. We're well stocked."

Will took off his jacket, revealing a barrel chest and biceps like cannon balls. His build reminded her of Kace, although Will wasn't quite as tall or broad. "Just black coffee, if you've got it."

"Of course. And for you ladies?"

The women looked at each other like they weren't sure how to answer.

Will snorted. "Do you have any sweets? They love sweets."

Charlie grinned. "Why don't you come into the kitchen with me, and I'll show you the sweets we have. This way."

Harper and Daisy followed after her.

Donna sat in the club chair adjacent to the big wraparound sofa. Finding out what was in her system was a relief, but knowing the same poison had played a part in the death of Reggie's fiancé cut deep.

Will took a seat on the far side of the sofa, putting the coffee table between them. "You all right, Governor? You look a little pale. Paler than usual for a vampire."

She shook her head. "Hearing about Reggie's fiancé is so upsetting. The drug makes it impossible for me to hide what I'm feeling."

He nodded. "Ah. I understand. Reggie's still not over it. Poor kid."

Hearing him call his grown daughter a kid made Donna want to smile. "I can't imagine the pain of losing the person you planned to spend the rest of your life with."

Will narrowed his eyes. "Your friend that was kidnapped... Is he someone special to you?"

"Rico Medina. He's a good friend. We're not romantically involved, if that's what you were asking. But he's been a great help in my life. I owe him."

"We're going to get him back, I promise."

"Thank you. And thank you again for your help. I know you don't really have an iron in this fire."

"Ma'am, when the fae killed Abraham, they took the light out of my little girl's eyes. I have all kinds of irons in this fire."

"That, I can understand. I have a daughter and a son. I believe I'd feel the very same way if something like that happened to them."

He smiled. "I didn't peg you for a mother."

"I've only been a vampire for a few short weeks."

His mouth parted slightly. "I just realized who you are. Were."

"Oh?"

"You were married to Joseph Barrone. The mobster. Or am I wrong?"

"No, you're right. I still am married to him, technically." She waved her hand like she could brush all that aside. "Long story short. He faked his death, so now I have to actually divorce him, but the paperwork's done. Just waiting on it to be official. And thankfully, he's in prison, where he belongs."

"That's good."

"It is." She exhaled. "With my help, Rico built the case that was instrumental in putting him there. Rico is the FBI agent who was going to help me get away from Joe when we were married. He pretty much kept me from losing my mind during the process."

"That's why the fae took him. To hurt you."

"Yes. I'm sure they figured he was the best, most available leverage they could get their hands on."

"Because of a dhamfir?"

"Also correct. The fae want her in exchange for Rico, but I can't do that. She's little more than a child, and they want to exploit her talents to hunt down my kind."

His expression grew steely. "If Fitzhugh was any kind of governor, he'd have rooted the fae out of his city long ago."

"You know the fae headquarters is in Manhattan?"

"Since Abraham, we know a lot about the fae. Reggie's built a dossier on them that you wouldn't believe. Being part of this raid is the first thing that's got her truly excited in the two years since Abraham's passing. My girl wants blood. As I'm sure you can understand."

"I do. Anything she can do to help us will be greatly appreciated. And rewarded."

"Your business is all the reward we need."

"Let's agree to disagree on that, Mr. Ferris."

"Call me Will, ma'am."

"Only if you call me Donna and lose the ma'am."

"Yes, ma'am." He laughed. "Starting now."

"When we're done here, I'll introduce you to the head of my security, Temo Danielson. He's putting the raid team together. We're also getting help from the New Jersey pack. Rico is the alpha's grandson. Do you know LV Medina?"

"I know of her, but we've never met. Her grandson, huh?"

"And the alpha-elect is his mother. I guess the fae didn't realize who they were kidnapping."

"I'm guessing not." He cracked his knuckles. The sound was like gravel crunching under a tire. "This is going to be one hell of a fight."

Donna sensed he wasn't human, but once again her inexperience left her without a better idea. "May I ask what kind of supernatural you are?"

He smiled. "Well, I'm a bit of a mutt, but the strongest blood in me belongs to only one kind. See, on my daddy's side, there's a lot of this and that, but mostly it's human. My mama's blood, however, was a hundred percent reaper."

Donna squinted. "Like the reaper on your jacket?"

"Well, that's my motorcycle club. But also, yes, like that. I'm a reaper. Which is why I ride with the Reapers."

"You mean like a grim reaper? The being that collects souls?"

He nodded, and for a second, his eyes went completely black. "I mean exactly like that."

Donna sat back. "Whoa."

His eyes returned to normal. "I didn't mean to frighten you."

She shook her head quickly. "I just wasn't expecting that. I've never met a reaper. I'm not sure I knew they were real."

"I promise you, they are."

"Do you collect souls regularly?"

"It's not my day job, no. But I can if called into service." He patted the hooked knife on his hip. "I never leave home without my scythe. Daisy's got one too. She takes after me. Her sisters take after their mama, may she rest in peace."

"So Daisy's a reaper too? I thought all three of your daughters were witches."

"No. She's a necromancer with a little witch in her. Harper and Reggie are full-on witches."

Donna made a note to find out more about necromancers. She knew they had something to do with the dead, but that was enough questions for now. "Wow. Today has been a real education for me."

Charlie, Harper, and Daisy came back in. Will's daughters had plates of cookies, candy, and other assorted sweets, plus drinks. Charlie had Will's black coffee. She put it on the table in front of him, then came back to Donna. "Anything you need from me, Governor?"

"We should let Temo know the Ferrises are joining us and make introductions."

"I'll text him to come up."

Jerabeth walked into the room. "Governor, we're ready for you."

"That was fast."

"Reggie knows her stuff. And we were able to use a lot of what I already had on hand."

Donna stood. "Excellent." She looked at Will and his daughters. "If you'll excuse me."

"Take your time, Governor," Will said. "And thank you for your hospitality."

"You're welcome." Donna left them to walk with Jerabeth back to the salon. Heat spilled through her. She started fanning herself. "Whew. Perfect timing. Another hot flash just started."

"That might be good. We'll certainly know if the antidote works."

They entered the salon, where Dr. Fox had the massage table moved to the middle of the room. The beauty cart had been transformed with a clean white towel and an array of medical instruments. An IV stand, complete with a bag of what appeared to be saline, stood at the ready, as did Jerabeth and Reggie.

"You look like you're setting up for surgery."

Dr. Fox smiled. "Not quite that serious, but I wanted to be prepared." He patted the table. "Please have a seat and lie down."

Donna hopped up and got into position. She glanced at the bag of fluid hanging over her head. "I need an IV?"

"Yes. Best way to counteract the drugs in your system is to go directly into that system. I'm going to monitor your vitals too." He started swabbing her arm with alcohol as he finished speaking.

"Am I going to feel it?"

Reggie came over. "You might feel something. Maybe a little queasy. Maybe a rush of emotions as the drugs fight back."

Maybe didn't instill a lot of confidence. Donna turned to see her better. "Have you ever tried this antidote on a vampire before?"

"No. You're the first one."

Doubt and panic nibbled at Donna's resolve. "How do you know it'll work?"

Reggie frowned. "I don't. But there's every reason it should."

With the arm that Dr. Fox wasn't putting an IV into, Donna reached for her crucifix. She needed the reassurance of its presence. "Is there any reason it could go wrong?"

Dr. Fox taped the IV into place. "That's why I'm here."

Donna blew out a breath as she began to feel queasy. "I don't feel so hot."

Jerabeth nodded. "Like you might be sick?"

"Yes."

"Nausea is another side effect of the tremetol. And a pretty strong indicator that it's winning complete control over you. This can't happen soon enough." Jerabeth looked at Dr. Fox. "It's up to you now."

He readied a syringe, then took hold of the IV port. "All right, Governor. I'm injecting the antidote now."

Donna nodded and said a prayer as he pushed the plunger.

A second later, pain jolted through her, followed by intense heat. She sucked in a breath as the pain increased. If the heat boiling inside her didn't do her in, the sharp jabs all over her body might. Were her bones breaking? She ground her teeth together as her fingers dug into the padding of the massage table.

Dying might not be such a bad option.

Chapter 16

Donna thrashed involuntarily as her muscles seized and spasmed. Hands held her down. She heard what she assumed were soft, reassuring words, but the haze of heat and pain swamping her drowned them out.

A low, keening sound broke through, and she was vaguely aware that it had come from her own mouth. Her skin felt covered in flames. Her bones ached, and her blood had turned to lava.

She wasn't going to survive this. Death had to be easier.

A new sensation welled up. The unbearable heat morphed into darkness, and a few seconds later, everything went black and still and cold.

Was this death? No, she was too aware to be dead. But the nothingness was a mercy. She wanted to stay there, floating and numb, for as long as possible.

She awoke to the soft beeping of a monitor and three very concerned faces peering down at her. She squinted at them, unable to open her eyes any more.

"She's awake," Dr. Fox whispered.

The room was freezing. For the briefest of moments, she wondered if she was in the morgue. "Did I die or pass out?"

"Just pass out. For about fifteen minutes." He cleared his throat. "How are you feeling?"

She took a quick inventory. "Good, actually." She blinked a few times, finally getting her eyes all the way open. "Why is the room so cold?"

"You spiked a fever of nearly 105," Jerabeth answered, wiggling her fingers. "So I dropped the air temp." She tipped her head. "How do you feel emotionally?"

"Say something that might make me mad."

Dr. Fox chuckled. "Would you like for me to tell you the amount of my bill?"

Donna managed a little smile. "That won't make me mad."

Jerabeth narrowed her eyes. "Pierce is leaving you to go to work for Claudette."

"He'd never do that. But good try. I think I'm fine. The antidote must have worked." She went to sit up, got a hard dizzy spell, and lay back down. "Whoa. Super lightheaded."

"You need to do a little healing, which means you should feed again. Any blood will do now." Dr. Fox glanced at the monitor they must have hooked her up to while she was out of it. "Your blood pressure is a little low, but a feeding should fix that up. Should I have Mr. Harrison come in?"

"No, I'll go find him. I'd rather get unhooked

from all this stuff before I take care of anything else."

Dr. Fox nodded. "Right away." He went to work on removing her IV first.

Donna shivered at the cold. Jerabeth had really put the supernatural AC on. "Thank you, Reggie. I owe you."

Reggie's smile was brief. "Let me kill my share of fae, and we're even."

Dr. Fox removed the sensor from her temple and helped Donna sit up again. She weighed Reggie's request. "Any fae that don't surrender are fair game. In other words, if they're trying to kill you, have at it."

Donna tipped her head as she pondered her own response. "Huh. The poison's definitely out of my system. A half hour ago, I would have told you to kill them all. But when Temo and I met with his fae contact, I got the impression there are some fae who would turn against Dredward if given the chance."

Reggie frowned. "I'll believe it when I see it."

"Me, too, but someone on the inside is still talking to him."

Dr. Fox coiled up the wires from the monitor. "There you go. All free."

"Thank you." She got off the table but kept a hand on it until she was sure she wasn't going to go wobbly again. "Jerabeth, where are you with the potion that will allow us to see the stronghold?"

"I need another hour. Maybe two."

Donna glanced at the wall clock. "That's about all you have. It's almost time for us to leave."

The witch nodded. "I'll have it done."

"Go, then."

Jerabeth took off.

"Reggie, thank you again for the antidote. I owe you. Your family is in the living room. Charlie will get you anything you want to eat or drink while you wait."

"You're welcome. Some food sounds good. Spending magic always leaves me in need of fuel."

"I'm sure."

Reggie left too.

Donna turned to Dr. Fox. "Thank you again."

"You're welcome, Governor." He pointed at the massage table. "I may take a nap while I wait for your safe return."

"There are guest rooms. You're welcome to use one of those."

"The table is good enough for me. Now, go feed. Get yourself strong again."

"I will. See you later." She left in search of Pierce.

She found him in his room, typing away on his laptop. She knocked on the open door. "Sorry to interrupt."

He smiled as he hit a few more keys, then looked up. "You're never interrupting. Are you all fixed?"

"I am."

His smile broadened. "And judging by the look in your eyes, you're hungry."

"That too."

"Well, come on in. I have just what you need."

Twenty minutes later, the mutual exchange was over, and she felt like a million bucks. Ready, as much as she could be, to face the fae and rescue Rico from their clutches. She dressed in a long-sleeve black tee, thick winter leggings, and black boots. Her leather coat, iron bracelets, and sword were the only additions she needed.

After dressing, she went straight to the conference room. Pierce walked with her from the kitchen.

Charlie and Rixaline were already there. So were the Ferrises, along with Temo, his cousin Penina, and Kace. Jerabeth, presumably still working on the magic necessary for them to see the stronghold, had yet to arrive.

There were a few other less familiar faces too. Men and women, all supernaturals, who'd helped with security before and had been completely vetted by Temo.

Neo was there too. A large black suitcase, with the word SKYNET stenciled on it, sat by the door. Her drone.

Donna took a look around the room and prayed that every single one of these people came back with her. Alive. "Thank you all for coming. And for willingly putting yourself on the line like this. Temo, how long before we leave?"

"Thirty minutes. I've texted Alpha Medina and Ishalan."

"Thanks." She surveyed the group. "You all need to know that a fae will be joining us. His name is Ishalan."

A few surprised looks greeted those words. She held her hands up. "I know it goes against everything that seems safe and sane, but he's made a substantial sacrifice to help us in this raid. It's because of his contribution that we'll be able to see the fae stronghold."

She glanced at Charlie. "What's Jerabeth's status?"

"I'm here," the witch answered as she hustled in.

Donna looked at her. "Done?"

She nodded. "Yes. Just."

Relief swept through Donna. Being able to see the stronghold was pivotal. "Excellent."

Jerabeth held her gaze for a moment longer. "I also have another potion for you. To protect you from the sun."

"Also very important."

Jerabeth handed Donna a little corked test tube of dark blue liquid. "Drink that down."

Donna did, noting the potion tasted very much like a familiar sports drink she used to buy for Joe Jr. when he'd played soccer. That probably meant Jerabeth failed to come up with something workable, but then a potion that would actually sunproof Donna hadn't been necessary. All that mattered was the appearance of being protected by magic. And in that, Jerabeth had done well.

Donna discarded the empty tube on the sideboard. "What about the vision potion? What do we need to do?"

Jerabeth put three small glass bottles on the table. Each rubber stopper had a pipette attached to it, barely visible in the murky reddish-brown liquid.

"Two drops in each eye. It's probably going to sting. You might even have a moment of temporary blindness, but that will pass."

Reggie grabbed a bottle before Jerabeth had finished speaking.

Donna picked up another one. "You're sure?"

Jerabeth nodded. "I've already tried it on myself with Rixaline as my subject. It works."

"What do you mean with Rixaline as your subject?"

The witch smiled ever so slightly. "The fae don't see each other the way we see them. Try it. You'll see."

"All right." Donna opened the bottle and squeezed the rubber stopper to fill the pipette with the potion. She tipped her head back and put two drops in each eye. It stung a little, but it wasn't bad. She squeezed her eyes shut for a second, then opened them. She looked at Rixaline, smiling at the girl. "Nothing different yet—oh. Wait."

Before Donna's eyes, Rixaline's sharp angles and dusky-colored complexion smoothed and softened, changing in such a subtle way that she was still clearly an otherworldly creature.

In fact, she was strikingly beautiful. More beautiful than she'd already been.

"It definitely works." Donna faced the group. "Everyone, two drops in each eye. And then we're ready to go."

In a few minutes, they were done, and their eyes were adjusting. Donna watched as they all stared at

Rixaline in amazement. "Jerabeth, how long will this last?"

"Four to five hours. If you think you'll need more than that, take a bottle with you."

Donna declined. "If we're still there after that long, we'll have bigger issues than being able to see the stronghold." She looked at those gathered in the room. "This needs to be a decisive strike. The longer we're there, the worse our odds become. We get Rico, we get out. Understood?"

They all nodded or answered affirmatively.

"I know some of us have deeper issues with the fae. I sympathize. But I don't want to lose any of you in the name of revenge."

More nodding. Except from Reggie. Donna understood. The woman's need for vengeance wasn't going to be turned off by a stern talking-to. But Donna wasn't about to call her out either. Everyone in front of her was an adult, save Rixaline. And she'd be in the car with Pierce and Neo.

Donna took a deep breath. "Temo, you want to go over the game plan one more time?"

"Sure, boss." He unfurled a large map of the wooded area in Central Park known as the Ramble. Rixaline had obviously helped him by adding the location of the fae stronghold. He tapped several spots around the park. "We're going in four vehicles. The Ferrises in their own, then the boss with me, Penina, and Kace. Then…"

As he continued, a strange sense of foreboding came over Donna, similar to the nightmare she'd had about Rico being served up as the main entrée at a fae banquet. But deeper and darker and far more troubling.

It was the kind of feeling that opened up a pit inside of her. The kind of feeling that left her unsettled and restless.

The kind of feeling that made her think they weren't all getting through this alive.

CHAPTER 17

The drive to Central Park took an hour. It was somehow the longest and shortest sixty minutes Donna had ever experienced. Maybe for Temo and Charlie, too, because they'd both been silent during the ride.

Donna understood. There was a lot to think about. A thousand emotions, thankfully all manageable now, raged within her. Everything from the anticipated joy of freeing Rico, to the terrifying fear of losing a friend.

Temo found a spot alongside the park. A block behind them was Pierce, Rixaline, and Neo. On the other side of the park were the two remaining teams.

Elsewhere, the wolves were either arriving or moving into position. She guessed Ishalan was doing the same. He remained a wild card in Donna's mind, no matter how much help he'd given her. If he turned against them, she wouldn't hesitate to take him down.

Bringing Rixaline had been a coin toss. Donna had wanted to leave her at the penthouse, but the girl had begged to come. Donna appreciated wanting to feel useful when the burden of responsibility weighed on your shoulders. No matter how many times she'd told Rixaline this wasn't her fault, she knew guilt clung to the girl like a black cloud.

Donna glanced out the window. The sky was still dark and would be for another half hour or so. The plan was to get into place and then, as daybreak came, launch their strike. The snow had stopped falling, but a coating of white blanketed everything.

There would be no hiding their tracks.

Temo turned the car off. He pulled something out of his pocket. "Here. Put this in your ear."

"An earpiece?"

"Yep. You, me, and Charlie are the only ones that have these. If you need me, I want to know."

She smiled. "Thanks, Temo." She put it in her ear. It was so small she barely noticed it.

"You got it, boss. Time to go."

They all got out, letting Donna lead by quite a bit. That was another part of the plan. She'd go first while the others stayed at a distance, in case the fae were watching. Hopefully, they'd think she'd come alone. She was not only all right with that, she'd suggested it.

This was her mission, so she ought to take the most dangerous spot. Even if the fae did kill her, so long as it wasn't a fatal strike through the heart, she'd still technically be alive since she could afford to die once. Another vampire perk.

With her hand on her sword and Rixaline's map in her head, she started through the winding paths of the Ramble. The snow soundproofed everything, making the woods eerily quiet and magnifying every sound. Every step left a print in the newly fallen snow.

The path was easy enough to make out, which was good because Donna's attention was on the forest around her and the sky above. She hadn't been in Central Park since Christina's class had come on a field trip here seven or eight years ago. But she swore she would have remembered the trees looking like something out of a scary movie.

The bare branches were dark and reaching, the bark twisted into whorls and snarls that looked more like scowling expressions than simple tree trunks. Was that fae magic? Intended as a warning to any who might approach? Maybe she could only see it because of Jerabeth's vision potion. The sound of flapping wings made her abandon that line of thought to take cover in a thicket of brush.

She glanced up to see three beautiful, graceful fae soaring overhead. Probably returning to the safety of the stronghold before sunrise and either unaware or uninterested in her and her entourage.

The sight sent a ripple of anticipation through her. Not only was Jerabeth's vision potion working, but Donna was close to the fae's headquarters. Which meant Rico wasn't far away.

She pushed to her feet and kept going. The sky was no longer black, but a muted blue gray. Sunrise was still a few minutes away, but it wouldn't be long. The gate had to be within a few yards. A little farther and she crested a hill.

The gate appeared out of the mist before her.

The thing was a crumbling, tumbledown arch of stone that vaguely resembled the larger, more refined marble version in Washington Square Park. Except that one didn't have snarling, drooling hellhounds guarding either side of it. She wasn't positive they were hellhounds, but it seemed plausible.

"Nice doggies," she whispered.

Their eyes glowed red, and they were simultaneously muscular and skeletal. One of the Great Dane-sized beasts pawed the ground with a clawed foot that looked like exposed bone covered partly in fur.

A shocking thought came to her. Were these the zombie version of hellhounds? Because considering what had been happening lately, that seemed like the only thing left for life to throw at her.

Zombie. Hellhounds.

The sky grew lighter still. The time to breach the stronghold was fast approaching. "Sorry, pups, no brains for you today."

She pulled her sword, holding it out before her, but indecision kept her in her spot. How should she handle it when the hellhounds tried to keep her from going through the gate? Take them on directly? Try to outrun them? And if they were indeed zombie hellhounds... Would her sword even be an effective weapon against them? Holy communion, she was still so out of her element.

It wasn't a decision she had to make. The hellhounds' heads came up, then they whimpered, cowering as they retreated a few steps.

Donna chanced a look over her shoulder. Every available space behind her was alight with pair after pair of gleaming blue werewolf eyes. Hundreds. Maybe thousands. As far back through the Ramble as she could see.

She faced the hellhounds again and saw that the eyes surrounded her and the gate. Wolves filled the woods on every side. LV and Toni had kept their word in the most stunning fashion possible. New courage filled Donna.

The hellhounds lay down, their heads between their bony paws, no longer a threat. Pale gray streaked the clouded sky. Dawn was imminent. Donna raised her sword over her head.

Behind her, a single howl broke the stillness and raised goose bumps on Donna's arms. Rico would know they were here now.

And so would the fae.

A metallic hum on her left made her dodge away, sword up, but it was only Neo's drone. Heart pounding ever so slightly, she gave a thumbs-up to the camera, and the drone took off again.

She raised her hand and gave the sign to go, a single finger pointed at the sky. Then Donna jogged toward the gate. No point in being quiet any longer. All around her, the woods came alive. Temo,

Charlie, and the rest of her crew appeared a few seconds later, breaking out of the pack of wolves.

She went through the gate, and the surrounding world changed. Thick mist permeated the woods, which were now darker, almost like daylight was being magically tamped down. There was no snow, only bare earth and a slate path. Clusters of lacy white flowers bloomed in patches around the trees.

Ahead of her in the distance, the stronghold rose like a behemoth from the mist, a massive, craggy fortress of stone and bronze that seemed like the architectural embodiment of brute force.

Torches burned all along the parapets, but there were no guards on patrol. None in the sky either. In fact, the fortress seemed oddly quiet.

Intentionally quiet. She got the distinct impression a trap had been set.

Temo joined her. "They can't all have gone to sleep. If they were vampires, I'd maybe buy it. But not the fae. I don't like this."

"Me either, but we have no choice. We have to go in."

"Boss, you should stay out here with Charlie and the wolves."

She slanted her eyes at him.

He shrugged. "Worth a try."

Kace joined them, then Will Ferris. Two wolves darted forward to meet them as well.

"LV? Toni?"

Both wolves responded with soft woofs.

"Amazing support, ladies. Thank you." She looked around. "Are we ready?"

Will nodded at Donna. "Jerabeth, Reggie, and Harper have just taken to the sky to patrol."

Donna frowned. "What?"

He raised his gaze and pointed. "There they are."

She followed his finger, and a woman on a broom went zipping past high above them. "Mary and Joseph. How about that. What about Daisy?"

"Daisy is coming in with another group," he answered. "You may see Reggie on the ground soon too. If the fae don't take to the sky, that is."

She nodded in understanding. Reggie needed to feel like she'd had her revenge. "Between them and the drone, plus the wolves and the rest of our team in the woods, we should be covered. Let's go."

"Not without me."

At the familiar voice, Donna turned to see a woman coming through the gate. Mist swirled past like a curtain billowing, but not enough to hide her chain mail shirt adorned with a bold crimson cross, leather pants, and long sword. For a moment, Donna imagined she might be Joan of Arc. But had Joan of Arc carried a crossbow on her back?

Donna's jaw unhinged as the woman's face came into clear view. Her dark hair was plaited back in a single braid. "Cammie?"

She nodded, stern and serious. "Here and ready to fight."

"With me, right?"

A brilliant smile lit her beautiful face. "With you."

She reached out a hand. "Whatever the consequences."

"Does that mean—"

"We'll talk about it later. Doesn't matter anyway. Family sticks together."

If Donna'd still had the poison in her system, she would have broken down in tears. Instead, she grabbed Cammie's hand and squeezed it. "Thank you."

"You're welcome, sis," Cammie said.

With a smile, Donna faced the stronghold again. As soon as they entered the stronghold, the wolves would pour through the gate and take up new, closer positions. "Okay, let's—"

Ishalan stepped out of the mist. With her eyes bespelled, he was a stunningly gorgeous creature. He had no weapons, no armor. He was dressed in a simple tunic and pants, his wings at rest behind him but glittering like a dragonfly's. He gave her an amused look. "Did you think I wasn't coming?"

The thought had crossed her mind. "I wasn't sure, but now that you're here, take us to Rico. We're wasting time."

"As you wish, Governor. But walking into the heart of the fae wearing that much iron is like banging a drum in the middle of the nursery and expecting the infants not to cry." He spread his long fingers, hands up. "It's your funeral."

Will snarled. "It's her funeral if she takes it off."

"It's Ishalan's if something happens to me." She held her hand up. There wasn't time for this. "I'll take the coat off. But I'm keeping the bracelets."

"Fine." Ishalan turned on his heel and marched toward the stronghold and the gothic arch that was the fortress' entrance.

She quickly shed the coat into Will's waiting hands and caught up to Ishalan. "Why is it so quiet?"

"Most of my brethren are asleep."

Mist swirled around them, making it hard to see more than a few steps ahead. "Really? Because it feels like a trap."

"They'll wake up soon enough, if that's what you're worried about."

"Why aren't you asleep? Why aren't you affected by the sun like all the rest of them?"

He shot a quick glance at her. "An interesting question from a vampire who should also be asleep in a safe, *dark* place."

"A witch's potion protects me." The fog seemed to thicken. "You?"

The ground changed beneath her feet. From dirt to wood. She looked down to see they were walking across a bridge that spanned a chasm. As far as she could tell through drifts of mist, there was no discernable bottom. The visual was enough to knot her stomach.

"Inside the gate, I am protected by fae magic. I've been here for hours, waiting in the woods for you and your friends."

She stopped looking at the chasm. "So the fae can be out and about so long as they're behind the gate? That would have been good information to have had already."

"My apologies. I thought your dhamfir would have told you that."

Maybe Rixaline didn't know. After all, she'd been held prisoner, not left to wander. Then a new thought came to Donna. "Wait. Does that also mean you won't be able to leave again until dark?"

"You're very perceptive for a vampire."

She didn't know how deep the woods inside the gate were, but after this, he'd be a target. Could he really hide long enough to get to safety? Or had he actually embarked on a suicide mission? That was quite a risk. Whatever his motivation for being there, it was *very* strong.

Despite the premonition she'd had earlier, something told her his end would not be today.

He glanced over his shoulder at the crew following them. "You turned a Venari to your side? Very impressive. Or is she here as a watcher?"

"A watcher?"

"To make sure things don't escalate, and if they do…" He slid a finger across his throat.

Was that why Cammie was here? Donna hoped not as she frowned and forced down the temptation to tell Ishalan that Cammie was her sister. Seemed an unnecessary sharing of information. "She's here to help."

That was all he needed to know.

They crossed onto stone again as they entered the stronghold. The interior was lit by more torches, the hall before them grandly paneled in wood and accented with copper and bronze and tapestry wall hangings depicting all kinds of scenes. Long wood tables paralleled the walls. Each had a pair of flickering lanterns on it, the light reflected in the finely waxed stone floors. It was beautiful. And empty.

The small hairs on the back of her neck pricked up. But maybe that was because she was in the middle of a fae stronghold now. Possibly the most dangerous place a vampire could be. Behind her, the team formed a small circle. All of them facing out. All of them in battle stance.

They needed to do this and get out. "Which way to the dungeons?"

Ishalan smiled. "Down, of course."

Chapter 18

If they had to fight on the stairs, they were in trouble. That was Donna's first thought as they descended the narrow passage that led to the bowels of the stronghold. It was dark and dank and smelled of death. The tinny, sweet odor of decaying blood permeated the air. Even for a vampire, it was an awful stench.

Her stomach roiled at first, finally settling a few moments later. She checked her crew. Except for Cammie, they all looked a little queasy. How used to this sort of thing was Cammie?

The raspy sound of fae voices reached them as they hit a landing.

Ishalan put his hand out, stopping the party in their tracks. Then he held a finger up for them to be quiet. He flattened his palm. He wanted them to stay.

They all nodded. He slipped a hand under his coat and withdrew a short dagger. "You must trust me, Governor."

They'd come this far. And if he tried anything, the

crew behind her would end him. She nodded. "Fine."

He held his free hand out to her. She took it, wondering what was about to happen. She didn't have to wait long to find out. He pulled her close, wrapped his arm around her neck, and held the dagger to her throat. "Play along," he whispered.

Behind her, she could hear the hiss of blades being pulled from their sheaths and soft, muttered curses.

"It's all right," she whispered to her team. All while hoping she wasn't telling them a lie.

"Ready?" Ishalan asked.

"Yes."

"Good. You take one, I'll handle the rest." He started down.

They hit another landing and went down two more steps. Three fae guards were shooting dice in front of a barred door. Rows of cells were visible through the bars.

She inhaled. And smelled wolf more strongly than she had since LV and Toni had joined them.

Ishalan tugged her along. "Brought a present for the king."

The guards looked up from their game. The one nearest the door started to rise. Ishalan released her, then threw his dagger into the man's throat.

Donna pulled her sword free and caught the middle one cleanly, lobbing off his head before he had a chance to speak.

At her back, Ishalan had the third up against the

wall, his hands gripping either side of the man's head. A sharp wrench left, the cracking of bones, and the last fae slumped to the ground. Ishalan bent and retrieved the keys from the man's belt. He dangled them on his finger. "Let's go get your wolf."

The rest of the team flowed down the stairs, but she stood there, a little numbed by the sight of the purple blood staining her sword. It wasn't the first time she'd killed someone. But it was the first time she'd done it with intent.

Her stomach twisted again.

Cammie caught her by the elbow. "Tuck it away for later. Those feelings aren't going to help you now."

She nodded. Compartmentalize. Temo had said she was good at it. Didn't feel that way right now, but she did her best.

Ishalan had already unlocked the door.

Donna lifted her head. "Right." With bravado she didn't feel, she wiped her blade on the dead fae's clothes and slid it back into its scabbard.

Ishalan pulled the door open and smiled. "After you, Governor."

"You first, fae," Cammie answered. She pointed down the long hall of cells with her sword. "Go."

Ishalan frowned but started walking. Donna followed, almost pushing him along to make him go faster.

"Rico," she hissed. No response. Was he unconscious? She glanced back to check on her team. Immediately behind her were LV and Toni, still in wolf form. Temo had stopped halfway. Kace, Will, and Cammie were at the door.

Ishalan slowed as they approached the end of the row, key ready in his hand. He looked into the last cell, confusion on his face.

Donna peered in. It was empty. She whipped around. So was the cell across from that one.

They were all empty. Rico wasn't in the dungeon.

LV and Toni snarled.

Donna turned on Ishalan, livid. Her fangs punched through her gums. "You set us up." She grabbed him by the collar of his tunic and shoved her arm against his throat so that her iron bracelet caught him squarely.

The sizzle of flesh rewarded her, as did his grimace of pain. "I had nothing to do with this. I swear on my wings."

"Then where is he?"

"I don't know."

A ripple of energy at her back pulled Donna's attention. She turned to see LV and Toni standing there in human form.

Toni was staring down Ishalan with the most murderous glint Donna had ever seen. "Let me kill him now."

Donna needed to defuse the situation. "Can either of you pick up Rico's scent?"

LV looked at her like she was a little crazy. "His scent is everywhere. It's like they deliberately put him in each cell. Add to that the stink of the fae, and finding him is impossible."

Donna turned back to Ishalan. "Where would he be?"

The fae swallowed. "There is one possibility."

"Where?"

"Dredward's chambers."

"Why would Rico be there?"

"Dredward has been known to keep high-value prisoners close during daylight hours as an extra precaution."

She glared at him, letting anger make her eyes shine bright. "More information that would have been useful earlier."

"I never assumed—"

She grabbed him by the back of the neck and pulled him close. Almost nose to nose. Her fangs were out, and she was almost snarling as she spoke. "What else haven't you told me?"

"Nothing. I swear."

"Where is Dredward's chamber?"

Ishalan raised a single finger to point skyward. "Main turret. Top floor."

Her lip curled back. "I could kill you now."

He nodded as best he could with her fingers digging into his neck.

She used her hold to steer him toward the entrance. "You're going to take me there. And if this is some kind of trap, I promise that I will take you down before I die."

As they rejoined the rest of the team, she yanked him to a stop. "Rico's being held elsewhere. I need cover."

Cammie nodded. "A distraction?"

"Exactly. Ishalan and I alone will get Rico. The rest of you raise havoc and draw all of their focus." She looked at LV. "Time to unleash the wolves of war."

LV stared daggers at Ishalan. "You bring my grandson back, or the wolves of war will pick this place down to the bones." Then she turned, and she and Toni shifted back to their wolf forms and ran out.

Cammie braced her sword on her shoulder and shot a look at Temo. "What do you say?"

Temo grinned. "One distraction, coming up." He clapped Kace on the shoulder as he glanced at Will. "Let's go, boys."

They all hustled out.

Donna kept her grip on Ishalan, doing her best not to look at the bodies they'd left behind. "How long before the guards file out?"

"When the alarm goes up? A minute. Maybe less. Dredward might keep a pair of guards, his personal ones, but that will be it."

"He'll be alone?"

"No. His paramour will be with him."

Donna struggled not to roll her eyes. "Remember how I just asked if you had any other important info to share and you said no?"

He frowned. "The paramour is unimportant. She might be Dredward's companion, but her loyalty is to herself first. She'll cower at the first sign of trouble."

A rumble outside shook the fortress. A chorus of howling followed, accompanied by a high-pitched sound like a siren going off.

"You have a banshee too? That's quite a distraction," Ishalan said. "Now wait..."

The thunderous beat of footsteps and shouts to rally rang out. The soldiers were leaving the stronghold.

Ishalan held up one long finger. Finally, the exodus seemed to be over, but the noise outside swelled. Fighting had begun. "Now."

He led Donna back up the steps, then straight through the grand hall to another set of stairs.

Her earpiece crackled. "Boss, it's going off out here. We're holding our own, but don't take too long."

"Copy." She poked Ishalan in the shoulder. "Faster."

He sped up. She kept his pace without a problem, and after what seemed liked a thousand steps, they arrived at a set of ornate wooden doors. No guards stood outside. Donna took that as a good sign.

Ishalan glanced at her, brows raised in question.

If he was asking her if she was ready, she was. She nodded, hand on her sword.

He held up three fingers, then two, then one. Shoulder lowered, he launched himself through the doors, breaking them apart in a shower of wooden splinters and copper fittings.

The fae Donna assumed to be Dredward stood at a window on the opposite side of the enormous space. He whipped around as they came barreling in, his gaze ricocheting from Donna to Ishalan. "You," he snarled.

"That's right, dear brother." Ishalan smiled. "I've come home."

A weak voice came from the right. "Donna?"

She glanced over and found Rico shackled in bands of silver inside a cage no larger than a dog kennel. "Rico."

Anger drove her. She grabbed the cage's door and ripped it off its hinges.

From the bed, a female voice shrieked. "Guards, guards."

Donna ignored her to get Rico out of the cage. He was dirty and smelled like they'd done nothing for him in the way of personal comforts. "I'm sorry it took so long."

He just stared up at her without much response, his lids drooping. Had he been drugged? Or was the silver in his restraints making him sick? Didn't matter. They'd figure it out. She grabbed him under the arms and got him out as best she could while bent over and trying not to hurt him further.

A blade whistled past her head and sank into the wood paneling behind the cage. She yanked Rico the rest of the way free and drew her sword.

Ishalan and Dredward were locked in hand-to-hand, so that wasn't where the blade had come from. She looked toward the bed.

A barely dressed fae woman with a handful of little knives stood on the bed. She threw another one as Donna was assessing the scene.

She dodged, *Matrix*-style, as the blade came soaring past her left side. As she twisted away, she came all the way around and used the momentum to charge forward, taking the woman down.

The fae screamed and kicked and snapped her teeth at Donna.

So much for cowering in fear.

Donna pressed her bracelet to the woman's throat just like she'd done with Ishalan. It had the same sizzling effect, but the woman kept bucking like a rodeo horse.

There wasn't much else she could do, so Donna clocked her across the jaw and knocked her out. Behind her, Ishalan and Dredward were wrestling on the floor, cursing each other and snarling like wild animals. Both were bleeding.

Fine with Donna. She needed to get Rico free of the restraints. She went back to him, grabbed the blade out of the wall and used it to pry off the shackles binding his wrists. Raw, oozing skin covered every inch the silver had touched. She worked on the ones around his ankles next, finally freeing him.

He moaned. She took it as a good sign. The time to get him out was now. Ishalan and Dredward were not her concern. "Can you walk?"

He nodded. At least she thought that's what he did. She pulled him to his feet, got his arm around her shoulders and hers around his waist, and started him out the door.

He felt lighter than she'd expected. Had he lost

weight? "Temo, Charlie, I've got Rico, and I'm on my way down."

A garbled mess of battle sounds, snarls, swords clanging, and shouting answered her. If Temo's response was an actual word, it didn't come through.

She got them to the steps and carefully began their descent. She prayed they didn't run into any guards, because Rico would be an easy target. She'd have no choice but to kill them, and she'd already realized that ending a life was a pretty traumatic experience for her.

What that said about her as a vampire, she wasn't sure. Of course, this was war. And she'd do whatever was necessary to protect herself and her friends.

They made the first landing without incident and kept going. The sounds outside grew louder as the battle raged on. Could the citizens of Manhattan hear any of that? The fae magic had to work as a sound barrier as well.

Rico turned his face into her neck. "Thank you," he whispered. His voice was raspy and dry.

"You're welcome."

"I take it you didn't trade the dhamfir?"

"No."

A hoarse bark of laughter wheezed out of him. "I knew you wouldn't."

"Save your energy. We still have a long way to go." The great hall lay ahead of them. She paused at the stairs' exit to make sure the space was empty.

A guard slumped near the hearth, purple blood covering him.

She listened hard, but there was so much other noise that detecting a heartbeat seemed impossible. Had he retreated to safety only to die by the fire? If he was still alive, he didn't seem like much of a threat.

"We need to go." She shifted Rico to the other side so that if the guard did come around and decide to attack, she'd take the brunt of it. The last thing Rico needed was more wounds. With more speed than care, they crossed the great hall.

About halfway and her earpiece came to life with Temo's voice. "Boss. The queen just showed up. Not sure if that's good or bad."

She tapped the button. "The queen?"

"Yep. Artemis."

Chapter 19

Artemis? Donna didn't have the time or mental energy to process that. Not right now. Plus, Arty was a big girl. She could look after herself. She'd said as much.

Donna held on to Rico a little tighter and picked up her pace toward the exit. They still had to cross the bridge with that gaping chasm below it. If she lost her grip on him, or he suddenly shifted... "Rico, how are you doing?"

A moment passed before he responded. "Okay."

He didn't sound okay. He actually sounded worse.

She could pick him up and carry him, but what if she got attacked? She couldn't risk dropping him.

Something creaked, followed by a small whistling noise. Pain erupted in Donna's thigh. She sucked in a breath as she glanced down to see a freakin' knife protruding from her leg. She looked up. The guard by the fire was glaring at her, but even as she watched him, his eyes rolled back in his head, and he listed to one side.

A second later, he collapsed all the way.

She glared right back. "You'd better be dead, or I will come over there and make sure of it."

She braced herself to support Rico so she could free one hand to yank the blade out. Pain radiated from the spot, a deep, throbbing ache that made her think the blade had been laced with something. The fae did seem to like their poisons. Blood oozed from the wound, a sure sign it wasn't healing with the kind of speed she'd grown accustomed to.

Good thing Dr. Fox was waiting for her.

She hauled Rico closer to the bridge, each step sending a jolt of pain through her. She eased him to the floor and propped him against the wall so she could check if the coast was clear.

It wasn't. Four guards near the end of the bridge were trying to keep a growling, ferocious pack of wolves from entering the stronghold.

She was so done with this. So. Freakin'. Done. Impulse took over. She yanked one of her bracelets off and tucked it into Rico's hand. "Iron," she told him. He didn't need more explanation than that. He knew what iron did to the fae.

He made a small movement that might have been a nod. His time was running out. She needed to get him help fast.

Blood covered her thigh, soaking her leggings. The pain blazed up and down her leg. She was going to need help soon herself. But first, she had to see this through. All rational thought disappeared, and she let instinct and anger take over. What she was about to do wasn't going to help her injury, but that could wait longer than Rico could. She squared her shoulders toward the bridge and charged.

She went low, catching the first guard around the hips and whipping him up and over the railing like a rag doll. New fire erupted in her leg.

To the fading sounds of his screams, she grabbed another guard and sent him flying as well. The advantage of surprise was gone. A sword hissed past her head, almost taking off her ear, but a wolf jumped on the guard's back and sank its teeth in the fae's shoulder. Will and Daisy were close by, battling a trio of fae, but holding their own.

Behind her, the remaining guard started screaming. Donna looked over to see him being dragged off by more wolves. A few other wolves still stood on the bridge. Breathing hard, she faced them. "Rico needs help. This way."

She led the small group toward their alpha's grandson. She crouched beside him, causing fresh blood to spill from her wound. "Rico, your pack is here."

Two of them shifted to human forms, turning into big, stocky men before her eyes. The oldest one, whose silver muzzle had turned into a gray beard, nodded at her. "We'll take it from here, Governor."

"Thank you."

"Thank *you*. Would you like us to carry you out as well?"

"No, I'm fine. Get him to safety."

"Yes, ma'am. Be careful with that leg."

"I will." She leaned against the wall to catch her breath.

Both men worked together to pick Rico up in a seated position and carried him out, a flank of wolves keeping the way ahead clear.

She watched them go, taking a moment to recover from the exertion of clearing the bridge. But a moment was all she could afford. Outside, the battle still raged. She tore down one of the wall hangings, cut a strip from it with a borrowed blade, and used the piece to tie a makeshift bandage around her still-bleeding wound. A metallic taste coated her mouth. That dagger had definitely been tainted with something.

She prayed she stayed upright until this was over. She started to leave, then realized the biggest tapestry that hung behind the royal dais depicted a scene in which a vampire was splayed out on a banquet table.

Much like what she'd seen in her dream, except Rico had been the one on the table. In a fit of rage, she grabbed a lantern off the nearest table and threw it into the tapestry.

It exploded in a shower of glass and fuel, setting the fabric ablaze. Good. That should keep any remaining guards busy.

She went back out to find her team. Thankfully, the bridge was still clear. If she was going to collapse, she didn't want to do it in the midst of the fae stronghold. Especially not while it was on fire.

The fighting seemed to be dying down. The

injured were everywhere, but she thankfully saw very few bodies. Losing some of the murderous fae was one thing, but to lose those who'd come to help with Rico's rescue was another. There also seemed to be scattered groups of fae with their arms crossed over their heads. Had they surrendered? If so, Ishalan had been right.

"Governor! Help me!"

She turned toward the voice. It belonged to Daisy. Donna started toward her, realizing a few steps in that the woman was kneeling beside her father. There was so much blood Donna couldn't tell where it was coming from. A sick feeling filled her. "What happened?"

"He took a sword to the gut and another to his shoulder." Daisy sobbed once, then inhaled hard. "He's dying."

"He's a reaper. How can he—"

"He's also half human. And all the fae blades are poisoned. You have to help him."

Donna shook her head. "I don't know how."

"Yes, you do. Turn him. It's the only way to save him."

Donna just stared at her. She'd never turned anyone. She had no idea how to do that. "I don't know how."

"The same way it was done to you. Please, you have to try."

Her turning hadn't been exactly textbook. She'd been bitten. And just as she'd felt like she was going to die, Claudette had showed up and revived her with blood from her wrist. Donna supposed she could do that much.

She leaned down. "Will, I'm going to turn you. Don't fight it."

The flickering of his eyelids was his only response.

With time running out, she lifted Will's wrist to her mouth and bit down. The flow was weak and sludgy with the murkiness of impending death. She drank sparingly. An image flashed in her head. Will, much younger, with a beautiful young woman in a white dress. The image vanished a second later, and she knew there was nothing left to take from him.

She bit her own wrist and held it to his mouth, praying there was no residual fae magic in her blood that might harm him. "Come on, Will. Drink."

Daisy held on to his arm. "Drink, Daddy, please."

Still no response. Donna's wrist had begun to heal over. She punctured her own flesh again, this time making a fist to squeeze blood out.

Nothing again. Then Will coughed. A second later, he latched on. Barely, but it was better than nothing.

Donna leaned in. "That's it." A few seconds later, she started to feel woozy. She didn't know how much blood he needed, but with what she'd already lost, she'd pass out if he took much more.

She reclaimed her wrist and looked at Daisy. "That's all I can do. Get him somewhere safe. Somewhere he can rest. He's going to need to sleep for a while." If she'd been successful. If not...she didn't want to think about that.

"I will. Thank you. We owe you."

"You owe me nothing." She got to her feet with real effort and took a good look around.

She spotted Temo and Kace a few yards from the bridge. They were looking up. So was most of the crowd around them, fae and supernatural alike. She tipped her head back to see what was drawing everyone's attention as she joined them.

About twenty feet up, Ishalan and Dredward had taken their fight to the sky. The two were engaged in a full-on battle, wings out, blades drawn, and it was something to behold. Even the witches, who were still patrolling the atmosphere, were keeping their distance from the battle. Neo's drone hovered about the same space away.

It was interesting, but Donna had other things to worry about. She nudged Temo. "Where's Artemis?"

"Not sure. She chased after a fae who tried to bite her. They both disappeared into the northside of the woods." He nudged her back, handing her the jacket she'd discarded earlier. "Better put this back on."

"Thanks." Donna tugged her jacket on as she glanced toward the northside in time to see a bloodied Artemis emerge from the trees, gold sword in hand. The blood covering her was purple, so Donna had a pretty good idea of how things had gone.

The queen was clad all in white leather. Perhaps thinking it would be good camouflage in the snow? Donna wasn't sure about that, but the getup was fierce.

Very much the Vampire Queen Goes to War.

But Artemis didn't look so much victorious as she did…feral. Her eyes glowed, and her fangs were on full display, but more than that, she had the look of a woman who'd been let loose. Had she really wanted to come after the fae that badly?

Artemis strode toward them, sheathing her sword as she did. It wasn't her only weapon. She was covered with them—a sash of small knives across her chest, throwing stars tucked here and there, a dagger strapped to each thigh, the sword at her hip and something else secured to her back.

Artemis turned to look up at the battle overhead, slowing her walk as she moved backward. "That's Dredward."

"Yes," Donna answered. "He's fighting with Ishalan, his—"

"Brother," Artemis finished. A curse slipped from her lips. At least it sounded like a curse. Donna didn't recognize the language. "This is the chance I've been waiting for."

She took a few steps away from them and reached for the weapon on her back. As she pulled it free and snapped it open, Donna realized it was a crossbow. Kind of like Cammie's, but not.

It had a handle like a shotgun. And the sash across Artemis's chest held short arrows, not knives like Donna had at first thought.

Without taking her eyes from the sky, Artemis loaded an arrow into the bow.

Donna kept shifting her view from the battling fae

to the vampire queen. Donna had a pretty good idea of what Artemis was about to do, and she didn't like it one bit.

A sudden feeling of trepidation went through Donna. She went after Artemis, knowing what she was about to say would probably not be well received, but she had to try. She had to do her best to keep a war from starting.

Artemis raised the bow.

"Your Highness, if I could have a word—"

"Not now, Governor."

"Please, Ishalan might be fae, but he helped us. I don't think—"

A soft snick and the arrow released. It shot straight and true, but the fae above were moving targets.

The arrow found a home in one of Dredward's outstretched, leathery wings. It sailed cleanly through, leaving a gaping hole in the iridescent skin.

Dredward cried out and shoved Ishalan away with such power that he hit the side of the stronghold. The resounding crack of bone sounded like a gunshot. He fell to the earth, his body crumpled and broken.

Despite the hole in his wing, Dredward seemed to have no issues staying aloft. He spread his arms. "Artemis."

She was already loading another arrow into her bow.

Dredward dove with a speed that made him blur. Her second arrow missed. Before anyone could react, he scooped Artemis up and took her skyward.

Donna grabbed Temo's arm. "I have to get up there. Get me up there!"

Kace turned to her. "I can take you." In an instant, he shifted, and his gargoyle form appeared before her, an enormous stone beast with wings. "Climb on."

His voice had changed, deeper and raspier. She had questions, but now was not the time to ask how a creature seemingly made of stone could fly.

She vaulted onto his back. He felt like stone too.

"Hang on."

She dug her fingers into the scaly ridges down his spine. "I'm good. Go."

He didn't take off so much as launch, nearly knocking her backward. Quick reflexes saved her. By the time she righted herself, they were ten feet in the air.

A few arrows zipped past them. Fae archers? One hit Kace but bounced off. She knew his skin was nearly impenetrable but wondered briefly if he'd end up with a bruise.

Kace flew directly after Dredward with a speed that had them catching up in just a few seconds. Donna couldn't fathom the physics behind Kace even being airborne; forget how he managed such speed. It was obviously magic. Magic she was very appreciative of.

She glanced down, then wished she hadn't. The fall would probably kill her. At least in the sense that it would end her need to breathe. She'd officially be undead then. She hung on a little tighter as the wind whipped past.

The witches on their brooms, more magic Donna still marveled over, moved in to flank them—Jerabeth and Reggie on one side, Harper on the other.

Maybe one of them would catch her if she fell. She leaned down, wrapping her arms around Kace's thick neck and putting herself in position to speak directly into his ear. Or where his ear should be. "Can you get under them?"

"Yes. Good plan."

She figured he'd understand. She glanced over at the witches, giving them each the thumbs-up.

Kace surged forward, and in a few seconds more they were beneath Dredward and Artemis. Dredward had one arm around her body, pinning her hands to her sides, and the other around her neck, a knife at her throat. She was struggling against him all the same, her glowing eyes defiant.

If the queen had a plan, Donna couldn't figure out what it was, but there was no time for worrying about that. Donna's plan would work. It had to work. In one smooth motion, Donna sat back and unsheathed her sword. "Now, Kace."

He rose, bringing them within inches of Dredward and his prisoner.

Donna raised her sword, very aware they were going higher and higher. "Release her safely to me, Dredward."

The fae glared down at her. "No vampire tells me what to do."

"Now, Dredward."

He laughed, a sick cackle that filled Donna with fear.

But the distraction had allowed Artemis to wriggle free enough to grab her gold sword. She yanked it from its scabbard as best she could, but without being able to move much, that meant she sliced through her leather breastplate as she did.

A glint of light off the blade caught Dredward's gaze. Surprised, he seemed to freeze as Artemis swung the sword toward his arm. He scowled, bared his teeth, and sank them into her throat. As he did that, he pulled his arm back.

With a blur of movement, he took his teeth from her neck and plunged the knife into the queen's heart.

Artemis stiffened, eyes wide in understanding. She held the sword toward Donna and opened her hand, letting it fall free.

Then she dissolved into ash.

Chapter 20

Somehow, Donna caught the gold sword. The hilt was still warm from the queen's touch.

Mouth dripping with Artemis's blood, Dredward tipped his head back and laughed, teeth bared, eyes wild. "Where's your queen now, vampire?"

Small flakes of gray drifted through the air, swirling and eddying on the currents.

White-hot, blinding rage pushed Donna to her feet on Kace's back. The pain in her leg disappeared. There was no thinking. Just action. Dredward had to pay. She leaped into the air, gold sword raised, and brought it down with every ounce of strength she could muster. The blade sliced Dredward in half from ribs to hip.

His eyes went wide and round.

And then he, too, went to ash.

A moment passed where time stood still. Then it started up again. Donna kept her grip on the sword as she felt herself falling toward the earth, pain spreading in her leg.

Artemis was dead.

Maybe she would be too.

A rock-hard clawed hand snagged her wrist and stopped her fall. Kace. He descended until her feet touched the ground. Her knees buckled, but she clutched the sword with every bit of strength that remained. Cammie and Temo caught her.

"Boss, you okay?"

Her gaze stayed fixed on the last spot Artemis had occupied. Flakes of ash continued to fall. The queen's? Or Dredward's? There was no way to tell. Donna moved her head slightly back and forth. "I don't know."

In the moment, she didn't care. She closed her eyes. The pain in her leg had taken over the lower half of her body and was creeping up her torso like a fungus. Her chest was starting to hurt. Even breathing was difficult. "Is...Rico okay?"

"We think so." Cammie took Donna's free hand. "Sis, you don't look so good."

"Ishalan...needs...help." The ash seemed to be clouding her vision. "Get him...safe."

"*You* need help."

"Yeah." Maybe she did. "Don't...feel...so good."

"Temo." Cammie's voice held a desperate urgency. "We need to get her out of here. *Now*."

And then the pain became too much, and darkness swept her into its welcoming arms.

Donna woke to a gloomy gray light a few shades above total blackness. The shapes around her were familiar. In another moment, she recognized her bedroom. Soft beeping meant she was hooked up to a monitor again.

She'd slept, but for how long? And how much of what she remembered was real and how much of it had just been a dream?

Her leg throbbed, and the rest of her body felt like death. Was she dead? Maybe. Who cared? Things had gone so wrong. She reached for her crucifix and found an IV in her hand. She took hold of the crucifix and prayed that Rico had survived.

That all of her team had survived. Someone had, obviously, because they'd brought her back here.

Tears leaked from her eyes and slid into her hair. She let them fall. The queen was dead. Artemis. Gone. And it was all Donna's fault. How many centuries had Artemis endured? Only to be turned to ash because of a course of events that Donna had set in motion.

She felt like an open pit of sorrow and bleakness. She wished she could fall into that pit and disappear.

The bedroom door opened a few inches, and Dr. Fox slipped in. He went to the monitor and looked at the readout, shaking his head a little.

"Am I going to live?"

He glanced over. "You're awake."

She turned her head away. "Yes."

He came over to stand by the bed. "You're going to live. You were poisoned again. A different, much stronger toxin. Quite a bit faster acting. I don't know how it didn't stop your heart. Perhaps the thing that you think protects you from the sun actually protects your life."

She didn't really care about herself at the moment.

"How's Rico?"

"As of yesterday, he's doing very well. He was dehydrated and had some severe burns from the silver, along with some bruises, but those will heal."

"Good. Glad to hear—wait." She looked at him again as his words processed. "As of yesterday? How long has it been?"

"Two days." He clasped his hands in front of him. "How are you feeling?"

That was easy to answer. "Miserable." She sniffed. She didn't want to cry in front of him, but her emotions were paper-thin.

"Physically? Or emotionally?"

She swallowed at the knot forming in her throat. "Emotionally, but also not all that hot physically."

"Some of that emotion is the toxin. The fae seem to love that kind of psychological warfare. But I'm sure some of it is also because you're grieving."

She pressed her head back into the pillow and stared at the ceiling. "The queen is dead." Her voice wavered. "Because of me."

"That's not true. Yes, it's a terrible loss for the vampire nation, but no one blames you. You didn't force Artemis to show up. Only a fool goes into battle acting like they think they're bulletproof. And at her age, she knew the risks better than most." He paused for a moment. "It might even be said that she planned this."

"What?" Donna pushed to a sitting position.

"Forget I said anything. Please, lie down. You need to rest.

"Dr. Fox, explain."

He shrugged. "She's now a martyr. With her death, Artemis made it open season on the fae. Before this, a vampire killing a fae would have sparked a war." His eyes narrowed slightly. "Now, there is already a bonfire blazing. Another death or two or ten won't change how hot it burns."

Donna shook her head. "You really think she'd do that?"

"With Artemis, anything is possible." He smiled. "Please don't feel responsible."

She let out a long sigh. "It's hard not to. Even if she allowed herself to be a martyr, my actions created the opportunity."

"I understand."

"Was anyone else killed?"

"I believe a wolf died. A good number of injuries as well."

The news didn't help her mood. "Any word on Ishalan? The fae who helped us? I think he was pretty badly injured." If not dead. She didn't know how resilient fae were, so she couldn't guess how he'd fared after his treatment at Dredward's hands.

"I'm sorry, but I don't know. Would you like to see Charlie? Or Pierce? Or your sister? Or anyone else? Everyone's here."

"My sister is still here? After two days?" Donna nodded. "Send her in. Please."

"I will. And now that you're awake, you should feed."

"I can do that with the toxin inside me?"

"The toxin's been mostly flushed out of your system. You're just recovering from the effects at this point. Feeding will speed that up."

"Okay. But just from a glass. I'm not up for more than that right now."

"Understandable." He glanced at the monitor one more time before he left.

A few moments later, the door opened again, and Cammie stuck her head in. "Hey."

"Hey."

Cammie entered, wearing jeans and a simple gray sweatshirt, her hair back in a low ponytail. "How are you feeling?"

"I'll live. Apparently. I'm surprised you stayed. I thought you'd go back to the convent."

Her smile was strained as she sat on the edge of the bed. She smoothed a wrinkle in the coverlet. "I can't go back."

"Why not?"

She glanced at her hands. "The order forbade me to return." She looked up again, smiling tightly. "I pretty much knew that would happen."

"Wait, back up. You knew that would happen? Why?"

"Because I came to help you."

"Oh, Cammie. Can you protest the decision? That's ridiculous. There's no way you deserve—"

"It's okay. I knew what I was doing when I made my choice."

Donna's heart clenched at the sacrifice her sister had made on her behalf. "You're staying here with me, then."

Cammie took a breath and smiled. "That's a very kind offer, but I don't know how it would go over for the vampire governor of New Jersey to have a former Venari hunter living with her."

"Screw how it goes over. You're my sister."

"Donna—"

"Camille, I'm not arguing with you. You're staying here. There's plenty of room."

"I'll stay for a little bit. But just until I figure things out and get my own place. I have some money."

"How much could you possibly have?"

"Not much, but—"

"And what will you do to support yourself?"

"I have skills."

"I know you do. But I don't see a lot of ads in the paper for vampire hunters."

Cammie laughed. "You're just looking in the wrong papers."

Donna could tell Cammie meant that, but nothing really surprised her anymore. "So you'd freelance?"

"It's a possibility."

"Wow. I didn't know that was a thing."

Charlie peeked in. "Governor? I have your dinner."

"Come on in."

Charlie came to the bedside and handed Donna a big, warm mug. "Good to see you awake."

"Good to be awake." She took the mug and drank the contents down without stopping. The surge of power and well-being was almost instant. "That definitely helped. You said dinner. What time is it?"

"Around 5 p.m." Charlie answered. "Are you going to rest some more?"

"No." Donna pulled the covers off and swung her feet to the floor. Someone had put her in a nightshirt. She still had her underwear on, but not her bra. "Someone got me out of my battle gear, I see."

"I did," Cammie said.

"Thanks. Charlie, will you send Dr. Fox back in? I want this IV out, then I'm going to take a shower, and then I want a full briefing on everything I missed."

Charlie nodded. "I'll be in the office waiting."

"I'm assuming you have things to brief me on?"

"Oh," Charlie said. "More things than you can imagine."

"Good or bad or—" Donna held up her hand. "Don't tell me. It can wait until after the shower. Baby steps."

"I'll go get Dr. Fox." She hesitated. "Will made it, by the way."

"Will?" Donna gasped. "Will Ferris? I actually turned him? I thought that was a dream. He survived?"

"He did. You sired your first vampire. Congratulations. See you in the office." She left.

Donna shook her head. "I made another vampire. How do you like that?"

"It was bound to happen sooner or later." Cammie stood. "I'm just glad you didn't die."

"Me too. I'm really sorry you got kicked out of the order. But I appreciate you coming to help me more than I have words to express. I was feeling pretty sad about how things were between us."

"Same," Cammie said. "That's why I made the decision I did. You didn't choose to be a vampire, but I did choose to be a Venari. And so I made another choice. I don't regret it."

"I love you."

"I love you too." Cammie grinned. "Use extra soap. You're pretty ripe."

"Thanks." Donna smiled.

Cammie laughed. "Just teasing."

Dr. Fox entered.

Cammie hooked her thumb toward the door. "See you out there."

"Yep." Just like that, things had returned to normal between them. But Donna suspected that it would take Cammie a bit to adjust to this change. How could it not? She'd been a nun, and apparently a vampire hunter, for nearly all her adult life.

Dr. Fox unhooked her from everything. "You're free. How are you feeling since you fed?"

"Good."

"Leg still hurts, I'd imagine."

"It does. But that can't last forever."

"Maybe another day or two. If you don't need me..."

She sat up a little straighter. "You've been here the whole time, haven't you? Go home. I'm sure you need some rest. And your family must miss you."

He smiled. "Call if anything changes."

"I will. But it won't. I'll be fine."

"Don't overdo it. You still need rest."

"Right. Order received, loud and clear."

With a little wave, he left.

She got up and walked gingerly into the bathroom, babying her leg. She flicked on the light, almost afraid to look at herself. Despite having just fed, her skin was pale, and there were dark circles under her eyes. Her hair looked oddly dull too.

She ran her hands through it, combing it into place.

A few small, gray flakes drifted free.

Ash.

Donna leaned on the counter and cried.

Chapter 21

She stood under the hot water for an inordinate amount of time, as though the deluge could somehow wash away the pain of Artemis's death. It couldn't, obviously. Just like it couldn't remove the purple and yellow bruise that stretched from her hip to a few inches above her knee. The whole thing was tender to the touch, although the puncture wound on her hip had healed.

She soaped up anyway. Pain was a reminder she was alive.

She was also bone-tired. There was no other way to describe it. Not tired of being governor, but tired of all the chaos. The weight on her shoulders had never felt heavier. Her life with the mob hadn't been this hard. Had it?

Maybe that was hindsight through rose-colored glasses. But boy, could she use a week or two when the most stressful thing that happened was deciding which TV show to binge-watch.

She finally dried off, got dressed, and went to the office so Charlie could bring her up to speed. She ran into her admin halfway down the hall, distress marring her pretty face. Not a good sign. "What's wrong?"

"Governor, we have a problem."

"Of course we do. We were running low." Donna sighed. "What now?"

"Fitzhugh has filed a formal complaint against Pierce for punching him at Francine's party and against you for allowing it."

Donna just stared at her for a moment. "That was almost a week ago. You have got to be kidding me."

"I wish I was."

She did her best to stay calm. Even took a deep, cleansing breath. But her leg was throbbing, and the queen's death continued to weigh on her, and she was just about done. "Does he know about Artemis?"

Charlie nodded. "That's pretty common knowledge now."

"I see. Why do I think these two things are somehow connected?"

Charlie's mouth thinned to a hard line. "Because you're a smart woman, and you know what an opportunist Fitzhugh is. I believe they're connected as well. The queen's death has left a powerful vacancy. One that Fitzhugh would very much like to cram himself into as quickly as possible."

Donna rolled her eyes. "Can you imagine him as the vampire king? That wouldn't be good for anyone. Except him." She sighed. "But why come after us?"

"All I can guess is that he wants to discredit you

while trying to make himself look like the victim. Earn some sympathy votes. All while causing you trouble."

Donna snorted. "I can barely handle being governor. If he thinks I have any desire to be queen, he's a dumbass. Well, a bigger one than he is currently."

Charlie laughed. "No argument from me on that assessment. But I have to say you're doing an exceptional job as governor. But the truth is, it's unlikely you'd be offered Artemis's position anyway."

Donna exhaled, not realizing she'd been holding her breath. "Good. You know what? Get Fitzy on the phone. It's time for us to have a come-to-Jesus meeting."

Charlie's brows lifted as amusement bent her mouth. "Right away, Governor." She turned and went back to the office.

Donna followed and got punched in the gut by an unexpected sight as she walked in. The armory doors were open, and Artemis's gold sword had been hung on the back wall. It gleamed softly in the light. Almost like a memorial.

A soft half sob left Donna's throat before she could stop herself.

Charlie looked over. "I'm so sorry. I meant to close those."

Donna swallowed. "It's okay." She walked closer. "I didn't know that her sword had come back with me."

"It took Temo and Pierce both to pry your hand open to take the sword from you. I cleaned it and thought it should go somewhere safe."

Donna stared at the gorgeous, deadly weapon. The blade was worked with a faintly Egyptian pattern. Or maybe it was something older. She nodded. "It should. Until it can be returned. To wherever it belongs."

"It's the royal sword, so it'll go to whoever takes over."

Donna frowned. "I really don't want to see that in Fitzhugh's hands."

"I don't think there's a chance that could happen. Although...who knows?"

"How do they pick the new king or queen?"

"The Immortus Concilio will nominate a panel of possible successors. Then the Prime makes the final decision. I'm sure they're already squirreled away somewhere, coming up with a list."

Donna arched her brows. "The Prime?"

"He's the oldest known vampire in existence. Some claim he's the grandsire of almost every vampire. And he's the final word when it comes to big decisions like this. Any major vampire decision, really. He's essentially the leader of the entire vampire nation. Legend says if he was ever to be killed, vampires would cease to exist. But legend also says his age has made him truly immortal."

"What's his name?"

"He just goes by Prime."

"Why am I just hearing about him?"

"For one thing, he keeps a very low profile. I don't think more than a handful of people outside of the council have ever seen him or even know where he lives. Although I would have thought Claudette or Artemis would have mentioned him to you. Okay, maybe not Claudette, but someone. Pierce, maybe? But then, we have been a little preoccupied."

"True statement. So who do you think the council will nominate? And who do you think the Prime will pick?"

"There are a few likely candidates, but typically, he chooses the oldest vampire. Not always, but most of the time. Makes sense. The older the vampire is, the more powerful and skilled they are."

"I can see that. I haven't even learned how to glamour people yet." Donna took a seat at her desk. "Who are the oldest governors?"

Charlie tapped a finger against her lip. "Governor Joseph of Idaho has been ruling for a little over three hundred years. I'd say he's got a good shot. Or maybe the governor of Hawaii. She's also close to three hundred, but typically the council picks someone in the contiguous forty-eight states. The oldest governor is Governor Kitka from Alaska at nearly four hundred years, but he could have been king before Artemis and turned it down. I doubt he'll be asked again because of that. In fact, he might be why they only ask governors in the lower forty-eight." She shrugged. "But he might get a second chance. You never know with the council."

"You really know your governors."

"It's my job."

"I'm glad, because that's all great information. Where's Fitzhugh in that ranking?"

"He's a possibility, but a very distant one. Not as distant as you are, however." Charlie smiled as she went back to her desk. "You have nothing to worry about as far as being chosen. You're far too new."

"For once, that's a positive. Speaking of sires, I should probably get in touch with Will. See how he's doing."

"Daisy called this morning to say he'd had a good night. They've been keeping him well fed so there's no danger of...you know."

"Yeah, I do. What about the psychic connection that's supposed to exist between a sire and their...child? Is that the right word? Seems odd to think of that burly biker as my child."

"But he is, in a way. And yes, that's the right word. The psychic connection should be there. It's very possible he hasn't used it because he knows you're also recovering. He probably doesn't have a reason to use it either. I can definitely let him and his daughters know you're up and about now, though."

Donna nodded. "Do that. I'd like to go see him soon. I do not want to leave him dangling like Claudette did with me."

Charlie's smile was small but sweet. "I don't think you have to worry about that. Will and his daughters know as much about vampires as anyone. I doubt anything about this turning will surprise him."

"I guess that's a good thing." Donna gestured at

the phone. "Go ahead and get Fitzhugh. I want this dealt with now."

Charlie picked up the phone and dialed. "Charlene Rollins calling on behalf of Governor Barrone. Is Governor Fitzhugh available? Very good. Transferring to Governor Barrone now." She gave Donna a nod.

Donna picked up her phone. A little click could be heard, then Hawke Fitzhugh came on.

"Calling to apologize?"

"You're a broken record, you know that? No, I'm not calling to apologize, because I haven't done anything that requires an apology. Instead, let's jump right to the elephant in the room. Why are you filing charges against Pierce? You earned that punch, and you know it."

The other side of the phone went quiet. And stayed that way. Being called out apparently made him speechless.

Donna was happy to fill the silence. "If you think you're going to earn sympathy votes from the council and get yourself on the short list for king, you ought to rethink that. Getting punched by a human is one thing, but reacting to it so poorly that you file charges, to quote my daughter, that's weak sauce."

He finally responded with a derisive snort. "It's not my fault that you can't keep your assistant under control."

"There was nothing to control. He was protecting me. Your drunkenness, combined with your loutish behavior, was rightly perceived as threatening. How about you just man up and accept that you made some errors that night?"

Charlie cringed, and Donna wondered what she'd said to trigger that reaction.

Fitzhugh huffed. "You're a train wreck, Barrone. You and your whole administration. You should have never been made governor. Never."

"Well, I am, so—"

He hung up.

"He's such a jerk." Donna put the phone down.

"No argument there." Charlie had turned back to face her computer screen and was typing away.

"What did I say wrong that made you pull that face?"

"Nothing wrong, exactly. But I'm sure the 'man up' comment rubbed him the wrong way."

"He's fussier than a teething baby. I'm done with trying to coddle him and play nice. That goes for everyone who wants to cause trouble for me and my team. *Done*."

Admiration brightened Charlie's expression. "I hope it's not too forward of me to say I love you. If Claudette had had half of your strength—" She laughed. "Forget I said that. I much prefer working for you."

"I appreciate that, Charlie. I'm very glad you're my admin. Now, bring me up to speed on everything else that's happened. How is Ishalan?"

"You don't remember?"

A deep sense of foreboding went through Donna.

"Oh no, don't tell me he died."

"No. As you were passing out, you told Temo to take care of him. Which he did, by getting LV to take him in until he could recover. She did, too, probably because of the fae's assistance in getting Rico back. A bunch of the wolves pulled a tapestry out of the fortress and wrapped him up in it to protect him from the daylight. One of the tapestries that wasn't on fire, that is."

"Yeah, I might have started that blaze. But I don't remember them helping Ishalan at all. I'm very glad that happened, though. Ishalan might not have been as useful as I'd hoped he'd be, but I don't think that was entirely his fault. Plus, he took on Dredward. I'm not sure I'd have gotten Rico out if Ishalan hadn't done that. Hopefully, he'll continue to be an ally."

"I think he will. A surprising number of the fae surrendered almost as soon as the fighting started."

"I remember seeing groups of them with their arms over their heads when I came out of the stronghold." It gave her hope too. "How about Neo?"

"That drone of hers was amazing. She probably took out more fae soldiers than anyone else."

"Get out of here. Wow! I wish I could give her some kind of award, but she's not even my constituent."

"You still could." Charlie smirked. "But I'm pretty sure she's about to become one of your constituents rather soon. She and Temo aren't showing any signs of cooling down. And she's an hour away. That's too far when you're head over heels."

"Well, I'd be happy to have her closer. What about Kace? He got hit, right?"

"He did, but the blow had no effect. Really, the only casualty on our side was a single wolf. The fae took the brunt of it. Their magic may have allowed them to be out during daylight hours, but they definitely weren't at full strength. And with the wolves, we outnumbered them."

"And now Dredward's dead. What does that mean for them?"

"Much like for the vampire nation, they'll have to find a new leader. If they haven't already. I'm sure all the royal ministers are fighting over the throne as we speak." She shrugged. "I'm sure we'll hear something soon, but we don't exactly get a fae newsletter."

"Right. Everyone else is fine? Pierce? Rixaline? Will's daughters?"

"All good."

"That's a relief." She slumped back in her chair. "What day is it, by the way? I feel like I've lost track."

Charlie laughed. "It's Wednesday. Almost 6 p.m. now."

"Did I miss the funeral for the wolf? I'd like to send flowers. Actually, I'd like to attend. Not just to pay my respects, but to show LV and Toni that our joint effort wasn't just a one-time thing."

"It's tomorrow morning. But a vampire out in daylight, no matter how worthy the cause, will raise eyebrows. You'll have to use the potion excuse again."

Donna shook her head. "No. I'm not lying anymore. I don't care who knows that I'm immune to the sun. When I said I was done, I meant it."

Chapter 22

"Governor, you know that could put you in danger."

"Charlie, I've been governor barely three weeks, and I've already been shot, stabbed, and poisoned twice. Maybe if word spreads that I can daywalk, it'll instill a little fear into the next yahoo that wants to take a crack at me. Because a vampire who can daywalk isn't nearly as vulnerable as one restricted to evening hours."

Still looking rather unsure, Charlie sighed. "You're not wrong."

"I hope not, because I'm tired of being thought of as an easy target. Being new doesn't help that. Look how Fitzhugh treats me. Has any other vampire come out as a daywalker?"

"Not any governor that I know." Charlie frowned. "There have been rumors of daywalkers but never a vampire who was really known for it. Outside of Astrid. But I think she's more of a legend than a real vampire. Hard to say."

"Who's she?"

"A Viking shield maiden who was supposedly unkillable. This led to the belief that she was a daywalking vampire."

"I see. If she was unkillable, is she still alive?"

"No one's sure. If she is, she's changed her name and reinvented herself. Happens a lot in the vampire world. Being the same person gets old after a few centuries."

Donna sat up straighter as a new thought came to her. "I bet Cammie would know about daywalkers. Considering her former profession and all."

Charlie nodded. "Talking to her is a good idea. In fact, I don't want to overstep, but I think your decision to be honest about your ability is something we should all discuss. At least you, me, Temo, and Pierce. It affects us too, in that we're around you and if you become a target, we could become collateral damage."

Donna nodded. "You're right. Text everyone and have them come to the conference room in an hour. I want Cammie there and also Jerabeth. She's part of the team, and she already knows, so we might as well include her. Although she may not feel like coming back for the meeting. We could just telecom her in. That would be fine."

"I'll work it out."

"Thank you. Now, speaking of funerals. What are the plans for honoring Artemis? I'm assuming it's going to be a major event."

Charlie shrugged. "Vampire memorials don't always work that way. Especially when there's no body. Anyway, I'm not sure yet. I expect there will be something, but I haven't heard anything from her deputy, Marcus. Or any of her team."

"Do you think that's because they blame me and they don't want me to be present? Or is it because they haven't organized anything yet?"

"I don't think they blame you. More likely they're all still in shock. Although Marcus isn't the kind to let grief sway him from his duties. He's more the kind to soldier through and get everything handled, then collapse. I'll reach out to them and see what I can find out. I'm assuming you'd like to attend that as well. If there is a memorial."

"Yes, I would." Donna glanced toward the armory, her guilt over Artemis's death still clinging to her with a tenacity that caused her almost physical pain. Maybe it would get better in time, but right now, it felt impossible to shake. She pushed to her feet. "I'm going to talk to Cammie. I'll see you in the conference room in an hour."

"One hour."

Donna headed for the guest rooms, where she hoped to find her sister. She did. Cammie was sitting in a chair by one of the windows, just staring out and looking very much like Donna felt. A little lost and unsure. "Hey. Can I talk to you?"

Cammie looked over, seemingly happy for the distraction. "Sure. Change your mind about letting me stay?"

Smiling, Donna shook her head. "Never. But I need your advice."

"About what?"

"About what the Venari would do if they found out I could daywalk."

All traces of amusement left Cammie's face. "That's a bad idea. Them finding out."

Donna sat on the end of the bed. "Why? Tell me specifically what they'd do. Please."

Cammie took a deep breath. "It would certainly bump you up on their radar."

"Is that a bad thing? So what if they're more aware of me? I'm not doing anything wrong."

"I'm no longer in the Venari loop, but I know they're not thrilled about the battle that just went down."

"You said that would happen." With everything going on, Donna had pushed the consequences out of her mind. "Do you think they're going to go forward with the kill order?"

"No, but I can only imagine their reaction to how it ended. I mean, two fairly stable supernatural nations have been thrown into leaderless chaos because of you."

Donna blinked hard. "Hey, now. I haven't heard about any chaos. And new leaders will be chosen soon."

"I'm just telling you how the Venari will perceive it. Things were...okay, not *good* between the vampires and the fae, but it was relatively peaceful. And a known quantity. Now it's not. Things could change drastically, depending on who takes over for the fae. And the vampires. I'm sure the Venari are watching very closely."

"Dredward wasn't exactly Mother Teresa, you know."

"No, he wasn't. But Artemis was enough of a pacifist to keep things from escalating."

"Artemis was a pacifist? She was trying to kill Dredward when she died."

"I understand that. But as queen, she was perceived as a pacifist, and that's how she ruled. She kept the peace. And very well too. At the battle, I think she just reached a point where she'd had enough."

"I know the feeling." Donna rolled her head back and forth. Maybe a massage would help. Bliss her out long enough to give her a break from the weight of everything she was carrying. But that wouldn't do anything to alleviate the number of things that still needed her attention. "Can you get me a meeting with the Venari? Someone with enough influence to matter?"

"Yes. But are you really going to tell them you can daywalk?"

"I'm tired of keeping it a secret." She leaned back on the bed, propping herself up with her elbows. "Have you ever known a vampire who could?"

"I was sent to…dispatch one once."

"Dispatch. That's a nice word. Hardly seems death-related at all."

Cammie frowned. "I was doing my job. And the

vampire in question lived in a residential area where several people had gone missing. Once we had irrefutable evidence, that was that."

"How was this vampire able to daywalk?"

"I don't know. That wasn't my job."

Donna sat up. "But that has to be something the Venari would want to know, right?"

"That's above my pay grade. Or was. I was just a hunter. You want to know about vampire physiology, you'd have to talk to one of the researchers. That's who I turned the ashes over to."

"Then you must know one?"

"I know several, but they won't have anything to do with me now. When you're out, you're out. Talking to me could cost them their positions as well."

Donna sighed. "Well, that's no help. Do you know of any other daywalkers?"

"I've heard rumors. Again, the Venari would know, specifically the data keepers. But just like the researchers, they won't speak to me either."

Donna thought a moment. "How does the Venari keep records?"

"Like any other big organization. On computers. Although they probably do more paper backups than most."

Donna got to her feet. "I need to talk to Neo."

"She's the techie one, right?"

"Yes."

Cammie's eyes narrowed. "What are you going to do?"

"Probably better if you don't know."

"I'm not dumb. You're going to get her to hack in."

"I will neither confirm nor deny—"

"Won't work. Their security is impeccable."

Donna shrugged. "I'm sure it is. That's what security is meant to be, after all." She grinned. "I'll let you know how it goes. By the way, there's a meeting in the conference room in forty-five minutes. I'd like you to be there."

Cammie sighed but nodded.

Donna went back to her bedroom to grab her phone, which she'd left charging on the nightstand, and dialed Neo.

A sleepy voice answered after four rings. "Whassup?"

"Sorry to wake you. I need your help. Well, really, I need you to move closer. Manhattan is too far away."

"Mm-hmm. Seems that way to me, too, these days. What do you need help with?"

"A computer thing. I don't want to say more than that on the phone."

"Oh. *Oh.*" A little rustling of bed linens. "You want me to come up? I mean, over?"

"Yes, please."

"Cool. I'll be there at sundown."

"Perfect. See you then." Donna hung up and looked at the time on her phone. Sunset was in less than an hour. There was no way Neo would make it that quickly. Especially when she couldn't travel during daylight. Whatever. Donna chalked it up to her being sleepy and not thinking straight. Or she was downstairs with Temo again.

Smiling at that thought, Donna called LV.

"Good evening, Governor. Very good to hear from you."

"Good evening, Alpha Medina. It's good to be heard from. I was so very sorry to find out that one of your wolves didn't make it."

"Thank you. We are in mourning, for sure, but he was a brave man who died in an honorable way. He will be celebrated."

"That's good. May I ask how your grandson is doing?"

"Very well. We expect Rico to be released from the hospital this evening."

"That's great."

"How are your injuries, if I might ask? The last I saw of you, you were surrounded by your team and didn't look well."

"After two days of rest and care from my doctor, I'm doing pretty well. A little bruised, but then, I'm guessing we all were."

LV laughed softly. "A small price to pay for Rico's safe return. And I am not sorry about Dredward's end, though I am about your queen. Artemis was a fair ruler. Her loss must be very hard on all of you."

Donna took a breath. "It has been. But vampires have been around since time eternal. We will continue."

"Any word on her successor?"

"Not yet, no. I'm sure we'll hear something soon." Donna didn't want to delve any deeper into that topic, so she shifted the conversation. "LV, I hope it's not too forward of me, but I don't want our collaboration to be a one-time thing. I would like very much if we could consider ourselves permanent allies."

LV's voice held a smile. "I accused you of kidnapping my grandson, and not only did you not hold it against me, you orchestrated his successful rescue. Donna, the New Jersey pack will be your ally as long as there is a Medina serving as alpha. Hopefully beyond that."

"Thank you. And the same to you. As long as I'm governor, you can count on me. In fact, if you have no objections, I'd like to attend the funeral tomorrow."

"I have no objections, but isn't that a little impossible? It's at 10 a.m."

"I'll make the necessary provisions. Like I did for the raid." Donna wasn't willing to say differently than that just yet.

"If you're able, you are very welcome. I'll see you there."

"Good night, LV."

"Good night, my friend."

Donna hung up and went out to the kitchen. She was actually starving for real food. Pierce was sitting at the counter with the same idea, based on the sheaf of takeout menus in front of him.

He smiled when he saw her. "Hey, how are you feeling? It's good to see you up."

"It's good to be up. I feel decent." She took the seat next to him. He put his arm around her shoulders for a quick hug, accompanied by a kiss to her temple. She leaned into the embrace, taking comfort in it.

"I'm glad to hear that." He let her go and spread the menus out a little more. "Hungry?"

"Starving."

"Do you need more than food?"

"No, I'm good. I had a mug when I first woke up. Now I want real food. Something delicious and bad for me. And then I want to disappear into a good movie." She picked out a menu and opened it up. "How about cheesesteaks? With fries. And onion rings. And pie for dessert."

He grinned. "That sounds perfect. You want me to let everyone know? Or is that what the meeting is about?"

"No." She looked at him. "It's about me going public with my daywalking secret."

His smile vanished. "Are you sure that's a good idea?"

"Not at all, but then again, maybe it is. Maybe it would make me seem a little less vulnerable to my enemies. You know what I mean?"

"I do. But I worry that it could also make you more of a target."

"You mean more than I am now?"

"Point taken. Still, I worry it would bring a new

element out of the woodwork. Those interested in finding out exactly how you're able to daywalk."

"Do you think we're not equipped to handle that?"

He seemed to weigh that. "I'm sure we could. I think. Temo would have to be the final word on that."

"Well, that's what I want to discuss. The pros and cons. What everyone thinks about it. Because this decision definitely affects all of us."

"Have you talked to Cammie about it?"

"Yes. I've asked her to set up a meeting for me with the Venari so I can talk to them about it. I figure being proactive would be a step in the right direction." She ran her finger down the crease in the menu. "Have you ever heard of a vampire who could daywalk?"

"Just the legend about the Viking shield maiden. My brother used to talk about how lucky she was."

Donna nodded. "You miss him, don't you?"

"I do. But it's gotten easier since I've come to work for you."

She smiled. "That's kind of you to say."

He turned in his seat to face her a little more. "Are you and Kace going to start dating?"

She laughed. "That came out of nowhere."

He shrugged. "I know he likes you. I wouldn't be surprised if you were attracted to him. He's young and handsome and well built. I'm not blind."

"There are no plans for any such relationship. Although I think he'd be okay with it."

"He'd be an idiot if he wasn't. You're the hottest woman he's ever seen, that's for sure."

She snorted as she shook her head. "I don't know about that, but you are so good for my ego." She put her hand on his arm. "Will you come with me to the funeral tomorrow morning? For the fallen wolf?"

"I'd be honored." He narrowed his eyes. "Is that why you want to announce your ability? So you can attend without questions?"

"No. I want to do it because of what I told you. I'm tired of hiding it, and I'd like to make my enemies think twice. But I wouldn't announce it before the funeral anyway. That would draw too much attention to myself, and it needs to be about the fallen hero. Besides, they're all under the impression that I used a potion by Jerabeth to keep me safe during the raid. I've already hinted to LV I'd be using it again. No reason they can't keep thinking that's what's making me immune."

"That works." He patted her hand, then picked up a menu. "If I order now, we could all eat together in the conference room. And then have our pie with the movie."

"I'm in. I'll go see what Charlie wants to eat."

Pierce was right. The food came about the time everyone was sitting down. He and Charlie passed everything out. Neo had joined them, arriving a few minutes before Temo, but smelling very much like his cologne, which probably meant she'd gone to see him first.

Or had already been downstairs, as Donna had suspected.

Either way, it didn't matter. Donna liked them as a couple very much. And if being closer to Temo meant Neo moved to New Jersey, Donna heartily approved.

She let everyone eat for a few minutes and get the small talk out of their systems.

When the food was mostly gone, she dunked a French fry in ketchup, ate it, then looked at her friends gathered around the table. Neo, Temo, Charlie, Pierce, and Cammie, plus Jerabeth via a laptop. "Thank you all for joining me."

"Thanks for dinner," Temo said.

She smiled. "You're welcome. I appreciate all of you very much. And I am so grateful you all came through the raid on the fae safely."

"You too," Neo said. "I would have had to waste a lot more of them if they took my girl out."

Donna laughed. "Thank you for having my back."

"You know it."

She took a moment, her thoughts focusing on the reason she'd called them there. "I have something on my mind. Something I want to discuss. And I'd like your honest opinion, so please don't hold back. Understood?"

Everyone nodded, expressions ranging from serious to curious.

"Neo, everyone else knows this already, but I've been keeping a pretty significant secret. I trust that you'll help me keep that secret, should this conversation not go as planned."

She crossed her heart. "Until I turn to dust."

"Thank you." Donna knew Neo meant that. She'd become a good friend and a valuable asset. "Shortly after I was turned, I discovered I am immune to the sun."

CHAPTER 23

Neo's mouth fell open. "Are you for real?"

Donna nodded at her friend. "Yes. I understand it's an extremely rare occurrence, although not unheard of. But sharing that secret with all of you isn't really why I asked you here. What I really want to talk about is making that secret public. I'm tired of having to hide it. I'm tired of a lot of things."

Charlie nodded. "You've had a heavier burden to bear than any new governor in a long time."

Temo nodded. "For sure."

"That's all part of why I want to reveal this," Donna continued. "My hope is that knowing about my ability would make my enemies think long and hard about coming after me. But I understand it would also likely make me a target and thereby put you all in that line of fire. So I want your opinion on whether I should do it."

They all just stared at her for a moment.

Pierce spoke first. "I worry about *you* becoming a target. But I've seen what you're capable of. And

I support whatever decision you make. There's a part of me that thinks it would absolutely make someone think twice about coming after you."

Temo nodded. "I feel the same way, boss. And if we need to bump up security, we will."

"Do it," Neo said. "Who's going to come after a daywalker? No one with a brain, that's for sure."

"You don't think it'll cause problems?" Donna asked.

Neo nodded slowly. "Is there any decision in life that doesn't make someone unhappy? Blowback happens. Doesn't mean anyone will act on it. Plus, people know you're not alone. They know you have a killer team around you."

"Yeah, they do," Temo said as he popped a fry in his mouth.

On-screen, Jerabeth raised her hand. "Governor, would you rather tell people that I've come up with some kind of permanent spell that allows you to daywalk?"

"Thank you for the offer, but no. I fear that would only make you the focus for other vampires who'd want you to re-create it for them. And there's no need for you to be in danger."

She nodded. "I should have thought of that."

Cammie hadn't touched her food since Donna had started talking. "I was against this initially, but I've been thinking. It absolutely could work in your favor. Consider this. If I was a vampire, and another of my kind came out as a daywalker, I would definitely consider them more powerful than I was.

And that would make me wonder what else they were capable of."

Neo nodded. "She's right. I mean, if you're bold enough to reveal that, what haven't you talked about? What else you got up your sleeve? Know what I mean?"

"I do," Donna said. "I'd like to think others would see it that way too."

Cammie's eyes narrowed slightly. "How would you make the announcement?"

Donna glanced from her sister to Charlie. "I guess sending out a press release on the governors' loop would be the best way."

Charlie finished the bite of cheesesteak she'd taken. "An official notice would be the easiest. After that, the entire vampire world—and probably most of the supernatural one—would know within twenty-four hours. Probably less. News like that will travel like wildfire."

"Okay, then that's how we'll do it." Donna looked around the table again. "Anyone opposed?"

Temo shook his head. "If you're good, so am I. When are you going to do this?"

"Soon. But not before the funeral tomorrow. I don't want to draw attention from the man being buried. For now, I'm just letting the wolves think I'm using the same potion Jerabeth provided me with to get through the raid. I may tell LV and Toni in private, if the opportunity arises, but I'm not making an issue of it."

"Smart," Pierce said.

"I also want Neo to see if she can hack into the Venari's database and find info on any other daywalkers that might have existed."

Neo's brows shot up, and she looked at Cammie. "You approved this?"

Cammie snorted. "Of course not, but I'm not Venari anymore. And Donna can make her own decisions. She is the governor, after all."

"True." Neo shrugged. "I'm not confident I'll be able to get through their security."

"You won't," Cammie said.

Neo wiggled her brows. "You don't know my skills."

Cammie laughed softly as she shrugged one shoulder. "I know Venari security. You won't be the first to try. And fail."

"Any tips?"

"No, sorry, that wasn't my department. I was never even issued a passcode."

Donna interjected. "I'd just like to know more about other daywalkers. From any source. Specifically, what happened to them after the information became known."

"You mean," Temo started, "if they had problems with other vampires because of it."

"In a nutshell, yes." Donna didn't want to share her secret if every daywalker before her had died a horrible death at the hands of a jealous rival. Or the Venari.

Neo wiped her hands on a napkin. "I'll start on that tonight."

"I can ask around," Temo said. "See if any of my sources have heard anything. Don't worry, I'll keep things on the DL."

"Thank you." Donna took a sip of her water.

Charlie folded up the paper her cheesesteak had been wrapped in. "We can start drafting the letter tonight."

"You know what?" Donna gave a little shake of her head. "No to any work being done tonight. Tomorrow is soon enough. Tonight, I want to veg out in front of a good movie and have a slice of that pie Pierce ordered. Maybe two. I need to not think about all of this for a while. I'm hoping you'll all join me. I'd certainly enjoy the evening more with your company, and we could all use a distraction."

Jerabeth laughed. "I should have driven back."

"I'm in." Neo looked at Temo.

He smiled back. "Yeah, me too."

Shocker. Donna smiled. "Cammie?"

A little reluctantly, her sister nodded. "Okay."

It had to be hard for her to go from the austere, focused life she'd known to living in a penthouse with a crew of supernaturals. Hopefully, the transition wouldn't be too difficult for too long. Cammie deserved to be happy. In whatever way that meant.

Charlie's phone chimed. She ignored it. "Sorry. Just an incoming email. I meant to put it on silent."

Donna looked at her. "It's okay if you want to check it."

"I'm sure it's nothing important." Charlie glanced at the screen. And kept staring. Then she picked up the phone and tapped it. A low groan emanated out of her. "You've got to be kidding me."

"What now?" Donna asked. "Are zombies arising from their graves? Because it's probably about time."

Charlie swallowed. "Fitzhugh has just sent a letter of his own to the governors' loop."

Donna braced herself. "And?"

Everyone around the table was silent.

"That power-hungry idiot." Charlie looked up. "He's claiming you're responsible for the death of Queen Artemis. He's calling on the council to investigate. Which they'd do anyway. The death of a queen isn't a small matter. But he's pushing it."

Donna quelled the urge to curse. Or flip the table.

Pierce did the cursing for her. He pushed back from the table with such force that his chair fell over. "That's enough. I'm not going to stand for this. It's one thing to come after me for something I actually did, but to make up lies about you? No. He needs to be stopped."

Donna felt the same, but those were easy words to speak. "I'm not arguing with that, but how exactly do you propose we do that? And honestly, my actions did set things in motion."

Charlie sighed. "There will be a council hearing. There's no way around it. And Pierce won't be able to represent you, because he's already involved in a dispute."

"Fitzhugh is a no-account scrub with a big feeling about himself." Neo was practically twitching with anger. "I'm done being one of his constituents. I'm moving to Jersey. And I'll tell you what else I'm doing. I'll hang with you for the movie, but I'm also going to work *tonight* on hacking into a different computer. *His.* I'm gonna get some dirt on him. He wants to fight dirty? Fine with me. I grew up on the street. No one knows how to play dirtier than me."

"Neo, as much as I appreciate that, hacking into his system is illegal. Let's table that for now. I don't need another charge brought against me."

"Okay." Neo's voice held some reluctance. "But if you change your mind…"

"I'll give you the word." Donna appreciated the enthusiasm, but Fitzhugh's public accusation stung. She was furious and hurt and on the verge of snapping. Slowly, she got up from the table. "I need a minute."

She walked out, leaving them stunned and silent, but they erupted in conversation before the door had closed.

She went straight to the balcony and stepped outside into the bitter night air. Her gaze fixed on the cityscape across the river. How could something so beautiful be under the care of a man as ugly as Fitzhugh?

Why did he hate her so much? Was this all because she refused to treat him like a god among men? Because she'd rejected his offers? What was his problem?

She didn't know. But this continued animosity was going to make it impossible for her to go forward.

Something had to change. *Fitzhugh* had to change. But how? She ran both hands through her hair, stopping about halfway to massage her scalp. No answer came.

"You've dealt with men like him before."

She glanced over her shoulder at her sister. She was standing by the open slider, looking chilly.

Cammie pulled her cardigan a little tighter. "Joe. Big Tony. Every lunk that ever traipsed through your house expecting you to make him a sandwich and bring him a beer. You handled all of them." She smirked. "And once you did, they knew better than to try anything with you again."

That wasn't entirely true. They hadn't really all expected her to make them a sandwich. But Donna understood what Cammie was saying. "This is a little different."

"How? Because he's a vampire? So are you. Because he's a governor? So are you. On top of that, you're a mother and a survivor. What's he ever done besides boss people around?" She shook her head. "He's playing head games with you, Donna. That's Mafia 101 right there. You need to get in the action, or you're going to lose."

"You're not wrong. But how do I do that?" Right now, the only idea she could come up with was putting a stake through his heart, and while effective, there would undoubtedly be repercussions. Killing your political rivals, even if they were jerks, wasn't approved behavior. Which was probably to her benefit considering Fitzhugh's attitude toward her. "Without involving the council any more than they already are?"

Cammie smiled like Donna hadn't seen her smile since she'd arrived. "Well, you have a vampire hunter living with you…"

Donna came back inside so her sister wouldn't freeze to death. She pulled the slider shut. "I'm listening. What are you proposing?"

Cammie's eyes narrowed, gleaming with a curious light. "Let me pay him a visit."

"To do what?"

She lifted one shoulder nonchalantly. "Have a little chat with him."

"Yeah, I don't think that's a good idea. He's a vampire, Cammie. You're human. I know you have a sword and a crossbow and some great armor, but you'd need it. He's not going to want to chat with you, and I don't want to have to avenge your death. Plus, if anything happened to you, it would kill me. Not to mention the kids would be inconsolable."

Cammie frowned. "Do you have any idea how many vampires I've confronted? I may be human, but I've been anointed by the church. Just because the Venari kicked me out doesn't mean I've lost my powers, my protection, or my skills."

"What kinds of powers and skills? What kind of protection? Don't you normally do your hunting in a group?" Donna knew her sister meant well, but what could she really do alone? What had she done at the raid? Donna hadn't seen much of her after she'd arrived.

Cammie poked Donna in the shoulder. "You don't need to know specifics. Just that I do. And nothing will happen to me. Especially because he'll think I'm still Venari. Trust me, a little warning that the Venari are watching him, and he'll straighten right up. Besides, he doesn't know that I'm your sister."

Donna thought it over. Cammie did look pretty impressive in her gear. "I don't know…"

Cammie leaned in. "How about if you go with me? Not to the actual meeting, but you can watch from a safe distance. That sort of thing. Just so long as he doesn't know you're there. I don't want to risk him figuring out we're related."

"Okay, the invite makes it tempting." Donna chewed on her bottom lip. "You really think this would work?"

"Ask Neo what she'd do if a member of the Venari showed up on her doorstep and told her she was being monitored."

"Pretty sure Neo would attack them with her drone. But that's a good idea. Let's get Pierce's opinion. He's a little more levelheaded and has been around vampires a lot."

He walked into the kitchen behind them, hands up apologetically. "I wasn't eavesdropping, but I heard my name. I can go."

She didn't really care if he had been listening. "No, stay. I need to know something. If you were a vampire and Cammie showed up at your door in full Venari regalia and told you to chill or be permanently put on ice, what would your reaction be?"

He looked at Cammie, then back at Donna. "I'd do my best to be a good little vampire. The Venari are no joke."

Cammie tipped her head in a very *I told you so* kind of way.

Donna rolled her eyes. "All right. Let's find out where Fitzy lives."

Chapter 24

Turned out, Fitzhugh lived in the Upper East Side version of Wellman Towers called Montevetro. Donna knew enough Italian to make out that the name kind of sort of meant "mountain of glass." Seemed mostly fitting for the angular glass and metal monolith that probably cost God's salary to buy into and looked like some kind of modern Danish saltshaker.

Charlie had told them the New York governorship owned the top three floors.

Donna tried not to let it bother her that Fitzy had one more floor than she did, but she couldn't fake it. That extra floor bristled. But then, with an ego his size, he probably needed the space.

Or he was overcompensating.

Temo had driven them but dropped Cammie off a few blocks away so she wouldn't be connected to them. Once they'd arrived in Fitzhugh's neighborhood, Temo had parked on the side of Fitzhugh's building. They could see into the lobby, but the doorman's back was to them.

Temo moved to sit in the back with Donna as well. The SUV's dark-tinted windows would keep them from being seen.

It was early evening, but the city was relatively quiet. Donna thought that might change if anyone looked too closely at Camille.

She'd dressed in her battle gear again. Leather pants, chain mail shirt with the cross, sword strapped to her hip, crossbow on her back, and this time, a leather cowl pulled up to hide her face. The cowl felt vaguely like a cross between her nun's wimple and an executioner's hood.

It was a total mood. One that was clearly meant to intimidate. But would it work on Fitzhugh? He was so cocksure, Donna had her doubts.

Temo had also fitted Cammie with an earpiece, like the one he'd given Donna for the raid, so they'd be able to hear the conversation. It would also give Cammie a way to call for help should she need it. She'd assured them she wouldn't, but Donna didn't trust Fitzhugh one iota, so if nothing else, it made her feel better.

"Here she comes," Donna said.

Cammie strode through the lobby doors like she owned the place and had just decided to tear it down. She went straight to the front desk. "Hawke Fitzhugh."

The doorman got to his feet. His back was to Temo and Donna, but his voice had a wariness to it. He already sounded smarter than Fitzhugh. "And you are?"

"A reckoning. Get him down here now."

"Miss, ma'am, I need your name and—"

A gleam of light and Cammie's sword was at the man's throat. "Fitzhugh. Now. I won't ask again."

Donna sat up straighter. "Mary and Joseph. I didn't know she could move that fast."

Temo nodded. "You should have seen her at the raid. Your sister's got skills, boss."

"She did try to tell me that."

The doorman had the phone in his hand. "Governor Fitzhugh? There's someone in the lobby who'd like to speak to you. Yes, sir. I don't think so. Very good, sir."

He put the phone to his chest. "He's unable to come down, but if you leave your name and number—"

"I will burn the building down if he's not in this lobby in two minutes."

An audible gulp could be heard. The doorman put the phone back to his ear. "Sir, if you could just come down... Yes, sir, I understand that, but...as you wish."

The phone returned to his chest. "Governor Fitzhugh is unable to—"

With her other hand, Cammie whipped out the crossbow. The end of the notched arrow burst into flames a split second before she shot it into the wall next to him. It twanged home in an enormous oil painting hanging there, setting it on fire.

"Governor Fitzhugh, get down here now, or I will file a complaint against you with the co-op." The doorman slammed the phone down and grabbed a fire extinguisher from under the desk. As he went to work putting out the growing inferno, Cammie returned both her weapons to their rightful places.

Donna's mouth was open. She looked at Temo. "You're seeing this, too, right? She just shot a flaming arrow into that painting?"

He nodded. "She did. Good thing she didn't break those out during the raid. Remind me never to get on her bad side."

"I hear you."

A soft ding brought their attention back to the lobby. The elevator had arrived.

A moment later, Fitzhugh walked into the middle of the lobby. He was in sweatpants, a faded T-shirt, and bedroom slippers, which made him look more like someone's grumpy dad than the vampire playboy he loved to play at. Granted, the slippers were Gucci, but still.

Donna lifted her phone and took a few pictures. "Wait until Charlie sees him in that getup."

Fitzhugh took a quick look at the smoldering painting. He managed not to react too much. He put his hands on his hips and stared at Cammie. "What's this all about?"

Cammie approached him. "I am a noble knight of the Venari, and I have come to issue you a warning, Hawke Fitzhugh."

He swallowed and dropped his hands to his sides. Then he raised his chin slightly. "So what? The Venari don't scare me."

Cammie made a slight hand movement, and a ball of fire exploded at Fitzhugh's feet. He lurched away. She kept talking. "Pay attention, vampire. This warning won't be repeated. Your behavior is being monitored. Your actions and decisions may have less-than-desirable consequences."

"My actions and decisions?" He barked out a weak laugh. "You're bluffing. You don't have a clue what—"

"You have contacted the Immortus Concilio twice in as many days, have you not?"

He blinked, but said nothing.

"As you know, the Venari never bluff."

He scowled at her. "I've had enough of this. You can tell whoever sent you that they need to stay out of my business. Out of all vampire business."

Then he turned and strode back to the elevators.

Cammie stared after him. "Mind yourself, vampire. If I have to return, it will not end well for you. And ashes make such a mess."

He spun around and gave her the finger.

She faked a lunge toward him. He jerked back with a whimper and ran into the wall behind him.

Cammie walked out. Donna couldn't see her face thanks to the leather hood, but Donna had to guess she was smiling. That had been a pretty impressive display. Cammie headed away from the building, back the way she'd come.

Temo hopped out and got back into the driver's seat. A few minutes later, he pulled alongside Cammie.

He came to a stop, and she got in, pushing her cowl off her face. "That definitely gave him something to think about."

"Well, it gave me a lot to think about. That was very impressive. I had no idea."

Cammie shrugged. "There's more, but that seemed like enough. Not sure this matters, but he reeked of French perfume, so he either had a woman upstairs or had just been with one. More likely, she was upstairs. Which might explain his reluctance to come down."

"Doesn't surprise me. He likes his companionship." Temo looked at them in the rearview mirror. "What I want to know is how you did that flaming arrow."

"There's a trigger switch that ignites the tips of a certain kind of our arrows." Cammie stripped off the crossbow and sword and leaned over the seat to put them in the back before buckling in. "I preloaded a fiery one in anticipation of needing it. I could have used it as just an arrow too."

Donna shook her head. "That's ingenious."

"The Venari have a lot of tricks." Cammie stared out the window. "Keep all that between us, though, all right? I might not be Venari any longer, but that's on me, not them. And I don't need to burn any bridges. No wordplay intended."

"Not a peep," Temo said.

"None," Donna answered.

"Thanks." Cammie leaned back now that she could without the encumbrance of the crossbow. "I guess we'll see soon enough if that worked. Are you still going to share your secret?"

"Why? Do you think I shouldn't now?"

Cammie was silent for a bit. "He's a slimeball. I'm a little worried what he'd do with that information. But then again, maybe it would get him to back off. Hard to say."

"Yeah, I don't know. He won't like it. I'm sure about that. But again, don't you think it might make him a little more leery of coming after me?"

Cammie pursed her lips in thought. "He wasn't nearly as afraid of me as he should have been. Which means he's either stupid or has more tricks up his sleeve."

Temo snorted. "I vote stupid."

"I don't know," Donna said. "He seems to do basically anything he wants without fear of retribution. Not saying what you did back there won't be effective, but then again…"

Cammie nodded. "I have my doubts too. It's like he thinks he's untouchable."

"He definitely thinks that," Temo said. "Look how he acted at Francine's party."

Donna's mind started working. "Should I file a complaint against him for that? The way he basically tried to disparage me at the party? Is there any kind of code of ethics for the governors?"

Temo shrugged. "Charlie would know that. That's her department. But I've never heard of anything like that."

Cammie twisted toward Donna. "You know you can file a complaint with the Venari. It's considered a pretty scummy thing to do for one vampire to turn in another, but it happens a lot more than you'd guess. No one ever talks about it, that's all."

"It does sound pretty scummy. But then, you just acted like a Venari to intimidate him on my behalf, so...maybe I've already crossed that line."

"Hey, what's a little playacting in the name of peace?"

Donna gave her sister a look. "Except Fitzhugh doesn't know you aren't Venari."

"That was the point." Cammie tipped her head back and closed her eyes. "We'll see tomorrow if it worked, I suppose."

Donna nodded slowly. "Maybe by the time Pierce and I get back from the funeral, Fitzhugh will have pulled his complaints. Or at least one of them. That would be something."

Temo glanced up. "Am I driving you to that, boss?"

"You don't have to. Pierce can drive."

"If I drove you, I could go too."

"Do you want to come with us? You're welcome to."

He nodded. "I think Charlie would too. It's a good idea to show support. The wolves turned out in a big way. I know Rico is one of theirs, but even so, they really gave us numbers."

"That, they did. Without them, we would have been hosed. It would be great if you both came."

Cammie yawned. "I'll stay at the penthouse. There are a few wolves who might take exception to a Venari attending. Namely those who have extremely close relationships with vampires."

"That's all right," Donna said. "Rixaline won't be going either. She can't. Daylight. And that works out, because I'm not crazy about her being alone in the apartment anyway."

"You don't trust her?"

"It's more about her being a teenager at this point. I don't trust them. Not that she's given me a reason to think she'd do something dumb." Donna laughed. "Speaking of, remember that time Joe Jr. convinced Christina she was adopted?"

Cammie grinned and rolled her eyes. "Or the time she used a pair of his underwear for her science fair project?"

Temo chuckled.

Donna sighed. "I'm glad they're such good friends now. There was a time when I wasn't so sure that would ever happen."

Cammie nodded. "Too bad Dad didn't stick around to see what great grandkids he ended up with."

"Yeah, well, I was twelve, and you were fourteen. I don't think grandkids factored into his decision to ghost us." Her phone chimed. She checked the screen to see a text from Charlie. She read it, then shared the info. "Hey, Charlie says LV just messaged her to say Ishalan is awake, and his first words were to ask how Temo was."

Temo let out a soft breath. "How about that? Maybe being part of a team was good for him."

She texted Charlie back. *Thanks, I'll tell him. Home soon.* Then she put her phone away. "You going to go see him?"

"I could. After the funeral."

"Maybe not a bad idea. It would be a nice thing to do. And it would certainly keep your relationship strong. No telling when we might need a fae ally again."

"Right." Temo nodded. "I'll make sure it happens."

Donna settled back after that, her mind stuck on the fae and the prospect of who would become their king. Or queen. She wasn't sure how the politics of all that worked in the fae world, but they'd have to have a leader soon.

Just like the vampires. She hoped that whoever was chosen to succeed Artemis would be level-headed and smart and fair. That definitely left Fitzhugh out.

But she didn't know enough about the other governors to wish for one of them specifically. Her hand went to her crucifix. All she could do was hope and pray.

Then her mind went back to Fitzhugh and the problems he was causing. If Cammie's attempt to rein him in didn't work, Donna would have to come up with a new plan.

Or...what? Would the council remove her from her position if they found her guilty? Or would they pass the same sentence on her that they'd passed on Claudette? Death.

Donna wrapped her arms around herself. If that happened, she was in serious trouble, because unlike Claudette, she had no one to pardon her. And with Artemis gone, no one in power was on her side.

Death wasn't an outcome she could accept. Not with her kids to think about.

Her only choice would be to run.

Chapter 25

For the funeral, Donna topped her simple black dress with a long black coat, finishing the outfit with low heels. She'd also added a single strand of pearls and a pair of diamond-stud earrings, keeping things understated and respectful.

She adjusted her coat as she got out of the car, dark sunglasses protecting her eyes from the sun's sharp glare.

At Pierce's suggestion, he held a large black umbrella over her to give the impression she wasn't completely at ease being out in the sun, but she was glad for it. The sun seemed brighter than she remembered, and there was very little cloud cover.

Temo and Charlie, now out of the SUV as well, joined them.

"Ready?" Pierce asked.

She nodded. The sleeve of her jacket hid the single iron bracelet she had, a reminder that she needed to get a replacement for the one she'd pressed into Rico's hand at the stronghold.

The cemetery overflowed with mourners. A

strange thing to find comfort in, but Donna did all the same. It was such a testament to the strength of the wolves' commitment to one another, and if that wasn't comforting, what was?

With Pierce next to her and Temo and Charlie behind them, they approached the graveside gathering. She stopped by a large cluster of evergreens. "This is close enough, don't you think?"

"Yes," Pierce said. He closed the umbrella now that they were in shade.

"I would like to offer my condolences to LV and Toni." Donna scanned the crowd for the two women, finding them quickly. "I'll be right back."

She headed toward them. A tall, handsome man joined them as she approached, causing her to suck in a breath. Rico. He looked good, all things considered. Maybe like he could use another day or two of rest, but the fact that he was at the funeral was so him.

She knew he'd have been miserable if they'd kept him away.

He looked up and saw her. And smiled. He said something to his mother, then started in Donna's direction.

He met her halfway, taking her hand as soon as he reached her. "It was nice of you to come. Means a lot to my mother and grandmother, I can tell you that." He glanced at Pierce, Temo, and Charlie, still under the tree. He gave them a wave. "It was nice of all of you."

Pierce waved back.

"Of course." Donna smiled. "It was the least we could do."

Rico stared at her like he was searching for words. "Thank you for...everything."

She wondered if that's really what he'd wanted to say. Or if he wasn't willing to speak plainly in front of all these people. "You would have done the same for me."

He nodded. "I would have." He dug into the pocket of his suit. "This belongs to you." He laid the other iron bracelet on her palm. "Can we talk soon?"

"Sure. You know how to find me." She slipped the bracelet onto her bare wrist.

"I do." He hesitated, just looking at her. "I need to go speak to the family."

"And I need to speak to your mother and grandmother."

"I'll see you soon, then. I'm very sorry about Artemis."

She gazed up at him, wondering what was going on that he wanted to talk to her. "Thank you."

He left, and she continued on to Toni and LV, waiting her turn to speak to them.

Toni smiled at her when the crowd broke. "Governor. Thank you for coming."

"I'm so sorry for the loss of your pack member."

"Thank you."

LV joined them. "Good to see you, Governor."

"You, too, Alpha Medina."

"The fae we were caring for disappeared last night. Left a note of thanks, but that was it. He's gone."

Donna glanced back at Temo. He was talking to some pack members. "I'll let Temo know. He was hoping to visit Ishalan after the ceremony, to keep things strong between us."

LV nodded. "Wise. But no longer possible."

"He must have been feeling better."

Toni shrugged. "I don't know much about fae, but they must heal fast. We had a doctor taking care of him, and according to Dr. Ritter, Ishalan had several broken bones, badly torn wings, multiple contusions, and a deep cut across his cheek. I don't know what he looked like before he left, but I can't imagine all of that had healed."

"Wow. He was in worse shape than I was. But then, I didn't get thrown into the side of the stronghold and fall thirty feet to the ground."

LV's eyes were hidden behind sunglasses, but she looked unmoved. "It's my understanding he wasn't the easiest of patients."

"That doesn't surprise me." Donna frowned. "He wasn't exactly fun to deal with when I was negotiating with him before the raid."

"I'm grateful you managed that, however you got it done." LV smiled. "I am very glad to have my grandson home."

"Yes," Toni said. "We are all very happy about that. You have nothing to worry about when it comes to us being allies."

"I'm glad." Maybe they hadn't heard about the recent news then. Donna was happy to keep it that way.

"So am I. Fitzhugh may not like it, but then he already doesn't like you from what I hear," LV said.

"I guess that means you heard about his complaint against me." Donna sighed.

Toni looked at her mother, then back at Donna. "What complaint?"

"Governor Fitzhugh has filed a complaint against me with the Immortus Concilio claiming that I'm responsible for Queen Artemis's death."

Toni gasped. "That lying son of a mongrel. He wants the kingship. He'd do anything to get more power. Everyone knows that."

LV looked disgusted. "If you need us to testify on your behalf, just say the word. We aren't fans of his, as you know. And unlike him, we were actually at the raid."

"Thank you. I appreciate that." The offer lifted her spirits considerably. "I don't want to keep you any longer. Your pack needs you."

Toni put her hand on Donna's arm. "Please, keep us informed on how things are going."

"I will." With a smile and a nod, Donna walked back to her crew. They were all looking at something behind her. Maybe the ceremony was about to begin.

She joined them and turned.

On the other side of the large crowd, Fitzhugh and Claudette were walking through the tombstones.

She stared at them for so long she forgot to blink. They were both under large umbrellas, their bodies completely covered and their faces an odd, pasty white. "How are they out in the sun? Does an umbrella and gloves really keep the sun off that well?

Pierce came closer. "They can if they're very thick fabric. But they appear to be using some kind of thick sunscreen too." He squinted. "They could have gotten a spell or potion that made this possible. If not, they won't be able to stay out here for long."

Charlie glared at them. "He has a lot of nerve showing up here. This isn't his state. And he had nothing to do with that raid. He's doing this for show. Or he knew you were going to be here and didn't want to be left out."

Donna looked at her. "You think he knew we'd be here?"

"It's possible. But this is some stunt. He wasn't included in the raid, so now he's making his presence known."

Donna frowned. "I wish I could have sent Neo after him."

They watched in silence as Fitzhugh and Claudette paid their condolences to LV and Toni. Neither woman seemed overjoyed to greet him.

Temo grunted. "I wondered what had happened to Claudette. Never figured she'd gotten back with him."

Donna snorted. "No wonder Cammie said he smelled like French perfume last night. Claudette didn't stay at her studio in the village very long, did she?"

Pierce nudged Donna gently. "You think she's behind his recent council complaints?"

"After I saved her life, she'd better not be."

Charlie blew out a breath. "I bet she's not discouraging him. In fact, I bet he's got her so twisted up that she somehow believes you're the bad guy. He's such a rat. Of course, Claudette's not exactly an angel either. They're so well suited."

"That's an understatement," Pierce muttered. He leaned in. "Do you want to leave?"

Donna arched her brows. "And let him think he intimidates me? Not a chance."

Pierce smiled. "Good. Because I was going to argue to stay."

She laughed softly. "He ought to worry about you punching him again."

Pierce gave her a wry smile. "He really should."

The ceremony began, and Fitzhugh and Claudette found a spot at the edge of the gathering under the scant shade of a few bare crepe myrtles. The reverend's voice traveled easily over the quiet crowd.

Donna listened, her mind wandering to the last time she'd been at a funeral.

It had been for Joe. She hadn't known he wasn't really dead then, and that day had been extremely hard on her. Not because of her grief, but because of all the manufactured sympathy for a horrible man who'd spent his life breaking the law to get ahead.

The willpower and self-control that it had taken for her to get through that day had nearly pushed her to her limit. And then Big Tony, Joe's boss, had given her an order that had changed her life.

Do one last job for him, a job Joe had been unable to complete, and Donna would be free to live the rest of her life as she wished.

She should have known it was too good to be true.

Not only had it been a setup, but her side trip to Joe's gravesite had put her in the path of the rogue vampire who'd bitten her.

Thankfully, Claudette had saved Donna's life. And set her on the path she now walked.

Donna shifted her gaze from the reverend to the former governor. Claudette had her arm through Fitzhugh's and was leaning into him, their two umbrellas mashed together.

What was she playing at? She had to know about the complaints he'd made to the council.

At least he'd been smart enough not to bring Claudette to Francine's party. Or Claudette had been smart enough to stay home. Although referring to either of them as *smart enough* seemed odd.

Donna would not be the terrible sire Claudette had been. She'd called Will after returning home from Cammie's Venari visit to Fitzhugh, thankful to find the man in good spirits and grateful to her for saving his life.

He'd seemed perfectly at ease being a vampire. But then, he was already part reaper, so maybe there wasn't much of a transition for him to deal with. If so, he was lucky.

Claudette had basically left Donna to fend for herself. Which was how she'd ended up draining Yuri, the Russian gangster, to death and breaking her psychic bond with Claudette. Thankfully, Will had told her he had no plans to use their psychic connection unless absolutely necessary. Donna appreciated that, because how did you prepare for having a man's voice in your head?

She looked at Rico, his hands folded in front of him. Was that Russian lunk still in the FBI's deep freeze? Rico had covered for her with Yuri. That alone would have been reason enough to rescue him from the fae.

What did he want to talk to her about? She couldn't imagine.

A violinist played as the casket was being lowered.

Her attention returned to Fitzhugh and Claudette. Had they seen her yet? Did they know they weren't the only vampires here?

She didn't think so, because they weren't looking at her, and they weren't actively not looking either. They were far too relaxed.

The funeral ended, and the crowd milled about, talking to the family and gathering in small groups. Some went straight to their cars, presumably to head to the reception. Donna wasn't going to that. The last thing this man's family needed was more strangers in their house.

Temo looked over. "Ready to go, boss?"

"Not just yet." There was one more thing she wanted to do. Needed to do. "Don't worry about visiting Ishalan. According to Toni, he disappeared on them last night."

"Sounds like something he'd do. Thanks for letting me know."

"Sure." She looked at Pierce. "Keep the umbrella closed and stay near me. Everyone."

She started walking, Pierce at her side, Charlie and Temo behind her. She wound her way through the people, the not-unpleasant earthy scent of wolf wafting by every so often.

Her target was easy to spot. About a foot away, she stopped. Pierce stayed at her side. Charlie and Temo came around to flank them. She stood there, waiting.

Then Claudette turned around and gasped, causing her umbrella to jump.

Fitzhugh glanced back and grimaced, his lip curling before he could stop it. "What are you doing here?"

"Funny question, seeing as how I govern this state and you do not."

He pushed his sunglasses onto his head. Donna left hers in place. "I am paying my respects."

She looked past him. The woman behind him, the fallen wolf's widow, was already walking away with an older woman at her side. Good. She didn't want to interrupt their day with the business she needed to handle.

She stared at Fitzhugh again. "Did you lodge a

complaint against me with the council in the hopes of making yourself a better candidate for king?"

He jerked back slightly as if her bold question had caught him off guard. "I don't know what you're talking about."

"So you have no desire to be king, then?" She posed it as a question, hoping to force him to answer.

"Whoever the council nominates is up to them."

She took her sunglasses off to glare at him. "Then why make that claim against me? Why?"

"Because you're responsible for Artemis's death, and you should be held accountable."

She nodded like she was pondering that with all seriousness. When she spoke, she kept her voice calm and level. "You've made a grave error, Hawke. Coming against me like you have. But your real failure is your own arrogance. Pride cometh before the fall."

She shifted to Claudette. "I hope the sex is worth it, because when he falls—and he will—there's no way you're going to escape that disaster."

Claudette's mouth hung open.

Donna wiggled her finger at Fitzhugh's face. "Your sunscreen looks like it's melting a bit. Better get home before you burst into flames, Fitzy."

He slapped a gloved hand to his cheek.

Donna put her sunglasses back on and smiled at him, the white-hot desire to crush him into the ground mixing with her need to show everyone what a jerk he was. Patience, she told herself. His time was coming.

Still calm, she lifted one hand and flicked the edge of his umbrella with her fingers, making the silk quiver. "You take care now."

Chapter 26

The minute the car was moving, Donna spoke. "I want to file a counterclaim with the council. Against Fitzhugh."

Charlie nodded. "Absolutely. What do you want to lead with?"

"His drunken behavior at Francine's party. His disparaging remarks against me. But mostly his false claims that I caused Artemis's death. Pierce, what do you think?"

His eyes narrowed as he metaphorically put on his lawyer hat. "I'd start with defamation of character, but we could also add slander and libel." He paused. "It would be worth mentioning malicious prosecution as well."

Donna took her sunglasses off. "Can you work with Charlie to write all that up?"

"I'd be happy to." He winked at her. "We'll give Fitzhugh a lot to think about."

Charlie was smiling. "We'll do it this afternoon."

"Perfect." A phone chimed. It wasn't Donna's.

Temo pulled his phone from his jacket pocket and checked the screen. "Hey, it's Ishalan. He wants to meet with us. Says he needs to talk to you."

Donna leaned in. "Seems to be a lot of that going around. When?"

"Tonight." Temo grimaced. "At the stronghold."

"Yeah, that doesn't sound like a trap at all," Pierce said.

"I'll meet him on the mortal side of the gate, but I'm not going through. You can tell him that."

Temo handed his phone to Charlie. "Can you text that back to him?"

"Sure." She tapped away at the screen, then hit send. As she held the phone out for him to take, it chimed again.

"Just read it," he said. "I'm not supposed to be doing that while driving anyway."

"Okay." Charlie looked at the screen. "Ishalan says outside the gate is fine. He'll see you at sundown." She looked back at Donna. "Is that good with you?"

"Yes." Donna yawned, unable to stop herself. "I really need to get back on a regular sleeping schedule."

Pierce glanced at her. "I don't think it's that so much as you're still recovering from your injury. You need sleep now more than ever." He tilted his head. "In fact, you ought to go to bed as soon as we get home."

She smirked. "So bossy. But I'm not going to argue, because I'm not sure I could stay up much longer." Her leg was also still aching, but she kept that to herself.

"Well, good." He smiled. "You did what you needed to do this morning. You showed support for the wolves. And you got to confront Fitzhugh. After that, you've earned a rest."

And rest she did, going straight to her bedroom when they returned. She stripped down to her underwear, threw on a tank top, and got under the covers in her deliciously dark room.

Sleep came fast and deep and dreamless, which was a blessing. When she awoke hours later, she felt the best she had in a few days.

She got up and went straight to the bathroom, flicking on the light to look at her leg. The bruise was almost completely gone. There was no more ache either. She was finally almost whole. Now if she could just keep from being poisoned or shot or stabbed or bitten or anything else, she'd be in great shape.

Of course, she had a meeting with Ishalan in—she looked at the time—two hours, so what were the odds nothing else would happen to her?

She touched her crucifix and prayed the meeting would be peaceful. Then she added a request that the rest of the week would stay that way too.

After a quick shower, then putting on jeans and a sweater, she went out to feed and find out what everyone was doing.

Rixaline was in her pajamas, playing a video game on the living room TV. There was a bowl of cereal on the coffee table, and Lucky was lying beside her on the couch. Donna walked over and gave him a tummy rub but spoke to Rixaline. "How are you doing?"

"Good. How are you?"

"I'm doing better. Going to meet with Ishalan today. He's the fae that helped us at the raid."

Rixaline paused the game. "Do you want me to go?"

"No." Donna smiled. "Just mentioning it. Enjoy your breakfast. Lucky looks like he's ready for a nap."

"He's waiting for me to brush him, but I told him not until after I eat my breakfast."

"Did he eat?"

"Yep, fed him first thing."

"Thank you for taking such good care of him." Donna felt a twinge of guilt. Rixaline had pretty much become Lucky's favorite person since she'd moved in, but then, Donna had been a little busy, so it was actually a very good thing.

Rixaline shrugged. "I love him. And he loves me. Dontcha, Lucky boy?"

Lucky's only response was a single air biscuit.

Donna laughed. "See you later."

She went down the hall to the office, where Charlie was hard at work. "What's going on? Anything new?"

"The complaint to the council is drafted, just waiting on you to read it and make whatever changes you want. Same with the letter announcing your daywalker status. Marcus sent a formal announcement to the governors' loop that Artemis's memorial service will be held at midnight next Wednesday at her estate."

"Where is that?"

"Kansas."

Donna stared at her. "Artemis's royal estate is in Kansas."

Charlie nodded. "Lebanon, Kansas, to be exact."

"That seems...random."

"She chose it because it's the center of the United States. She felt it would give her the best access to everyone that way. Also, she was able to buy the entire town, so I think she liked that part too."

"Oh. Wow. Who gets the town now that she's gone? Her successor?"

"No, the town is part of her personal holdings, along with her estate, so I imagine it'll go to whoever she left it to. It's not like with the governor's holdings that go to the next person to take the office. Her successor can make their headquarters anywhere they want. That's part of why the Prime usually picks a vampire from the contiguous United States."

"Makes sense. Have you ever been to her estate?"

Charlie nodded. "Once. It's pretty amazing. Biggest house I've ever been in. Sits on a hundred and twenty acres."

"That does sound amazing. How does travel for an event like this work? Is there a vampire-friendly hotel or what?"

"Attendance isn't really expected. The service will be livestreamed. It's too difficult for most vampires to travel on such short notice. Not to mention that the logistics of keeping yourself safe from the sun during travel can be tricky."

"Five days is short notice?"

"It can be when you're a vampire who can't do daylight travel."

"So no one will be there but her staff?" That seemed sad.

"No, there will definitely be a good number who go. Won't just be vampires either. I'm sure there will be supernaturals of all kinds who want to offer their condolences."

"Can we attend if we want?"

"Of course. You want to go?"

"Artemis was my grandsire. That kind of connection makes me feel like I should go. And yes, I want to. I want to pay my respects. She helped me when Claudette didn't."

Charlie nodded. "Let me reach out to Marcus and see what her team is doing for those who want to attend."

"Great. Thank you." Donna turned on her laptop and found the drafted complaint and daywalking announcement in her email. She opened the file. "I'll read these drafts now. Thank you for doing that."

"Pierce really knocked it out of the park with that complaint. He's pretty good at stuff like that."

"Yes, he is." Donna started with that one. It was two pages of very official legalese but still pretty easy to understand. It laid out her complaints in bullet points, citing specific times and dates too.

Next she read the announcement. It was half a page and as straightforward as could be.

She liked both of them. But she had a nagging feeling that she needed to let them sit awhile before sending. "I don't really have any changes to either of them, but I don't want to send them just yet."

"Are you getting nervous?"

Donna twisted her chair around. "Not nervous, exactly. I don't know how to describe it except that I just need to let them sit while my brain works. I want to be completely sure that I haven't missed anything or overlooked something that could change what I'm about to do. Does that make sense?"

"It makes perfect sense. We've done this pretty quickly. There's no reason not to take a beat and let it settle. Once we hit send, they're gone, and the deeds are done. You take all the time you need."

"Thanks. And thank you for the great work on these." She glanced at Charlie. "Have you eaten?"

"I had some fruit salad and a bagel. Rixaline had some cereal."

Donna nodded. "She was still eating it. She's in the living room playing a video game with Lucky."

"I didn't know he could work the controllers."

Donna laughed, then shook her head. "What are we going to do with that girl? She can't live here forever. Is there a vampire foster program?"

"No, but we might be able to find her a place in a nest. Kind of like a vampire group home."

Donna sighed. "I hate for her to think I'm kicking her out, but this was never meant to be a permanent situation."

"I completely understand. And I think she will too. She might like being around other vampires more. Especially some closer to her age. As it is, she spends a lot of time alone now. Or with one of us. That can't be very exciting for a teenager."

"Probably not. But she hasn't complained."

"In that regard, she is not a typical teenager. I suppose any life is better than the one she had."

"True." Donna couldn't imagine life on the run, always being hunted. Except, that would have been her life if she'd tried to get away from Joe on her own. So maybe she did understand a little of what Rixaline had gone through. "I guess it wouldn't hurt to see what's available. But it's not a pressing problem either."

"She could always move downstairs with us."

Donna shook her head. "That's not really fair to you and Temo."

"Wouldn't bother me. And I don't think it would bother Temo either. She's a good kid."

"She is." A new idea came to Donna. "What are the chances the governorship could buy another apartment in this building? If there's even one for sale."

"I can tell you in just a second." Charlie turned to her computer and started typing. A new website popped up. "There's a three-bedroom on the sixth floor. A studio on the third. And an executive suite on the eleventh floor. That's also the most expensive, but it's the only one that could be linked to our two floors by elevator. If that's what you were thinking."

"What's an executive suite? And how expensive are we talking?"

"It's a three-bedroom, but also has a conference room and office space. Kind of like a mini version of the penthouse. Closer to what we have downstairs, but a little smaller. Price is three point five."

"You mean million, right?" What else would it be?

Charlie laughed. "Yes, I mean million."

"Do we have that in the budget?"

"We do. Are you considering adding that to the governor's holdings?"

"I am. Is that crazy?"

"Not at all. We could use the space."

"I know Neo wants to move out of the city."

Charlie's smile was sly and knowing. "You thinking about offering her the space?"

"Well, not the whole thing. But maybe she and Temo could take it over? Then Rixaline could move downstairs with you."

"That would give you and Cammie some more privacy."

Donna nodded. "I don't think my sister is finding the transition all that easy."

"I'm sure it's been tough. She's probably grieving the loss of the life she's always known. And until she gets through that, finding happiness in her current reality might be tough. Even though she's got you close by."

"Exactly."

"You want me to set up a viewing of the executive suite?"

"Yes. Tomorrow, if possible."

"I'll send an email right now." Her smile broadened. "Then Fitzhugh won't be the only one with three floors."

Donna stood up. "I swear that has nothing to do with it."

"I know." Charlie was still chuckling, though.

"I'm going to get something to eat. Pierce in his room?"

"No, he and Temo went to play racquetball, but they should be back soon since you have that meeting with Ishalan."

"Okay, thanks."

"You got it."

Donna went back to the kitchen and cut herself a piece of caramel apple crumb pie. It wasn't the most nutritious thing to start her day with, but sometimes comfort eating was more important than fiber and vitamins. Besides, it was partially fruit, which was totally healthy.

As she sat down to eat at the breakfast bar, Cammie came in, dressed head to toe in black except for her chain mail shirt, which seemed to have been turned inside out to hide the Venari cross. She had a leather bag slung over one shoulder, her crossbow on her back, and her sword at her hip. "You're not going to believe this."

Donna's fork stopped halfway to her mouth. If this was more bad news, she was going to lose it. "I'm almost afraid to ask. What won't I believe?"

Chapter 27

Cammie dropped her bag at her feet. "I answered an ad for a demon removal and got the job. It's in Queens, so it's not even that far. And the pay is good. More than enough for first and last month's deposit on a place."

"Demon removal? You can do that?"

"Absolutely. Been doing it for years."

"Wow, that's amazing. But makes sense, I guess. What's in the bag? Holy water?"

Cammie arched her brows. "Among other things."

"I'm happy you got a job and that it pays well." Donna was, genuinely. "But I really don't want you to move out. Please. I know it's a little crazy here, but things will calm down soon." She prayed that was true. "And I like having you around. Living in the convent made you pretty inaccessible at times. Maybe that's selfish of me, but there you are."

Cammie leaned against the counter, took the fork out of Donna's hand, and ate the bite of pie herself. She swallowed with a big smile on her face.

"Well, if you're going to have pie like this around, I guess I could stay for a while."

"Yeah?"

Cammie helped herself to another bite of Donna's pie. "Yeah. I'll be back as soon as the job is done. Don't wait up."

"Be safe."

"I will." She picked up her leather bag and turned toward the door.

"Hey, how are you getting there?"

"Public transport, why?"

"You have your driver's license, right? Take one of the SUVs. Temo can give you the keys."

"I don't know…"

"I do. If you need a fast getaway, you can't be waiting for a bus."

"If the job goes right, I won't—"

"Just take the car."

Cammie smiled. "Okay, I will. Thank you." She shifted directions toward the stairs that led to the apartment below.

"Hey, tell Temo I'm ready to go when he is."

"All right," Cammie called over her shoulder.

Donna finished the pie, put the plate and fork in the dishwasher, then went to get her boots and coat.

By the time she came back out, Temo was in the kitchen. He was scrolling through his phone but looked up when she entered. "We can leave a little early if you want. Sundown is subjective."

"Let's go, then. I'm really itchy to get this done for some reason. I wish I knew what he wants."

"I wish I could tell you."

Together, they went out to the elevator.

Donna zipped her coat. "Cammie got the keys from you?"

"She did." He made a little face. "You aren't worried about her side jobs?"

"In what way?"

He shrugged as the elevator arrived and they stepped on. "Demon removal sounds kind of dangerous."

Donna pushed the button for the lobby. "No argument from me, but she acted like it was just a standard thing. And she's been a hunter a lot longer than I've been a vampire, so who am I to say anything?"

"I guess so." He smiled. "I've never known a hunter before, but your sister's pretty cool. And after that display at Fitzhugh's, I guess I shouldn't worry."

"It's nice that you do, though. Hey, did Charlie tell you about the memorial service for Artemis?"

The elevator arrived, and they got off. Temo had already pulled the car up, so it was waiting out front.

He opened the door for her. "No, what about it?"

"I'd like to attend." She smiled. "I'd like for us all to attend."

He came around and got behind the wheel. "All of us? Meaning you, me, Charlie, and Pierce?"

She nodded. "Yep. What do you think? Charlie's looking into the logistics."

"I'm game." He squinted as he started up the car. "Wait. Is the memorial going to be in New Jersey?"

"Nope. At her estate in Kansas."

"Huh." He seemed surprised. "All I know about Kansas is that's where Dorothy and Toto got into trouble."

She laughed. "Well, I haven't been there either, so we'll have to figure it out together."

"You got it." He glanced over. "Boss, I'd follow you anywhere."

"Thanks, Temo." She wished she could tell him about buying the third apartment, but she didn't want to get him excited about something that might not happen. Instead, she kept the conversation light, asking him about Neo, which got him talking until they arrived an hour later at Central Park.

They got out. He locked the car, then joined her on the sidewalk. "Pretty sure I remember how to get to the gate. Do you?"

"I think so." Orange and pink streaked the sky, the last vestiges of the setting sun. But it was close enough to sundown that by the time they got to the gate, it would be. "If we can't find it, you can text him."

They started walking. He glanced at her. "Why didn't you bring your sword?"

"I have the short blades that came with the jacket. I thought this was a friendly meeting."

"It is." He stared into the woods. "But we're also going to be right outside of the fae stronghold.

You know, the one you set fire to?"

"Right. Did you bring a weapon?"

He pulled his coat out to show her the large blade secured to the lining.

"Good enough. You think Ishalan might try something?"

"No." Temo frowned into the distance. "But there's a lot more fae on the other side of that gate. And no sun to keep them behind it."

"Good point. Well, I guess we'll know how they feel about us soon enough."

They continued on, but the Ramble looked different without Jerabeth's special eyedrops. It seemed calm and serene, even in the growing darkness. Just an ordinary space filled with trees, a little underbrush, and footpaths.

She kept her voice low. "I'm not so sure we're going to be able to find the gate now. It all looks so...unmagical."

"I was just thinking the same thing."

Another minute or two of walking, and things seemed vaguely familiar. "We aren't far from where the gate should be. In fact, I think it was right over that little rise."

He nodded. "It was."

They kept going, down the little dip in the path, then back up and over the mound.

The only thing there was a bench. A homeless person had made a bed there, covering themselves in newspaper.

Donna sighed. "It's not here. You're going to have

to text him that we need to meet somewhere else. Or he'll have to come find us."

He pulled his phone out. "On it."

She kept looking at the homeless person. "Do you have a blanket in the car, Temo? Or an extra coat? It's going to be another cold night." She'd give them her coat, but it was the custom leather one lined with lead, and she wasn't sure what the magic would do if someone besides her put it on. "Maybe I could get them a hotel room."

While Temo texted, she approached the bench. "Sir? Or ma'am? Can I help you in some—"

The person sat up, throwing off the newspapers.

It was Ishalan. He grinned wildly, like he'd just made the best joke in the world.

She frowned at him. "Was that supposed to be funny?"

Temo put his phone away. "Yeah, man, not cool."

"Relax. It wasn't supposed to be anything but self-defense. I had to be sure you'd come without an army."

"Why would I bring an army? I haven't done anything to hurt you. Although I'm thinking about popping you in the mouth for your little stunt." She jerked her thumb at Temo. "Or maybe I'll get him to stomp his foot."

"Now, now, Governor." He got off the bench and stood up, brushing himself off. He was dressed in a sweeping velvet cloak with fine leather knee boots worked in all shades of teal and purple and fastened with bronze fittings. Sparkling silver chains hung from both ear tips. He looked oddly royal. Had he spent the money she'd given him on clothes? Or had he found a new position in the fae regime?

He could have set it all on fire for as much as she cared. "I see you've recovered from your injuries."

His expression turned serious. "Not entirely, but I am much better. For that, I owe you. I fear I would have been left to die had you not intervened."

In hindsight, she wasn't sure that was true. "What about all the fae who agreed with you? Who didn't approve of Dredward's ways? I know there were some who surrendered at the raid. Wouldn't they have saved you?"

"Perhaps, but I fear they would have been too worried about outing themselves as my sympathizers. It's one thing to give up. It's another to side with an infidel. Even with Dredward dispatched." He bowed. "Something else I am indebted to you for."

"He killed my queen. He gave me no choice."

Temo moved closer beside her, but in her peripheral vision, she could see he wasn't watching Ishalan so much as scanning the woods around them. Always on guard. Always protecting her.

Ishalan looked genuinely sympathetic. "I am sorry for Artemis's death. That was unfortunate."

"That seems like an understatement." But she wasn't here for small talk about the past. "Why did you ask to meet me?"

"I have a proposal for you. A peace treaty."

"You and I are already at peace, Ishalan. So as

much as I appreciate the thought, I don't really understand the point of it."

"I'm offering you an official peace treaty. Granted, it would only be between the vampires you govern and the fae in my district, but it would be a start."

She shook her head. "So it's broader than just us, which is great, but how can you guarantee a thing like that with everything that just went down?" Then the answer hit her, as plain as the fancy clothes he was wearing. "Are you working for the new king? Or queen?"

His smile was broad and toothy with a kind of smugness that made her feel like the punchline of a joke. "My darling Governor, I am the new king."

She blinked hard, unsure how he'd gone from outcast to king. "You are?"

Temo's mouth was open.

Ishalan nodded slowly. "Yes. I was Dredward's brother, after all. Had I killed him, that would have disqualified me, but you took care of that. As I said, I owe you."

"Then you really can offer us a peace treaty." What an amazing thing that would be. No vampire would have to fear the fae again. Not in her area, anyway. Although, getting her side to abide by that might be a little trickier. Still worth the effort, though. Peace would be a very good thing. She stuck her hand out. "Obviously, there are details to be worked out, but I accept."

He laughed. "You don't know my terms yet."

She dropped her hand. "What are they? I'm sure we can reach an agreement."

"I'm so glad you feel that way." He laced his fingers together in front of him. "There are some minor things to be worked out, such as vampires being willing to donate blood and—"

"Donate? In what way?"

"The same way humans donate to you."

"We use blood banks. A lot of humans don't know they're donating to vampires. Do the fae need vampire blood to live?"

His mouth narrowed to a thin line. "Do you need chocolate or wine to survive?"

"No."

"How would you feel if you had to give those things up for the rest of your immortal life?"

She answered honestly. "Cranky."

"It's a bit of the same thing with us. Although vampire blood is slightly more essential. Thankfully for your kind, we can survive on small quantities. A pint might last me two weeks. We're just asking that some provisions be made. If the fae have to go without, the treaty will not last. I can assure you."

"I can't promise you that will happen without speaking to my constituency as a whole." Could she do that? Charlie would know, but Donna assumed it was possible. There had to be a way to get a message out to everyone she served.

"I understand. This may take a few days."

"What else do you want? You said minor things, which implies there might be a major one."

He took a deep breath. "You don't miss much, do you, Governor?"

"I try not to. What else do you want?"

"I won't pretend it's a small request. But I need the dhamfir."

Chapter 28

Temo snorted, which was good because Donna was too shocked to react for a moment.

Finally, she found her voice. "You've got to be kidding. I'm not going to turn Rixaline over to you."

"You don't understand," Ishalan said. He flexed his hands in what appeared to be frustration, looking much less confident than he had a second ago. "I need her to hold the throne."

"Right." Donna looked at Temo. "We should probably go."

"Please," Ishalan said. "Hear me out."

She tipped her head. "Talk fast. I could be watching a *Golden Girls* marathon right now."

His face scrunched up. "A what? Never mind. Listen to me. With Rixaline at my side, supporting me, my position as king will be twice as strong. Maybe even stronger."

"Why? Because she's half vampire?" Donna shrugged. "I don't get it."

Ishalan sighed loudly. "Because if she supports me as king, it will quiet the remaining dissenters."

Donna leaned in. "I'm still waiting for the reason *why*."

He shook his head, making the chains dangling from his ears ring softly. "She is Dredward's child. His daughter. My niece."

Donna huffed with amusement. "Nice try, but her father was a guard named Rix. That's how she got her name. Her mother named her after the fae she fell in love with."

"All rubbish. That's just the story Rixaline's mother told the child to protect her from the truth."

"Where's your proof?" Temo asked.

"Good question." Donna waited expectantly. "You can't drop a bomb like that without showing me the fuse."

Ishalan stared at the sky like his answer might be there. Finally, he looked at them again. "I wasn't banished just for disagreeing with my brother. It was because I fought with him over Rixaline's mother. He kept her as a pleasure slave, using her for whatever appetite came upon him. She was too drugged to fight back most of the time."

A muscle in his jaw twitched. "I know you think very little of me, but I was raised much differently than Dredward. He was groomed to be king. I was trained to be a *sacardos*. A kind of fae priest. A keeper of ancient texts. A giver of blessings and curses."

This was all new to her.

"One of the first things Dredward did after ascending the throne was to declare all *sacardos* apostates. I was allowed to remain in the kingdom on the condition that I never put on my robes again and that I denounce the teachings I'd been raised with."

"So you did?"

He nodded reluctantly. "I spoke the words, but I didn't abandon my beliefs in my heart. When I found out what he was doing with Brielle, the dhamfir's mother, I couldn't stay silent any longer."

He told a compelling story, but Donna still didn't know if she believed him. She stared at him, searching her heart and mind for what to do.

"You doubt me. I don't blame you."

"It's hard to believe." And yet...was it? Now that she looked at him, there was a slight similarity between the shape of his eyes and Rixaline's. "Rixaline told me the guard's parents—that is, the fae she believes to be her father—that his parents don't want anything to do with her. That implies that he existed."

"He didn't. That was just something else she was told to keep her from searching them out."

"So there was never any fae named Rix? That was just a name her mother pulled out of thin air?"

"No." He swallowed, clearing his throat softly. "My middle name is Rix. She named the child after me. I suppose because I'm the one who helped her escape."

She glanced at Temo. He raised his brows as if indicating he didn't know what to think either. It would be quite something to have a dhamfir so close to the fae throne. "I need some time to process this."

"She would have a very good life. She'd be made a princess. And my successor, if that's what she wants. I would never harm her. Never force her to use her skills against her will. You have my word. My blood oath."

That gave Donna an idea. "I'll talk to her. That's all I can do. I'll be in touch as soon as she decides what she wants to do, but I have to go now."

"Thank you for listening."

She nodded. "Congratulations on becoming king."

He smiled briefly, then turned, took a few steps, and disappeared.

She grabbed Temo's arm. "Back to the penthouse immediately."

They hustled to the car, not saying a word until they were inside and on the road.

Temo spoke first. "You think he's lying?"

"I honestly don't know. What do you think?"

"I'm inclined to believe him."

"Yeah?" She thought about that. "You know, having Rixaline in the stronghold wouldn't be such a bad thing. She could definitely let us know if something was brewing. Not that I expect her to spy for us, but maybe just the occasional report. Although I can't imagine she'd want to go back there."

"She might, considering how different the circumstances would be. And she'd actually have family. An uncle anyway. Plus, she'd be a princess. That might be hard for a teenager to turn down."

"If Ishalan's claims are true. But yes, I can see how that would be appealing." Donna shook her head. "Can you imagine? From prisoner to princess. Sounds like a Lifetime made-for-TV movie."

He snorted. "Yeah, it does. So what are you going to do?"

"I'm going to tell her everything Ishalan just told us. It's her decision ultimately. I'm not her guardian."

"Maybe knowing Dredward is gone will help too."

"Maybe." Donna wasn't convinced of any of it, but she had an idea that might change that. "I need to make a few calls."

By the time her calls were made and things were put in motion, they were pulling up to the Wellman Towers. Temo parked, and they walked in together, but he got off the elevator one floor before her. "Let me know if you need me."

"Will do." She went up to the penthouse and straight in. Rixaline wasn't in the living room, but Donna found her lying on her bed, flipping through a clothing catalog. "Hey."

Rixaline sat up. "Hi. How was your meeting?"

"Very interesting. We need to talk."

Rixaline put the catalog aside. "Am I in trouble?"

Donna laughed. "No, nothing like that." She came in and sat on the end of the bed. "I have some news for you. News that will require you to make a decision, and that decision is totally up to you, okay?"

Rixaline's brows bent. "Okay. This sounds serious."

"It is. But again, the decision is yours to make, so don't feel overwhelmed until you know all the facts. You don't have to make any decisions right away either."

Rixaline nodded, still looking very unsure.

"Ishalan, the fae that helped us in the raid, has become the new king. He was Dredward's brother."

She pulled her knees up to her chest. "I heard rumors of that when I was in my cell. Not about him by name, but the guards used to talk about the king's brother like that was a warning not to go against him. How if Dredward would banish his own brother, he'd banish anyone. But they never said his name. Is that true, then? Dredward exiled him?"

"Yes. Ishalan went against Dredward, and the king forced him out. It seems one of the things they fought over was the treatment of your mother."

Rixaline's eyes went big. "Ishalan knew my mother?"

"It seems that way." Donna hesitated. "Seems that his relationship with her went beyond just knowing her. He says her name was Brielle. He claims to have helped her escape."

Rixaline whispered the name Brielle, then frowned. "That can't be. My father did that. A fae named Rix. The one I was named after."

Donna shook her head. "Ishalan says that was a story made up by your mother to protect you because…Dredward was your father."

Rixaline swallowed. "What?" she whispered. "That can't be—how is that possible?"

It was hard to look at her and repeat the things Ishalan had said. "He claims Dredward took advantage of your mother. That his treatment of her is what pushed Ishalan to the edge. And that before he was banished, he helped her escape. He said his middle name is Rix."

Rixaline stared at the coverlet and went quiet for a few long minutes. Donna let her be. The weight of the new information had to be pressing down on her with suffocating force.

"Could that be true? Is he really my...uncle?"

"I don't know. But I know a way we might find out. If you're willing."

She lifted her head. "How?"

"We have a sample of Ishalan's blood. We can compare it to yours."

She stuck her arm out. "I want to know the truth."

"I'm glad to hear you say that. I'd like to know too." Donna smiled sympathetically. "There's more to my conversation with Ishalan."

Rixaline put her knees down, crossing them and leaning forward. "What else?"

"He'd like you to come live at the stronghold. He talked about making you a princess. You'd be his successor to the throne."

She laughed. "Me? A princess?"

"That's what he said." She'd reacted the way Donna had expected her to. A little shocked, but also a little giddy at the possibility. "What do you think?"

She frowned. "I lived at the stronghold once before. It wasn't good."

"No, it wasn't, but I'd like to believe it would be a very different experience this time. If it wasn't, I wouldn't want you to stay there. He said you'd never be forced to use your skills either."

"That's good." She went silent for a moment. "But I'm half vampire, and the fae kill vampires."

"Not anymore. I hope. We're working on the details of a peace treaty. Sorry for not telling you that right away, but I thought the news about your mother was more important."

"Is my going to live with him a condition of the treaty?"

"I...don't really know. He would very much like for that to happen. He believes that having you at his side would add legitimacy to his position as king. The support of Dredward's only child and all that."

"I don't know. I never dreamed I had any family, outside of Rix's family that isn't interested in me."

"You need to know that Ishalan said the whole story about Rix is completely made up. So there isn't a family who's been ignoring you. They simply don't exist."

"But he might be my real uncle."

"He might." Donna couldn't fault her for being a little bit excited about that. Ever since she'd given Rixaline sanctuary, it was plain the girl felt a bit out of place. And while she might be half vampire, she looked more fae than anything.

A determined look came over her face. "Let's test my blood. See if he's telling the truth. I don't have to decide anything until that happens, right?"

"Right. And even then, you can forget we had this conversation if that's what you want to do."

"Really?"

"Of course. I'm not going to push you to do something you don't want. But if you do decide to try life at the stronghold, I have an idea."

Her brows lifted slightly. "What is it?"

"I would officially give you the title of vampire-fae liaison. And I would require daily check-ins to know that you're okay, that you're being treated well, and that Ishalan is keeping his promises. We could even have a code word that would be your secret way of telling me to come get you if you needed me to."

Rixaline smiled. "That would be cool."

The doorbell rang.

Donna tipped her head in that direction. "That's probably Dr. Fox. I asked him and Jerabeth to come over to do the blood tests."

"You knew I'd say yes?"

"I had a feeling. Come on, let's see if you really might be a princess."

Chapter 29

Rixaline's reaction to the blood test's confirmation was to take a deep breath, grin, and go off to her room to pack.

Temo got on the phone with Ishalan to let him know Rixaline was coming for a *visit*.

Because that's all it was right now. A temporary thing. Donna's idea and one she'd gently suggested so that Rixaline would have an easy way out in case things got uncomfortable for her. Charlie was even supplying her with a burner phone from the stash in the office.

Temo also explained to Ishalan that there had been no blood-donation agreement yet either. How could there be? There hadn't been enough time to begin making that happen.

Donna walked Dr. Fox and Jerabeth to the door. "Thank you both for coming on such short notice and getting these tests done so fast."

Jerabeth nodded. "I wouldn't have missed it. And besides, I had his sample, so you couldn't have done it without me."

"Nope."

Dr. Fox pushed his glasses back. "I feel the same. Wouldn't have missed it. All very interesting. But glad to see you're nearly healed too."

"Thanks." Donna's injury was little more than a memory. "I have to admit I had my doubts about Ishalan and Rixaline being related, but now that it's verified, Rixaline seems pretty happy about it. I'm still cautious and will be for a while."

"I would be too," Dr. Fox said. "But that's the parent in us." He gave her a fatherly pat on the shoulder. "Be well, Governor."

"I will. Have a good night, both of you."

"You too," Dr. Fox said.

Jerabeth nodded as she pushed the elevator button. "Night."

"Jerabeth, feel free to come in a little later than usual since you've just basically worked some overtime."

"I should be okay, but I'll see how I feel in the morning. Thanks."

The elevator arrived, and they both got on.

Donna closed the door and went back to the kitchen. Back to Temo, Charlie, and Pierce. They all had skeptical looks on their faces.

"What?" No one answered her immediately, but they didn't have to. "I know you're concerned about her. I am too. But I am not her parent or her guardian. None of us are. The girl deserves to test these waters if she wants to. And I'm going to put some safeguards in place."

"Such as?" Charlie asked.

"I'm making her the vampire-fae liaison for the New Jersey Governor's Office. If that requires paperwork or something, fine. But that way, if anything happens to her, it's more than personal. And I can act in an official capacity."

Charlie smiled. "That's pretty good."

"And," Donna continued, "I'm requiring that she check in with one of us at least once a day. That phone you gave her isn't just for emergencies." She lowered her voice in case Rixaline could hear her. "I want a daily proof-of-life kind of thing."

"I like that," Temo said.

"We're also going to have a code word. If she uses it with any of us, that's the signal something's wrong and we need to get her out."

Pierce nodded. "That's smart. I feel better about this. What's the word?"

"I don't know yet. She's still deciding." Donna exhaled. "Charlie, where are we on that other thing I asked you about?"

Charlie stared at her for a second. "Oh! We can, uh, take care of that tonight. Right now, actually. We're good to go."

"Then let's do it." She smiled at Temo and Pierce. "We'll be back."

Pierce looked amused. "What are you two up to?"

"You'll know soon enough. If it happens." She and Charlie went out to the elevator. She waited until the penthouse door was closed and they were alone in the hall. "You already got the key? Or is the Realtor meeting us?"

Charlie called the elevator. "Security opened the door for us. The apartment is currently unoccupied, so the real estate agency has a key with them. Also, I asked about connecting that apartment with the current two, and the penthouse elevator can have a stop added at that floor with a simple programing adjustment."

"That's great."

The car came, they got on, and about two seconds later, it stopped again.

As the doors opened, they exited. There were three doors off the small lobby.

Charlie went straight for the door on the right. "I did a little more digging and found out they could also open an interior stairwell between this floor and the one above. It already exists, actually. It's just been closed off since this apartment wasn't purchased as part of the original governor's package."

"I think that would be a good idea. And pretty much necessary."

Charlie nodded, her hand on the knob. "Considering the cost of the unit, the expense of that small alteration is rather minor." She opened the apartment door. "All right, let's see what you think."

Upon entering, Donna saw that the apartment had impressive views. Slightly different from the penthouse because of the lower elevations but gorgeous all the same. The space was smaller but luxuriously appointed. Donna hadn't expected less.

They walked through to the big, combined

kitchen and dining room. The kitchen had stainless-steel appliances, glossy dove-gray cabinets, and glittering white quartz countertops. Those neutrals carried through the rest of the space with touches of white, black, and brushed nickel.

"You're awfully quiet," Charlie said.

"Just thinking it's kind of masculine, but that could be changed with soft furnishings."

Charlie nodded. "The right touch would do wonders to add some feminine balance."

Donna opened the pantry door. Empty, of course. And very clean. "Who used to live here?"

"I don't think anyone was in it for long. It's currently owned by a supernatural security firm that used it as a safe house."

"Get out. Really? That's pretty interesting. Why are they selling it?"

"The firm's owner has retired and moved to Belgium, so he's divesting all his US properties."

"Belgium, huh? I hear they make great chocolate." Donna smiled and went back to looking through the three bedrooms.

Charlie followed, peeking in cabinets and closets, trying faucets. They did a sweep through the conference room and office space as well. There was an armory in the office and a large wall safe. It reminded Donna of the one Joe had installed in their walk-in.

Between the two of them, they kicked the tires pretty good. Finally, Donna opened the living-room sliders and stepped outside. Charlie joined her. She glanced at her admin. "I know what I think. What do you think?"

"It's a great space. Bright. Gorgeous views. Almost identical to what Temo and I share now, just a little smaller."

"It would be nice to add this square footage to our domain."

"Even with Rixaline leaving? Not trying to talk you out of it, just playing devil's advocate."

"She could still come back. And do you really want to live with Temo and Neo as a hot and heavy couple?"

"Good points."

Donna leaned on the railing, enjoying the night air even as cold as it was. "And let's say that things don't work out between them. Not that I want that, but just say at some point, things change. One of them leaves. This would allow you to continue to have your own space. I can't speak for you, but I like having my privacy."

Charlie laughed. "You have no privacy. You live in a penthouse that is constantly full of people."

"True, but it doesn't feel that way." Amused, she stared at the city across the river. "Maybe I'll move down here."

"You could move Pierce in with me after Temo moves into this place."

"Maybe." But Donna knew that wasn't going to happen. She liked having Pierce around, and he was one of the least intrusive people there was. "How long has this place been on the market?"

"Two months. This kind of price tag tends to make a property harder to sell."

"And the owner's already moved to Belgium?"

"That's the word."

Then he probably really wanted this apartment off his books. "Offer three million, but go as high as three point two if he counters. Contingent on a building inspection, of course."

"Inspection's been done already. I can show you the paperwork. There were a few minor things, but they've all been fixed."

"Even better. Make the offer, then."

Charlie pulled out her phone. "I'll do it right now."

She walked back inside, but Donna stayed on the balcony. It was impossible to look at the city and not think about Fitzhugh, but now when she looked at it, she'd be thinking about Rixaline too. Praying the girl was safe.

She was doing the right thing, wasn't she? Even if she wasn't Rixaline's guardian, she could probably persuade her to stay. But would that lead to resentment? Always wondering what if? That was no way to live.

Donna knew about growing up with resentment. She'd had to do without a father most her life, and although she didn't dwell on it, the wound was there. She thought Cammie probably felt the same. What girl didn't want a strong father figure in her life? A sense of someone to protect her?

Could Ishalan be that someone for Rixaline? If his

story was true, he'd already done that for her mother. As best he could, anyway.

Donna hoped he'd continue in that role. Because if he hurt Rixaline, Donna might have to kill him.

When they got back upstairs, Temo and Pierce were busy in the kitchen. Pierce was seasoning a big tray of steaks. A pot of potatoes bubbled on the stove, a colander full of green beans sat near the sink, and Temo was chopping veggies for a big salad. The savory aroma of garlic bread was just floating out of the oven.

Lucky perched on one of the counter stools, watching intently.

"Wow," Donna said. "What's all this?"

Temo smiled. "We figured it might be nice to do one last family meal before Rixaline leaves us."

She nodded. "I like that a lot." It would be a great send-off for Rixaline to remember when she thought about them. And an even better way for her to measure her new life. Donna hoped that was true about Rixaline's whole experience at the penthouse and that it would be the standard by which she judged how she was cared for.

She'd lacked for nothing while she was here. She'd been treated with love and respect too. And while they hadn't spent every waking moment together, they'd certainly had a few fun evenings of pizza and movies or just hanging out.

Would Rixaline have those kinds of evenings at the stronghold? Donna had no idea. And not knowing made her a little sad. Suddenly, she was missing her own kids *and* Rixaline, who hadn't even left yet, and feeling misty.

"Hey," Charlie said. "Are you okay, Governor?"

Donna nodded and managed a smile. "Just feeling very much like a mom right now."

Charlie put her arm around Donna's shoulders. "You know, I think that's a big part of what makes you such a great governor. You genuinely care." Then she leaned in slightly. "Rixaline's a tough girl. That's easy to forget, because she doesn't come on strong, but she's already survived more in her life than a lot of people three times her age."

"You're right. She has. And that is easy to forget."

Just then, Rixaline walked out with her bag, which looked barely big enough to hold a toothbrush and her pajamas.

Donna glanced at it. "Did you change your mind?"

"No. Why?"

"Where's all your stuff? Your clothes? Your leather jacket?"

She chewed on her bottom lip for a second, her shoulders hunching up a little. "You paid for all those things."

"Oh, honey. Those are yours to take. *Yours*. I bought them for you. After all the help you gave me tracking down Joe and giving us a map to the stronghold, you have more than earned those things. Besides, Lucky probably spent some good time getting cat hair all over that stuff so you wouldn't forget him."

She sniffed, her eyes suddenly luminous with tears. "I won't forget him. I won't forget any of you."

Unable to hold in her emotions any longer, Donna felt a tear roll down her cheek. "You know you can come back here anytime you want."

Rixaline nodded. Temo sniffed. Pierce cleared his throat. Charlie sucked in a breath that sounded more like a sob. They all stood still, as though they might break down at any second.

Lucky put his front paws on the counter, stood up, and meowed loudly.

They all burst into laughter. Pierce picked up the tray of steaks and headed for the grill top. "The boss has spoken."

Rixaline dropped her bag and picked Lucky up. "Hungry, boy?"

He butted his head into her chin.

She laughed. "Come on. Let's get you some dinner."

Charlie got dishes out to set the table, but Donna just stood there, soaking in the moment. For all that was going wrong, there were a lot of things going right, and she had amazing people in her life.

It restored her spirit and renewed her energy to fight. She couldn't let these people down.

No matter how big that fight or how many injuries she incurred.

Fitzhugh had better be prepared.

Chapter 30

After dinner, they said their goodbyes to Rixaline, then Temo and Donna took her into the city and walked her through the Ramble to meet Ishalan.

He stood waiting in front of the gate, two guards in royal armor visible on the other side.

He walked toward them as they approached. Donna watched Rixaline carefully for any sign that she might be changing her mind.

Ishalan smiled, bowing his head slightly. "Princess Rixaline. Welcome home."

She stared at him intently. "You're really my uncle."

Her sentence was more of a declaration than a question, but he answered it anyway. "I am."

"And you really helped my mother escape?"

"I did."

"Then I have a question."

"Ask me anything."

Rixaline narrowed her eyes. "What one thing did my mother leave with me at the orphanage to remember her by?"

Ishalan's gaze went thoughtful, and for a moment he seemed perplexed. He shook his head. "The only thing I can think of is a small wooden heart. I gave it to her right before she left. A little amulet for luck and safety. But I can't imagine that mattered enough to her to pass it on."

Rixaline dug into the pocket of her jeans, then opened her palm. "This heart?"

Ishalan stared at it for a moment. "She kept it."

"You really are my uncle." Rixaline exhaled and tucked the heart away. She reached for her bag that Temo was holding. "Thank you."

He nodded. "Anytime, kid."

She hoisted the straps over her shoulder, but Ishalan came forward. "Here, let me."

He took the bag from her.

"But you're the king," Rixaline protested.

"More importantly, you're my niece." He smiled. "We're the only family we have. We have to look out for each other."

This was a new side of Ishalan. A kinder, gentler side. Donna hoped it continued. "Does this mean the treaty is secure?"

Ishalan nodded. "We still have details to work out."

"I know. The blood donations. I need a little time."

"I understand that. Just let me know. Regardless, you brought my niece home to me, and for that I am eternally grateful. I'll send out a notice about the impending treaty tonight."

"Thank you." Donna smiled at Rixaline. "You know I'm always here for you."

Rixaline nodded, looking very much like she was going to tear up again. "Thank you for everything." She hugged Donna hard.

"You too." Donna squeezed her right back. "Take care."

"I'll talk to you soon." With a little wave, Rixaline walked through the gate with Ishalan.

The moment they passed through, mist obscured the sight of them.

Donna sighed.

Temo nodded. "I feel the same way."

They'd almost arrived back at the penthouse when Donna's phone chimed with a text from Rixaline. With a note saying everything was fine, she included a picture of her room, which was beautifully appointed. That eased Donna's mind a bit.

She went to bed as soon as they got back. She read awhile, hoping sleep might find her that way, but she got to the last chapter without much effort.

She turned the light off anyway and lay down. Sleep was a long time coming. Her mind was too busy. By the time she finally drifted off, the watery light of dawn was already seeping around the edges of her drapes.

Thankfully, she slept without dreams or nightmares. None that she remembered, anyway. She got up, wondering if she should sleep longer. But there was still a lot on her desk.

A hot shower got her moving, although coffee would help. She went out to the kitchen in leggings and an oversized hooded velour tunic.

Charlie was there, fixing a cup of tea and waiting for a bagel to toast. "Morning, Governor." She smiled. "I have some plain news and some good news."

"You do?"

The bagel popped up. "I do. The plain news is that it seems like the best way to get us all to Kansas is to rent some RVs and drive. There's a company that specializes in supernatural-friendly models. I've sent them an email to see what they have available."

"Road trip to Kansas. That should be interesting."

"I'm sure it will be. The first of the good news is Ishalan sent the treaty agreement out last night."

"Excellent. And fast. Which I find encouraging. I was sure he was going to drag his feet."

"Same here. He also issued a formal note of apology for the way vampires were treated under Dredward's rule."

"How about that? That seems like a big thing."

"It is." Charlie looked a little impressed herself.

"What's the second thing? You said the treaty was the first."

Charlie grinned. "The offer on the apartment was accepted at three point two."

"Yes! No one else knows, right?"

Charlie put the bagel on a plate and popped the top off the tub of cream cheese. "Just us."

"All right, excellent. I need to talk to Neo. And Temo. Maybe I should talk to Temo first." She rubbed her hands over her face. "Actually, first I need coffee."

Charlie picked up one half of her bagel, freshly schmeared with cream cheese. "Just tell me one thing."

"Sure, what?" Donna got a mug and a K-Cup out of the cabinet.

"Can we call them Nemo? Can that please be their couple name?"

Donna laughed so hard she almost dropped the mug. "I'm down with that."

Charlie smiled as she chewed. "Good, because I've been looking online at a big stuffed clown fish pillow for a housewarming gift."

Donna shook her head as she put the K-Cup in and got her coffee started. "I did not know you had such a devious side. I like it."

"Never get on my bad side." Charlie smirked as she took another bite of her breakfast.

"I don't plan on it, but thanks for the reminder." Donna eyed the bagels. "Would you put one of those in the toaster for me?"

"Absolutely. Any more thoughts about filing the complaint against Fitzhugh or the declaration of your ability to daywalk?"

"File the complaint. But I'm still not sure about the declaration."

"Totally up to you." She picked up her teacup and the plate with the rest of the bagel on it. "I'll be in the office if you need me. Going to file that complaint immediately. Temo's up if you want to see him."

"Thanks."

As Charlie left, Cammie walked slowly into the kitchen. Her right cheekbone bore a long red scratch, and a dark bruise was beginning to show on her jaw. Her bottom lip was split too. "Morning. Or afternoon. Or whatever it is."

"Almost evening, I think," Donna said. "Are you okay?"

"I look worse than I feel."

"Are you sure? I can get Dr. Fox over here."

"No, I'm good. Thank you though."

"You want coffee?"

"So much." She carefully eased down onto one of the stools at the counter.

"Based on how you look, I'm not sure if I should ask this, but how'd the demon removal go?"

"A little tricky, but I got it done."

Donna took her cup out from under the brewer and got another cup going. "I guess I should see the other guy, huh?"

She smiled, then winced. "Something like that."

Donna fixed her coffee and gave it to Cammie. She needed it more than Donna did. While waiting on the second cup, the bagel Charlie had put in the toaster popped up. Donna looked at her sister. "You want half of this?"

Cammie nodded. "Yeah, that would be good."

Donna passed over the coffee, then started

spreading cream cheese on both halves. "Rixaline moved back to the stronghold."

"Really?" Cammie looked amazed. "How did all that happen?"

Donna explained the whole thing, including the treaty, as she put Cammie's half of the bagel on a plate and set it in front of her.

"That's quite an accomplishment," Cammie said, picking up her bagel half. "But I'm glad you thought about doing the blood test to prove Ishalan was telling the truth."

"So am I. Gave me some peace of mind, you know? Although he seemed genuinely happy that she decided to come."

"Why wouldn't he?" Cammie took a careful bite of her bagel, using the side of her mouth without the split in her lip.

"Right, but I mean in a way that meant more to him than just securing his throne."

"Even better."

Donna nodded. "It is good. It means the treaty is really happening."

Cammie wrapped her fingers around the handle of her coffee cup but didn't drink. "I don't know that there's ever been a fae-vampire treaty before."

Donna sat beside her. "Well, it's not worldwide or anything."

"Doesn't matter. Still quite a feat."

"I guess it kind of is. You have a better perspective on things like that since you know more of the history, but I'll take whatever peace I can get."

Cammie sipped her coffee. "Speaking of, how are things with Fitzhugh?"

"By now, Charlie has probably already filed the countercomplaint."

"That'll be interesting."

"Yes, it will."

Cammie gently prodded the bruise on her jaw. "What's on your schedule for the evening?"

Cammie might not want Dr. Fox's attention, but she was going to get some from Donna. She got a frozen bag of peas out and wrapped it in a kitchen towel. "I have to talk to Temo, then I'm offering someone a job, then I have my support group meeting."

"The First Fangs Club?"

"Yep." She slid the makeshift ice pack over. "Here, put that on your jaw. What are you doing tonight?"

"Long soak in a hot Epsom salt bath followed by a look through available apartments in the area."

"Cammie." Donna frowned at her. "Don't be so stubborn. Stay here. Please."

"I appreciate the offer, but I'd rather leave before I wear out my welcome."

"You're a long way from doing that. A long way. And I'm already working on getting us some more space."

"What does that mean?"

"You'll see. Just don't do anything for a month, okay? If nothing else, that will give you a chance to save up some money. Plus, I could use the support with everything going on."

"You're surrounded by support. But I'll think about it."

"You'll promise me right now."

Cammie's eyes widened in amusement. "Well, look at you with the demands. Okay, *Governor*. One month."

"Thank you." She leaned over and kissed her sister on her uninjured cheek, then she went to work finishing her bagel. When that was done, she took her coffee downstairs to talk to Temo.

Usually, everyone came upstairs, but she wanted a chance to speak to him on his turf. She thought he might be more comfortable saying no that way.

The stairs led into the kitchen, just like they did in the penthouse. "Temo?"

"Morning, boss."

She turned to see him coming out of the laundry room, a basket of clothes tucked under one arm. "Laundry day, huh?"

He nodded. "Gotta do it. You need me?"

"I want to talk to you for a few minutes. If now is a good time."

"Sure. You want to go into the living room? I'll just put these on my bed and be right in."

"Great." She went to wait for him. He didn't take long.

He sat across from her. "What's on your mind?"

"Neo. I'd like to bring her on as part of the team. Not just to handle our cybersecurity, but also to help with all of our IT needs."

"Like when you want to hack into something?"

"Maybe." Donna laughed. "Let's just not say it that way."

"Right." He was smiling. "Having her as an official part of the team would be great."

"Yeah? You're okay with me hiring her?"

"Absolutely. I like her a lot."

His broad grin said he liked her more than a lot. "You'd be okay working with her on a regular basis, then?"

He nodded. "Yes."

"How about living with her?"

His brows lifted, but the smile went nowhere. "You're going to ask her to move in here?"

"Maybe. I know she's ready to move out of the city."

"She is."

"So...I bought the apartment below this one. It's a three-bedroom executive suite. I was thinking if you two wanted to make that your own..."

"Really?"

She smiled. "Yes. The penthouse elevator is being reprogrammed to add the stop, and that apartment will also get access to the stairwell."

"Boss, that's...amazing. I know you didn't do it just for us, but—"

"Eh, I kind of did. Don't get me wrong, it'll be great to have the extra space. That apartment has another conference room and office, which I have no doubt we'll use, but you guys plus Charlie in this apartment seems kind of cramped. Plus, this way, Charlie can have some more space too."

"It's a win-win." He got a curious twinkle in his eyes. "And now Fitzhugh isn't the only one with three floors."

She sat back, her smile widening. "There is that."

Maybe that was petty, but she didn't care. She was sick and tired of Fitzhugh thinking he was better than her.

"When are you going to talk to Neo?"

"I'm going to see if she can meet me a little early for group tonight. So as soon as possible."

"Good." He let out a little contented sigh. "She's going to be really excited."

"I realize that this could go poorly if things between you two don't end well."

He shook his head. "That's not gonna happen, boss. I like that woman way too much. Enough to think maybe someday I'd like to ask her to make things permanent."

"Glad to hear that." Smiling, Donna got up. "Now, let's see if she takes the job."

Chapter 31

Neo was waiting outside the New Manhattan Health and Wellness Center when Temo dropped Donna off. She walked up to the car as he got out to greet her. "Hey."

Neo lifted her chin. "Hey."

Donna came around the SUV in time to see her friend give Temo a quick kiss. She smiled but said nothing.

Temo, smiling sheepishly, took a step back. "You'll text me when you're done, boss?"

"I will."

"Okay." He grinned at Neo as he got back in the car. "See you later."

Donna wasn't sure which of them he was talking to. She stuck her hands in her coat pockets as she stood by Neo. "Thanks for meeting me early."

"Sure," Neo said. She watched Temo pull away. "What's up? Need help with something else?"

"Sort of. More like permanent help. I'd like to offer you a job as my IT person."

That got Neo's attention. She whipped around to

look at Donna so fast her braids went flying. "Get out. Are you playing with me?"

"Totally serious. Pay is great, you can still take care of your existing clients in your free time, and the position comes with room and board. If you want it."

"This after I failed to get into the Venari system. You should really let me dig into Fitzhugh and see what I can find."

"Not as long as that's still illegal. And Cammie warned us the Venari setup was impossible, so I don't consider that a mark against you."

The corner of Neo's mouth hitched up. "Thanks. Wait. You said room and board?"

Donna nodded. "The governorship has added another apartment to its holdings."

Neo's expression turned incredulous. "Any chance that crib is in the Wellman Towers?"

"Every chance."

"And that's where the room and board would be?"

"It is. I thought you and Temo could take over the new addition. If you're ready to take that kind of step with him. I'm not about to rush you into something."

Neo put her hand to her head. "I can't process all of this. It's too much. You're serious?"

"I wouldn't joke about a thing like this. You're already part of my team. Why not make it official and put you on the payroll? Besides, you said you were ready to get out of Manhattan. So are you in or what?"

Neo lunged forward and hugged Donna. Which was very unlike Neo. But the hug lasted only a few seconds, so Donna didn't have to wonder if her friend had been body-snatched. "Yes. I say yes. And thank you."

"Great. Temo will be so happy." Donna looked past her and saw Francine getting out of a sleek black sedan driven by her roommate/sire/boyfriend, Lionel. "Well, the party just arrived, so we'd better get upstairs. Hi, Francine."

"Donna! Neo! How are you?" Francine gave Lionel a wave goodbye, then came over to them. Tonight's velour tracksuit was emerald green with rhinestone trim. Her waist pack was gold lamé, which matched her metallic gold sneakers.

"Hey, Frankie." Neo gave her a fist bump, which Francine returned. "I'm good. How are you doing?"

"Better than I was at forty, that's for sure." Francine grinned at Donna. "I already know you're good, honey. I heard the news. Someone's been a busy vampire governor."

"What news? About the raid to get Rico back?"

"No, about the treaty with the fae. That's unbelievable. How on earth did you pull that off?"

"It wasn't really any one thing I did. Just a lot of pieces coming together at the right time."

"Regardless, well done. After losing Artemis, the vampire community needed a good thing like that." Francine held on to Donna's arm. Not because she needed it for stability, she was fine in that department. More like a motherly gesture. "You're smoking Fitzhugh in the points department, that's for sure."

Donna sighed. "I don't know about all that. He's filed two new complaints against me, which you might not know. Well, one complaint against Pierce for punching him at your party, and another against me claiming I'm responsible for Artemis's death."

Francine frowned. "What a putz. He's jealous. And trying to make himself look better because he knows the council is making up their short list of successors." She shook her head. "They're never going to pick him. Ever."

Neo wrinkled her nose. "They better not. Can you imagine?"

Francine sighed. "I can, and it's not good. We'd probably decamp to England if that ever happened. Lionel has an estate there. But speaking of Artemis, has anyone talked to Meghan?"

Meghan Murphy, the redheaded supermodel member of the First Fangs Club, had been sired by Claudette as well, so that made Artemis her grandsire, just like Donna. And it made Meghan and Donna blood sisters. Which wasn't something that had ever come into play despite how related it made them seem.

Donna shook her head. "I haven't. Do you think I should have reached out to her?"

"You could have, I suppose, but that responsibility really falls on Claudette." Francine made a face. "And you know that didn't happen."

"Hey, I did see Claudette." Donna's brows lifted

as she prepared to drop the rest of that juicy tidbit on them. "Pretty sure she's shacking up with everyone's favorite New York governor. She was hanging on him like a cheap suit."

"Shut up," Neo said. "How did you not tell me that?"

"I'm telling you now."

Francine's mouth was open. "Boy, she's a piece of work. Didn't take her long, huh?"

"No, it didn't," Donna said.

Francine's blue eyes twinkled. "I guess she missed being governor so much that sleeping with one was the next best thing."

Donna snorted as Neo waved to someone behind her.

Neo grinned. "Hey, LaToya. What's up, girl?"

The curvy woman joined them. "I am, baby." She stuck out her arm and pulled up her sleeve. "Look at this bracelet my new man got me."

The gold links gleamed in the streetlights.

"Ooh, that's gorgeous," Neo said. "He must be a keeper."

LaToya dropped her arm. "We'll see. But yeah, so far he's doing all right. What are you all doing out here?"

"Just gabbing. We should go upstairs," Francine said. "Dr. Goldberg will be wondering where we are."

"Well, let's go, baby." LaToya shifted slightly, pulled her big sweater coat tighter. "It's chilly out here."

Donna nodded. "It is. But at least it's not still snowing."

As they headed for the door, a voice called out, "Wait for me."

They all looked to see Bunni tottering down the street in zebra-print stiletto boots and a matching fake fur zebra coat. All of a sudden, she went slightly sideways as one of her ankles bent. With vampire speed and strength, she righted herself without falling, but not without a high-pitched yelp.

LaToya sighed. "That girl crazy." She put her hands on her hips. "You're gonna break something in those fool shoes."

Bunni reached them. "Maybe I'll meet a cute ER doc that way."

"Yeah, and when he tests your blood, he's gonna know there's something worse wrong with you than a broken ankle, baby." LaToya laughed. "But you do you, boo."

They all went up in the same elevator and straight to floor twelve, suite C, the group's meeting room.

Dr. Goldberg was already there. She stood at the credenza where the coffee service was set up, fixing herself a cup of tea. "Good evening, ladies."

They all greeted her in return and got themselves something to drink. Donna got a bottle of water and a couple of cookies from the array beside the coffeemaker.

As they were milling about, Meghan came in, gorgeous as ever in a sweeping plaid coat that made her look like a Highland goddess. "Good evening, everyone." She went right up to Donna. "I've been talking to my attorneys about your idea of setting up a foundation for people with sun sensitivity, and it's actually happening. Thank you for that. It could really be life-changing for me. Please tell me you'll come to the first event."

"You're welcome. And sure, I'd love to." Donna had made the suggestion about the foundation at the last meeting, which was also the first time they'd met. "I have to ask. How are you doing with the loss of Artemis?"

Meghan sighed. "It's been hard. I don't even know why. It's not like I knew her. I guess I thought she was somehow more immortal than the rest of us."

"I think I felt a little of that myself."

Meghan tucked a fiery strand of hair behind one ear. "How are you doing with it? I heard you were there."

"I was. I'm dealing with it. I'm going to the memorial. I feel like I need to."

"Oh, I wish I could go."

"Why don't you? You can travel with us if you'd like."

Meghan shook her head. "I don't know. I have to be really careful not to draw undue attention. The council frowns on that."

"I guess it might stir things up if one of the world's most famous supermodels suddenly showed up in Lebanon, Kansas."

Meghan exhaled. "It would. And I can't risk the

press digging into why I'm there. I will definitely be watching online. And sending a fortune in flowers. Still, it's not the same as being there."

Donna gave Meghan's arm a little squeeze. "If it makes you feel any better, she didn't die without a fight, I can tell you that."

Neo joined them. "And Donna took out the fae who killed our queen too. Their king, actually. I guess that's fair. A king for a queen. Sliced him right in half with Artemis's sword."

"You did?" Meghan's face brightened. "You're so fearless, Donna. I don't think I could ever do something like that. But then, there's a reason you're governor."

"I don't know." That reason had been more about the right place and time than anything Donna had done. "I think you'd surprise yourself with what you're capable of when the situation demands action."

Meghan shrugged. "The best I can do is stand in heels for eight hours without complaining."

"And you've been doing that since well before you were turned," Donna said, laughing. "If that's not a superpower, I don't know what is."

Meghan snorted.

"Ladies." Dr. Goldberg clapped her hands. "If we could take our seats."

Everyone got their refreshments and came over. Donna sat between Meghan and Francine, who was beside Dr. Goldberg. Rounding out the circle on the other side were Bunni, LaToya, and Neo.

"Full house tonight. Always nice to see." Dr. Goldberg smiled as she opened her notebook. "Let's get started, shall we? And I think the best way to do that is to acknowledge that this has been a hard week. The loss of Queen Artemis, regardless of how you felt about her, is a major stressor. Does anyone want to talk about how her death has affected them?"

LaToya raised her hand, making her new bracelet clink against her watch. "I feel like I need to do something, but I don't know what. I'm sad that she's gone, but that sadness has no real place to go. You see what I'm saying?"

"Uh-huh," Bunni agreed. "She was our queen, right? So we need to, like, show our support. But how? It's hard."

Dr. Goldberg nodded, teacup in hand. "Understanding grief and how to react to it isn't easy, you're right. What about you, Meghan? Or Donna? You were both related to Artemis by your sire. How are you doing?"

"I'm doing all right." Meghan smiled. "Actually, better now that I know Donna killed the fae who murdered our queen."

Dr. Goldberg nearly choked on her tea. "What now?"

Neo nodded as she crossed her arms. "She did. I was there. She sliced that son of—that dude right in half. And did you know fae turn to ash when killed, just like we do? Because I didn't."

LaToya let out a long, whistling exhale. "That's crazy."

Bunni nodded, penciled brows high. "Yeah, it is."

Dr. Goldberg was staring at them, lips parted but saying nothing.

Francine reached over and patted the doctor's knee. "It's okay, honey. I know you're dealing with some heavy emotions right now. You want to take a break?"

Besides being a great therapist and group leader, Dr. Goldberg was an empath. It's what made her such an outstanding therapist, but that gift meant she felt things much more deeply than most people.

Donna hadn't even thought about how she might react.

Dr. Goldberg took a deep breath and shook her head. "No, I'll be fine. I just didn't realize..." She looked at Donna. "Maybe you should start from the beginning. Just exactly how did you come to kill the fae king?"

Chapter 32

By the time Donna had finished the retelling of the raid, Dr. Goldberg, LaToya, Francine, Bunni, and Meghan were all staring at her in rapt attention with the occasional astonished glance aimed at Neo.

Donna's phone had buzzed once, but she'd ignored it to get through her story. She folded her hands on her lap. "And that's it. I was unconscious for the next two days, but as you can see, everything worked out."

Bunni popped her gum. "I can't believe you turned Will Ferris. He's, like, famous. Well, I mean, his leather jackets are. They're amazeballs."

Neo gave Bunni some hard side-eye. "Governor Barrone rescued a werewolf FBI agent, took down the fae king, then made peace with the new one, and your takeaway is that the guy she turned makes great leather jackets?"

Bunni made a face. "I can like what I like. You're not in charge of what I think is important."

"Hey," Donna said. "Both of you, chill out. I don't know about the rest of you, but I've had enough stress this week." Her phone vibrated again. "I don't need to come here and get more of it. Especially not from two women I consider friends. Whatever this thing is between you, get over it. Being enemies is pointless. We're all vampires. We all need to support each other. Fighting will get us nowhere."

Dr. Goldberg nodded. "Donna makes some great points. If there was ever a group of women that should support each other, it's this one. And you're all feeling the weight of this week's events. Whether or not you realize it, you will need to grieve."

"I agree," Meghan said. "I just don't think I understood that until you said it. I haven't cried. But maybe I should."

"I did," Francine said. "But I cry at all kinds of things."

LaToya leaned forward. "Maybe we could do something as a group. Maybe get together and watch the memorial?"

Dr. Goldberg jotted something in her notebook. "That's a wonderful idea, LaToya. I can ask if the room's available that night, if that works for everyone."

"I can't," Donna said. "I'm going to Kansas to attend in person."

Francine's eyes lit up. "That's even better. Let's do that."

Neo shrugged. "I'm in."

Donna started to respond as the door flew open, and Temo burst in. "Boss, I'm sorry to interrupt, but you weren't answering your phone."

A chill went through her. If he felt the need to interrupt, something had to have gone seriously sideways. "What's wrong?"

"It's not wrong, exactly, it's just that, well, your daughter landed at LaGuardia twenty minutes ago. She called Charlie for a ride. I guess you gave her that number?"

"I did." Donna stood up. "Christina's here? I thought—wait. Did I forget she was coming?"

He shook his head. "You talked about it but never firmed anything up, but she decided to come anyway. As a surprise."

"Good surprise." Donna put her hand to her heart. Her baby girl was here. She bent to pick up her purse. "Ladies, I'm sorry, but I have to go."

They were all smiling and nodding.

"Go 'head, baby," LaToya said. "Nothing like family."

"That's for sure," Meghan added.

"Have fun, honey." Francine gave her a little wave.

"I will, thanks. And listen, I'll be in touch about the trip to Kansas." She pointed at Neo. "This changes nothing."

She nodded, grinning. "You got it. Boss."

Donna hustled out the door with Temo. "Are we headed to LaGuardia, then?"

"Yes, as fast as I can get us there. Pierce and Charlie are making sure the penthouse is ready."

"What's there to do? It's not like it's a pigsty."

He lifted one shoulder as they got in the elevator.

"They just want everything to be perfect. This is your kid. They want her to like them."

Donna smiled. "She's going to love all of you."

His brows pulled together. "You think so?"

She nudged him with her elbow. "Temo, you're so easy to like, I don't know why you'd think otherwise."

He grinned. "Thanks, boss. Hey, did that exchange with Neo mean she took the job?"

"She did."

They got to the car, which he'd left parked in the fire lane, and he drove for all he was worth, smiling most of the way. How they didn't get pulled over for speeding, she had no idea.

But her mind wasn't really on his driving. She was texting with Christina, making sure she knew where to wait and how soon they'd be there.

Wasn't soon enough, even with Temo's incredible efficiency.

They pulled up to the airport, and Donna's heart skipped. "There she is. She doesn't see us."

Temo aimed for a closer space that had just opened up. "She looks like you. Very pretty."

"Thanks." As soon as he parked, Donna hopped out and ran toward her. "Christina!"

"Mom?" Christina turned. "Mom!"

Donna wrapped Christina in her arms. "Hi, baby."

"Hi, Mom." A second later, she was bawling.

Donna pulled back. "Honey, what's wrong?"

Sniffling, Christina shook her head. "I'm just happy to see you."

"Aw, I'm happy to see you too."

"You look amazing." She wiped at her eyes. "I mean, like *Real Housewives* good. Wow. Being a…you know is really working for you."

Donna laughed. "Thanks. Is that your stuff?" She pointed to the bags behind Christina. A suitcase, a duffel bag, a computer case, and her enormous purse.

"Yeah."

"Are you moving in?"

Christina rolled her eyes. "Ha ha."

Temo had already gotten out. "I'll get them, boss."

"Thanks." Donna put her arm around her daughter. "Christina, this is Temo Danielson, the head of my security, my driver, and an all-around great guy."

He nodded at her. "Nice to meet you, miss."

"Call me Christina." She looked at Donna. "Is that okay?"

"Of course. I'm the governor, not the queen of England."

"And you may call me Temo." He picked up all four of Christina's bags at once and carried them to the car.

She watched him go. "Wow, he's strong. Is he a…you know, like you too?"

"Not the same as I am. But he's more than human."

Christina nodded, a little wide-eyed. "Cool."

"Come on, let's get back to the penthouse."

Donna opened the rear passenger door. "I can't wait to introduce you to everyone. Oh! I have a surprise for you too."

"You do?" Christina climbed in and scooted across to sit behind Temo, who was closing the rear gate.

"I do." Donna took her seat and shut the door.

Temo got back behind the wheel. "All set?"

"All set."

With a nod and a grin, he pulled out and started for home.

Christina poked Donna in the leg. "What's the surprise? Tell me."

"Aunt Cammie is at the penthouse, too, so you'll get to see her as well."

For a second, Christina didn't look quite as happy as Donna had anticipated she would. Then a fresh smile bent her mouth. "That's awesome."

But it clearly wasn't. Not entirely. And Donna had no idea why. She wasn't about to dig into that in the car, however. Or maybe at all. Whatever the reason for Christina's surprise, Donna didn't want to ruin the happiness of the moment.

"So, do I look that much different?" Donna asked.

"You do and you don't." Christina shook her head. "You look like a supermodel version of yourself. I still can't really believe you're an actual vampire."

"Believe it. I am."

"Can I see your teeth?"

Donna smiled widely.

Christina smirked. "That's not what I mean."

"You mean the fangs I use to drink the blood of my hapless victims?"

"Mom, you don't really—okay, very funny."

Donna snorted, followed by a similar noise from Temo. "Ready? I don't want to freak you out."

"I've seen all the *Twilight* movies, you know."

Donna shook her head slowly. "This is nothing like that."

"Just show me. Please?"

"All right." Donna called down her fangs and let a little glow into her eyes. "How's that?"

Christina reared back, eyes rounding. But a second later, she chilled out and leaned forward again. "Okay, that is *freaky*." She reached out like she was going to touch one of Donna's fangs.

Donna pulled them in. "Don't. They're really sharp." She quickly changed the subject. "How's school?"

"It's good. Busy. Tons of work. I'm always in the library."

Donna wasn't so sure about that. Christina was a good student, that much was true, but she'd been a very social creature in high school, and Donna couldn't imagine that had changed. "That sounds a little boring."

Christina laughed. "I'm not always in the library. But I do spend a lot of time there."

"Are you any closer to deciding what you want to be when you grow up?"

She shrugged, her smile suddenly going coy. "Maybe I'll be a vampire like you."

"That's not a profession. And let's not even start that discussion."

Christina's expression went thoughtful. "I don't know. Would you be mad if I decided I wanted to be a housewife and have kids and just do the whole stay-at-home-mom thing?"

"If that's what you really wanted, no. I'm never going to be mad at you for doing something you want to do." It wouldn't surprise her if that's what Christina wanted. She'd always had a deep maternal instinct. "You have to follow your heart. Being a mom isn't easy. It's one of the hardest jobs you'll ever have, actually."

"It was hard for you, wasn't it?"

Donna took a moment as her past rushed back in waves of memories. "It was hard at times."

"Because of Dad."

"Yes. He was…mostly a good father, but at the same time, the worst one possible." Donna took a breath. "I was always afraid he might hurt you. Or do something that would cause you to get hurt."

"You did a great job of protecting us. You really did."

"Thanks, honey. Sometimes I think I should have tried to get you kids away from him sooner…" She'd always have doubts about that. "But if he'd come after us, I don't know that I could have kept you safe. I'm sorry about that."

"Mom, you did the best you could do. And it was more than a lot of people could have done. You have nothing to apologize for."

"Thanks." Donna wondered what had brought all this up. Was Christina struggling with something? They hadn't even talked about Joe this much at his funeral. Didn't matter. Donna would do whatever she could to help her children. No matter what age they were, or what they were going through. "Everything okay with you?"

Christina nodded. "Yeah, everything's good. Or will be."

That was a slightly cryptic statement. But Donna got the sense Christina didn't want to go deeper than that with Temo listening.

Christina grinned and let out a little laugh. "I can't believe you're a vampire. It's one thing for you to tell me that, but to see you... There's no denying it now."

"Nope. I am definitely a vampire."

"Did it hurt? Being turned?"

"Not really." Donna didn't want to frighten her with the gory details.

Christina grimaced. "But you have to drink blood?"

"I do. I know that sounds awful, but it doesn't to me. It's what keeps me going. The same as air to you, I suppose."

"Can I see your fangs again?"

Donna laughed. "Sure." She brought them down and curled her lip back so Christina could see them more easily.

"I want to touch one."

"They're teeth. Like all the rest of my teeth."

"Mom, they are literally not like all the rest of your teeth. The rest of your teeth don't retract into your jaw."

"True. Okay, fine. But be careful."

"Why? Does the sight of blood drive you uncontrollably mad?"

Temo snorted softly.

"No," Donna answered. "I just don't want you to hurt yourself."

"Mom. Please." She stuck a finger out and poked at one of Donna's fangs. "Huh. They're hard just like teeth."

What had she expected? Donna sighed and shook her head.

Her fang sliced across Christina's finger.

"Ow." Christina snatched her hand back, but not before a drop of blood fell.

"I told you." Donna retracted her fangs and frowned. There was something off about the metallic taste of the blood. An underlying innocence that was both wonderful and out of place.

Understanding came a second later. Donna sucked in a breath as she looked at her daughter. "Holy Mother. You're pregnant."

Chapter 33

Introductions were short and sweet at the penthouse, probably because Temo assisted in getting everyone to give Donna and Christina some alone time. Thankfully, Cammie wasn't there, as she'd gone out to talk to some potential customers. Donna didn't want to have to explain just yet why Christina's beloved aunt was no longer a nun and was now freelancing as a supernatural bounty hunter.

Not when there was a much bigger topic to discuss.

She closed the guest room door and faced her daughter, who sat on the edge of the bed, arms crossed and looking like she was about to cry or scream. Donna took a breath and made herself stay calm. "Does the boy know?"

Christina relaxed slightly. Had she been expecting Donna to yell? "He does, and he's super supportive. In fact, that's why I came home this weekend. I wanted to tell you all this in person. I didn't think you'd find out before I could say something."

A thousand different thoughts and emotions swirled through Donna. She turned the chair around from the dressing table and sat. Then she asked a question she felt like she already knew the answer to. "Are you going to finish school?"

"I'd like to. It's part of our plan, anyway. I'm so close, you know?"

Our plan. Donna's intense distaste for that phrase surprised her. Maybe because it illustrated how keenly she'd been replaced in her daughter's life. But that was how things went, wasn't it? "Yes, you are close. What is the plan?"

Christina twisted her fingers together. "We're going to get married."

Donna's mouth opened, but forming words took a second or two longer. "Married." She blew out a long breath.

After everything she'd been through in the last couple of weeks, a little unplanned pregnancy should be a breeze. But it wasn't. The word *pregnant* had caused every dream Donna had ever had for Christina to disappear like...ash on the wind. "I see. Tell me about him. About how he's going to support you and the baby. About how you're going to take care of a baby and a husband and finish school. About how—"

"Mom. I know you're mad. I know this isn't what you wanted for me. It wasn't what I wanted for me either, but it happened, and now I want to do what's best for all of us. We love each other, and we want this baby."

Donna nodded, her throat constricted with a knot the size of a softball. *All of us* didn't seem like it included her anymore, but that was selfish, and she knew it. She couldn't stop herself from feeling it, though. "Go on," she whispered. "Tell me the plan."

"He's got some money. He's been working since he was a kid. And his parents are going to help. We're going to—"

"His parents already know?" Another cut to the heart. Donna had been second to find out.

"It wasn't intentional. We'd already decided I was going to talk to you before we did anything, but we were there last weekend, and somehow his mom just guessed." Christina put a hand to her stomach. "I'm not even that far along."

A small comfort, but Donna couldn't shake the sense of numbness that had seeped into her bones. "The plan?"

"Right. We're going to get a little off-campus apartment, and we're going to make it work. He loves me, and I love him very much." She smiled. "It's all going to be fine. You'll see."

The confidence of youth was a staggering thing. "How old is he?"

"He's twenty-three. He's working on his master's." Christina lifted her chin ever so slightly. "He's very smart."

"Not smart enough to keep this from happening."

"Mom. It takes two people to make a baby."

"I'm well aware." Donna sat back. "Let me guess, if one of you has to drop out, it's not going to be him."

"No, it won't be. But if I have to drop out, I will go back. I'm only three semesters from graduating. And the way I see it, I should be able to get through next semester without any issue, have the baby this summer, then be good to finish my last year. And if that doesn't happen, and it takes a little longer, so be it."

Donna wondered if that could actually work, but having had two babies, she was pretty sure it wouldn't. "What's he studying?"

"Hospitality management. His family owns a restaurant chain, and he plans to open his own location after he graduates." Christina paused. "His dad is also the mayor of their town. His parents are great people."

"What town?" Donna was fast getting a sense of these people, but she didn't know if she could trust it. She wasn't exactly in a warm and fuzzy place.

"Timberville, Indiana."

Donna had never heard of it, but she did know Indiana was on the way to Kansas. "What kind of restaurants?"

"Barbecue. Called Big Dog's. We don't have them around here. I mean, obviously. But they have seven locations in Indiana. Eight after Noah opens his location."

"Noah?"

Christina's smile was big and bright and instant. "Noah Miller. That's his name."

He certainly didn't sound Italian. In fact, he sounded as middle American as all get-out. And about as far away from the life Christina had growing up as could be.

Noah Miller wasn't the name of a guy who would ever think about breaking the law as a means to an end. He'd probably been a Boy Scout and captain of the football team and maybe even prom king. He undoubtedly never drove more than five miles over the speed limit, definitely ate all his vegetables, and more than likely thought the mob was mostly a Hollywood construct.

Or at least that's what Donna hoped. Except Noah Miller had still managed to get her daughter pregnant. "Does he know about...your father?"

Christina's smile faltered. "He does. His parents don't. Yet. I mean, it's bound to happen. They know my last name."

Donna nodded. "I wouldn't be surprised if they're already suspicious." Especially since Joe had been in the spotlight recently thanks to his faked death and arrest by the FBI. No wonder Christina had been so upset by that news coming to light. "How long have you been seeing this boy?"

"Almost a year."

"And I'm just hearing about him?"

"We were taking it slow."

That was a good sign, right? Except things sure weren't slow now.

"We were kind of hoping you might want to meet his parents. I know that's an inconvenience, but we figured if they got to know you, then finding out about my family might not be such a big deal. You know, if they could see what a regular person you are."

"Except that I'm a vampire, which is about as unregular as a person can be. Does Noah know about that?"

"*No.*" Christina's eyes widened. "I don't think that's a good idea at all."

"Neither do I. So it needs to stay that way."

"Right. Totally."

"I'd be very interested in meeting his parents. I'd like to see what kind of people they are too. And it just so happens, I'm going to be driving through Indiana next week."

"You are?"

"Yes."

"Why?"

"I have a funeral to attend in Kansas, and driving is the easiest way for everyone involved."

"Who died?"

"No one you know. The vampire queen."

"Get out. The vampires have a queen?"

"They did. But back to you. Are you sure about all this? Sure about this boy?"

"Mom, you can't keep calling him a boy. He's a man."

Donna did her best not to snort. "He's going to have to prove that to me."

"He's marrying me, isn't he?"

"Yes, but I married a man who turned out to be very different than what I expected."

"But you got Joe Jr. and me out of that marriage."

Donna smiled. "Yes, I did." She sighed. "I'm not mad at you. Disappointed, yes, but not in you so much as in this turn of events. I hope that makes sense."

"It does. I wasn't jumping up and down when I found out. I took five pregnancy tests because I didn't want to believe the results. But they were all positive. And then campus health confirmed it." Her mouth quirked up a little. "Can you be a vampire and a grandma at the same time?"

"I guess I'm going to find out." Donna shook her head. Nonna wasn't a title she thought she'd take on for a long time to come. Funny how life worked out.

"Do you mind if we don't tell Joe Jr. for a little bit? I can only take so much sharing at once."

Donna smiled. "It's your news to share. Although I have no doubt your brother will be thrilled to find out he's going to be an uncle."

"I'll tell him soon, I promise." She glanced over at her luggage, still stacked by the door where Temo had put it. "Do you have anything to eat or just blood?"

"Sweetheart, this penthouse is loaded with food. And if there's something you want that we don't have, we'll get it." Donna got to her feet and opened her arms wide. "I love you, you know."

Christina almost fell into her mother's arms. "I know. I'm sorry about all this." She was on the verge of crying again.

Donna didn't want that. Being pregnant was hard enough without feeling like you were doing it on your own. "Hey." She pulled back and cupped Christina's face in her hands. "It's going to be okay. You're not in this alone. And I don't mean Noah. I'm here for you. Okay?"

She sniffed and smiled. "Thanks, Mom."

Donna embraced her again, kissing her head and hugging her tight. "I can't believe you're making me a grandmother before I'm fifty."

Christina laughed, the desired response. "You'll be fifty before the baby comes."

"Just barely." She let her daughter go. "What would you like to eat?"

"Steak. And a lot of it."

"We can handle that."

"Can you also help me tell Aunt Cammie? I'm afraid she's going to be so disappointed in me. I'm sure the convent won't like her having a niece that got knocked up before getting married."

Donna put her arm around Christina's shoulders. "I wouldn't be so sure. There's something I need to tell you about Aunt Cammie…"

Chapter 34

An hour later, they were all seated at the dining room table, finishing off the steak dinner that Pierce and Temo had happily jumped in to cook for the second night in a row. Even Cammie, who'd thankfully returned in time to eat with them, seemed to be enjoying herself.

And that was with full knowledge of her niece's impending bundle of joy, which she'd reacted to with all the love and enthusiasm Donna could have hoped for.

In fact, the meal almost seemed like a celebration of Christina's news. There was laughter and storytelling and such happiness that Donna could almost pretend Fitzhugh wasn't out to destroy her.

Maybe the prospect of becoming a grandmother had already changed her. Donna was already feeling much better about this new impending stage of her life. A baby was a gift, even if the timing wasn't perfect. The truth was, despite Donna's initial reaction, it really did seem like Christina had a great handle on things. But then, she'd survived having

Joe for a father. She ought to be able to manage just about anything after that.

And if Noah turned out to be a jerk, well, Donna wouldn't hesitate to put a little fear into him. In whatever way necessary. She wasn't about to let her daughter suffer because of a bad decision.

She was already thinking about setting up an account for Christina in case she needed money for anything. Even getting out. Noah's parents weren't the only ones with means. Donna wasn't about to let them control the situation with money either.

The whole thing certainly had Donna thinking about her own upbringing.

Donna's mother, Rosa, had basically turned her back on Donna not long after she'd realized who Donna had married. Rosa was Sicilian, a devout Catholic, and had been raised with an almost debilitating fear of the Mafia.

Because of that, Donna forgave her just a little. Rosa had been taught to give the Mafia a wide berth. But life would have been much easier if Rosa hadn't basically shut Donna out.

Donna would never do that to Christina or Joe Jr. And she'd never disappear on them the way her father had done to her and Cammie. She'd thought about it once not too long ago when going into witness protection had seemed like the best way to get Joe and the Villachis out of their lives, but she couldn't do it.

She couldn't leave her kids behind. They were her life. And family was everything. These people around this table were just as much her family as those who shared her blood. Donna raised her glass of wine. "I love you all. I want you to know that. I consider you all family."

Pierce raised his glass a little higher. "I think I can safely say we feel the same about you."

"Hear, hear," Charlie said.

Temo looked over at Cammie. "I never thought I'd be related to a nun."

"Former nun," Cammie corrected with a smile. "And I never thought I'd be related to a demigod."

"Wait a second," Christina said. "You're a demigod? I'm going to need that explained right now."

Temo's smile was sly. "You sure you wouldn't rather hear about how your aunt became a vampire hunter?"

Christina's mouth fell open. "Aunt Cammie. Is that true?"

Cammie looked down the table at Temo with a teasing glare. "You're like the little brother I never wanted."

More laughter erupted, but it couldn't drown out the sound of the door chime. Charlie started to get up, but Donna put a hand out, gesturing for her to stay in her seat. "Stay. I'll get it. I was going to get another bottle of wine anyway."

"Governor, I can—"

"Don't worry about it." Donna was already up. "It's probably Neo."

With a smile, she headed to the door. Christina

was going to love Neo. And Neo would flip when she found out about the baby.

Donna opened the door, but the vampire standing there wasn't remotely who she'd expected.

"Good evening, Governor Barrone. I'm Richard D'Angelo, emissary for the Prime. I've come to speak with you concerning some recent allegations that may have bearing on your ability to remain a nominee to succeed Queen Artemis."

Donna stared at him, her heart pounding with such ferocity that there was no way he couldn't hear it. But her heart wasn't thumping because he was an emissary for the Prime or because he'd basically just told her that she was on the short list to become queen, but because even without introduction, she knew who he was.

Granted, she hadn't seen him in nearly thirty-seven years, but his wasn't a face she would ever forget. How could she? His face hadn't really changed since the last time she'd seen it. He still looked exactly like the yellowing photo tucked in the envelope that held her passport and birth certificate. But then, becoming a vampire did have a tendency to freeze a person's looks at the age they'd been turned.

She swallowed as she tried to gather her thoughts and form an answer, but her head was a jumbled mess. How was this possible? Was it possible? Obviously, it was. Could she be wrong? No. Not with that same little scar running through his eyebrow.

"Did you hear me, Governor Barrone?"

"Yes," she whispered. She cleared her throat, finding a little more strength in the anger that had begun to well up inside her. "You'll have to forgive me for being a little overwhelmed, *Emissary*."

He nodded. "I understand the possibility of becoming queen might certainly—"

"Nope, that's not what did it. Not even close." She stared at him. Hard. Wondering if he was really going to pretend that he didn't know who she was. Because Donna wasn't about to play that game. "It was more the fact that the man I'm looking at now is the same man who used to be such a big part of my life. The same man who turned out to be such a huge disappointment."

She held her arms tight at her sides, fists clenched as she practically seethed with resentment. "The same man I used to call Dad."

Want to be up to date on new books, audiobooks and other fun stuff from me? Sign-up for my newsletter on my website, www.kristenpainter.com. No spam, just news (sales, freebies, releases, you know, all that jazz.)

If you loved the book and want to help the series grow, tell a friend about the book and take time to leave a review!

Other Books by Kristen Painter

PARANORMAL WOMEN'S FICTION
First Fangs Club series
Sucks to Be Me
Suck it up, Buttercup
Sucker Punch

COZY MYSTERY
Jayne Frost series
Miss Frost Solves a Cold Case: A Nocturne Falls Mystery
Miss Frost Ices the Imp: A Nocturne Falls Mystery
Miss Frost Saves the Sandman: A Nocturne Falls Mystery
Miss Frost Cracks a Caper: A Nocturne Falls Mystery
When Birdie Babysat Spider: A Jayne Frost Short
Miss Frost Braves the Blizzard – A Nocturne Falls Mystery
Miss Frost Chills the Cheater – A Nocturne Falls Mystery
Miss Frost Says I Do: A Nocturne Falls Mystery

Happily Everlasting series
Witchful Thinking

PARANORMAL ROMANCE
Nocturne Falls series
The Vampire's Mail Order Bride
The Werewolf Meets His Match
The Gargoyle Gets His Girl
The Professor Woos the Witch
The Witch's Halloween Hero – short story
The Werewolf's Christmas Wish – short story
The Vampire's Fake Fiancée
The Vampire's Valentine Surprise – short story
The Shifter Romances the Writer
The Vampire's True Love Trials – short story
The Dragon Finds Forever

The Vampire's Accidental Wife
The Reaper Rescues the Genie
The Detective Wins the Witch
The Vampire's Priceless Treasure

Shadowvale series
The Trouble with Witches
The Vampire's Cursed Kiss
The Forgettable Miss French
Moody and The Beast

Sin City Collectors series
Queen of Hearts
Dead Man's Hand
Double or Nothing

STAND-ALONE PARANORMAL ROMANCE
Dark Kiss of the Reaper
Heart of Fire
Recipe for Magic
Miss Bramble and the Leviathan

URBAN FANTASY
The House of Comarré series:
Forbidden Blood
Blood Rights
Flesh and Blood
Bad Blood
Out For Blood
Last Blood

Crescent City series:
House of the Rising Sun
City of Eternal Night
Garden of Dreams and Desires

Nothing is completed without an amazing team.

Many thanks to:

Cover design: Janet Holmes
Interior formatting: Author E.M.S
Editor: Joyce Lamb
Copyedits/proofs: Chris Kridler

About the Author

USA Today Best Selling Author Kristen Painter is a little obsessed with cats, books, chocolate, and shoes. It's a healthy mix. She loves to entertain her readers with interesting twists and unforgettable characters. She currently writes two best-selling paranormal romance series: Nocturne Falls and Shadowvale. She also writes the spin off cozy mystery series, Jayne Frost. The former college English teacher can often be found all over social media where she loves to interact with readers.

www.kristenpainter.com

For More Paranormal Women's Fiction Visit:
www.paranormalwomensfiction.net

Made in the USA
Coppell, TX
09 March 2021